Also by K. L. Parsons

Stranded in Leavenworth Series
Love by a Landslide
Love Under Snowfall
Love on a Ledge (Coming February 2025)

Love Under Snowfall

Stranded in Leavenworth, Book 2

K. L. Parsons

For all my winter weather warriors:
I hope my words convey an accurate love, passion, and wonder for
snow and snow sports because, well, I'll be honest...
I hate the snow.
Don't ignore the wanderlust.
(Even if you choose to wait 'til spring.)

K. L. PARSONS

Trigger Warnings: profanity, explicit sex scenes, loss of loved ones, mentions of past experiences of child neglect.

This book is intended for mature audiences.

While it may be my deepest desire for everyone to read and LOVE my book, I am aware that some content may not be suitable for everyone. If any of the above are triggers for you, Love Under Snowfall may not be the right fit. Take care of your mental health—Frankie and Benjamin still get their happily ever after whether you read through to the end or not. Take care!

LOVE UNDER SNOWFALL

Author's Note:

Much of Love Under Snowfall takes place in a fictitious college called Northwest Washington University. While there may be some similarities to any number of institutions in the greater Seattle area all accounts are made up and for fun. I received my Master of Jurisprudence from the law school at the University of Washington, and while the building may bear some resemblance to where Frankie attends, my academic experience was vastly different. The program I completed was full of supportive professionals who wanted nothing more than to see students succeed. There wasn't a single Professor Clark or Dean McCaffery in the bunch!

Contents

Chapter One

First day of fall quarter, Seattle: Frankie

Frankie Miller lumbered down the vacant hallway with an off-kilter gait that made her lower back cringe. She'd brought too much with her. There was no way she'd need the laptop, notebooks, and what must have been a fifty-pound casebook on day one. But odds were, if she left any one of those things at home, she'd probably end up needing it, and that was an embarrassment she desperately wanted to avoid.

Especially since she was already running late.

You might want to explore a little, the voice of her soon-to-be sister-in-law, Lucy, taunted at the back of her mind. *It sure would suck to be late on your first day.*

The weekend had been a last-minute scramble. Between finding all the necessary supplies, standing in line for her student ID, and moving into her new place, she had barely a moment to breathe, let alone take a tour of the 750-acre campus. Setting an early alarm seemed like the responsible thing to do but selecting p.m. instead of a.m. in her drowsy haze sabotaged her attempted timeliness. So instead of a two-hour headstart to get her bearings, her amber, sleep-sandy eyes popped open with twenty minutes 'til go time.

The flimsy strap of her crossbody bag dug into her exposed shoulder, causing her to regret the racerback tank she'd thrown on in her haste to leave her apartment. Her flip-flops weren't the best option either. She'd nearly eaten it a couple of times as the foam soles repeatedly caught on the cobblestones of the main square. Sneakers would have been much better, but since she fell asleep last night before taking the time to unpack, the flimsy footwear was all she could find.

Frankie reached a junction, scanned the large plague of room numbers, and continued waddling down the long corridor.

Room 120.

Room 123.

Her phone buzzed in her back pocket. She knew exactly who the text was from, but he would have to wait. A quick glance confirmed her suspicions and filled her with alarm as she spied the current time.

Crap!

Showing up late would be a bad look. But it was the first day of the quarter. Surely, she wouldn't be the only straggler on day one. Perhaps she'd be able to sneak in unnoticed and find a seat in the back. Slide under the radar before the dusty old professor had a chance to look up from his notes.

Finally, room 127 came into view, the placard gleaming like a chrome beacon of salvation. Her messy bun bobbled at the crown of her head as she scurried across the hall. She breathed a sigh of relief and gently pushed through the double doors. Making herself as small as possible, she attempted to creep around the perimeter of the room in search of a seat.

"Can I help you?" a deep voice rumbled with mild annoyance as the door sighed shut behind her.

Busted.

Frankie's eyes snapped up to the front of the room. She was ready to plead her case and ask for a little understanding, but then she froze. Standing behind the podium, instead of the seasoned educator she expected, stood a man not much older than she was.

And he was devastating.

His immaculately tailored suit—the exact color of his navy eyes—hugged the broad expanse of his shoulders. Perfectly coifed black hair upped the ante of his sharp, stern features, giving him a near-sinister vibe. His lips were the only soft thing on him, and even they were pulled tight in a perturbed scowl.

Mouth hanging open, Frankie willed herself to speak.

Say something.

Anything.

Really, anything will do right about now.

But all words—even the notion of language—escaped her, and all she could manage was a pretty spot-on imitation of a statue in the entryway.

"Are you lost, miss . . .? he prompted, speaking louder and slower this time.

"I'm Fra—" she croaked then cleared her throat. "Francesca. Miss Francesca, er, Miller. I'm Francesca Miller, so I guess that would be Miss Miller."

"Glad we finally got there. What are you doing in my classroom?"

"This is family law, right?"

"It is."

"I'm in this class."

"You're late." His level tone matched an equally flat expression aside from a muscle clenching at the back of his jaw.

"Only by ten minutes—"

"Twelve."

Frankie cringed as she glanced around the room in search of a clock. The small auditorium held around eighty people, and every single set of eyes took in her disheveled state. Some smirked, but most had *glad I'm not you* scrawled across their pitying faces. Her heart raced and she struggled to swallow the boulder-sized lump stuck in her throat.

"I'm sorry I'm late. My alarm didn't go off, and I got somewhat lost." She chuckled nervously and gestured to her feet. "And the flip-flops slowed me down, and—"

"And you are wasting everyone's time." His intense glare finally broke as he shuffled around a few papers then scribbled a note at the top of one.

Was he dismissing her?

Should she leave or find a seat?

"Well?" the intimidating man prompted. "Are you going to grace us with your presence from a seat or the doorway, Miss Miller?"

"A seat," she blurted then turned and scanned the crowd for an open spot to slink off to.

"You're in luck. There is one chair that remains open." Sweeping his arm out in front of him, he gestured with flourish. "Front and center."

"Thank you," she said with a curtsy because her lizard brain had completely taken over at that point and she had no control over her body. Ignoring a few snickers, she slinked to her seat, cringing as her footwear *slap-slap-slapped* her heels with each step.

Professor McMean'n'Scary shuffled his papers once then cleared his throat. "Oh, and Miss Miller?"

Frankie looked up, and the cold, deep ocean of his eyes again captured hers. "Yes?"

"Arrive late again and you're out of my class. The waitlist is a mile long and full of students hoping that someone like you will wash out quickly so they can take your place. I do not tolerate tardiness. Is that clear?" The terse cadence matched the bristly expression, each sentence punctuated by a clench of his clean-shaven jaw.

"Yes. Um, sir."

"Yes, Professor Clark," he corrected her with a low rumble.

Her ears flamed with embarrassment, and she wished desperately that her hair flowed loosely around her shoulders to cover them.

"Yes, Professor Clark," she parroted quietly.

Can the world open up and swallow me already?

He finally released her from his petrifying focus, settled a pair of black-rimmed glasses on the bridge of his aristocratic nose, and resumed the lecture.

Frankie couldn't focus on a single word he said as she scrambled to pull out her laptop and textbook. Her classmates turned their attention back to the front. Many typed furiously, trying to capture every word the professor said, while others sat back, nodding smugly everything he discussed was common knowledge. She wished she could pull off that level of aloof confidence—pretend or otherwise.

"Let's examine the cases assigned for today's reading," Professor Clark announced loudly, breaking through Frankie's shame haze.

The what now?

"We will start with *Griswold v. Connecticut.*"

Assignment? It's the first day.

He scanned a sheet of paper and said, "Let's hear from . . ."

No. No no no. Please, anyone but . . .

"Miss Miller."

Crap.

"What?" Frankie's stomach dropped, and her cheeks flushed crimson to match her ears. The rustling sound of her classmates turning to watch her crash and burn was deafening.

"Miss Miller, tell us what the holding was for *Griswold.*" He stepped out from behind the podium and removed his glasses.

"The what?"

"The holding," he demanded, brows raised expectantly. Again with that bland expression and piercing eyes.

She was dreaming. She had to be. There was no other way to explain this particular brand of humiliation. Unfortunately, an inconspicuous pinch to the thigh did nothing but make her leg hurt. Perhaps she was in hell.

"Miss Miller, are you still with us?" His exasperation showed as he heaved out a sigh.

Around the auditorium, she felt eighty sets of eyes boring into her with intense scrutiny, just waiting for her to say or do . . . something.

"I'm sorry, but I was unaware that we had a reading assignment on the first day."

"I see," he clipped, running his tongue over straight, white teeth. Replacing his glasses, he picked up the list again. "Miss Landry, please tell Miss Miller and the rest of your colleagues what the holding was for *Griswold*."

"Gladly, Professor Clark," she purred, wearing a haughty smirk. "In *Griswold v. Connecticut* the court held that the state of Connecticut violated the 14th Amendment when the state imposed a law that prohibited the use of any form of contraceptive drug or device."

"And, Mr. Jacobs," he continued without affirming Miss Landry's response. "What was the basis of the court's decision?"

"Well, professor," a thin redhead of maybe twenty-two began speaking with the same air of cockiness as Miss Landry.

The rapid-fire questions and answers gave Frankie whiplash as she tried to keep up and swallow her panic. She reminded herself that she deserved to be here, and it would take a lot more than a rocky start to scare her away from something she'd worked so hard for.

Chapter Two

Frankie

The class continued (painfully) the same way for the following two hours, and Frankie was utterly lost the entire time. Every other word, in the context of the cases, was new to her, and when they were finally dismissed for the day, she had a list of nearly fifty terms to look up.

Watching her peers pack up, she noted the mix of expressions ranging from overwhelmed—like hers—to arrogantly unfazed. Despite the fleeting reassurance that others were almost as dazed as she, everyone else had at least appeared to have done the reading. But the perk of being the only student flopping around at rock bottom was that the only direction to go from there was up.

Or out.

The waitlist is a mile long and full of students hoping that someone like you will wash out quickly so they can take your place.

She held back until the last student left the auditorium and approached the lectern, where her terrifying instructor huddled over some documents.

Clearing her throat, she asked, "Excuse me, Professor Clark?"

He didn't bother to look up. "Miss Miller."

Frankie wrung her hands together. The session had been brutal, but this class was crucial to her studies. She had a lot to gain, and it wouldn't be easy. But instead of bolting with her tail between her legs, she summoned the bravery to say, "I want to apologize again for being late to class today."

He didn't look up.

"And for not reading the assigned cases."

He continued to study the papers laid across his podium. The heat of frustration began to overshadow her nerves and gather in her belly. She was trying to apologize, and the least he could do was make a little eye contact.

"I had no idea there was reading for the first day of class," she continued.

Shoulders tense, he clenched his jaw yet carried on scanning and scribbling, not bothering to give her the time of day. "How does an L2 not know there would be cases assigned for the first day of class?" he scoffed.

Professor Clark's pen halted abruptly, and he looked over the rim of his glasses and up through his thick black eyelashes and brows. With his chin still dipped low, his appraisal of her was intimidating, sending another prickle of discomfort up her spine to the roots of her hair.

Suddenly aware of her disheveled appearance, Frankie cursed herself again for oversleeping. She'd intended to put a little effort into what she wore the first day. At the very least, she could have put on an unwrinkled, fresh-from-the-dryer shirt instead of something from her floor that barely passed the sniff test. And while her light boyfriend-cut jeans with a few too many holes were perfect for moseying around Leavenworth on a Saturday, they didn't exactly scream, "Take me seriously."

Professor Clark, on the other hand, was groomed immaculately. His suit was sculpted by the gods, under which he wore a pressed white button-down and expensive-looking tie a few shades lighter than his eyes. Frankie could practically smell the fresh shower on him, mixed with clove and cinnamon. He'd clearly shaved—his skin had that moisturized gleam to it—but the five o'clock shadow was already starting to peek out.

How is this guy real?

"Miss Miller," he scolded.

What had he asked? She shook her head, clearing the cobwebs.

"Sorry, but what's an L2?"

His eye twitched, but only once. "A second-year law student."

"Oh, I'm not a law student."

"Then what are you doing in my class?" His voice rumbled low in his chest, displaying the loosening grip he held on his already dwindling patience.

"Dean McCaffery approved my request to take this class. I'm in the master of social work program, and he agreed that family law would be helpful to my studies," Frankie explained. She'd been so excited when she got the ok to attend. She knew firsthand how confusing the legal system was—especially for foster kids—and having a decent grasp would give her a leg up after graduation. The dean had been ecstatic when they'd finally met after she'd submitted her formal request; something about *co-mingling disciplines* and *the dawning of a new era.*

Professor Clark appeared to consider this new information for a moment while his expression gave little away.

"I have no intention of making this class easier for you. I expect you to keep up. No touchy-feely vibes like what you'll undoubtedly experience in the rest of your MSW courses. Law classes are cutthroat. Students are ranked against each other, and the weak are culled. As I mentioned earlier, there are a lot of talented students on the waitlist who would kill to take your seat in the class." A bit of nostril flaring emphasized his words, and then he returned to his notes.

"Yes, sir—er, Professor Clark. I have every intention of

keeping up. It's just . . ." Silence and tension crackled in the air.

"Out with it, Miss Miller, I have another class in fifteen minutes."

"Well, there were so many terms that felt foreign to me. Is there a book or something you can suggest for me to catch up with the rest of the class?"

"You mean a book that will substitute for an entire year of formative law classes?"

Frankie chuckled nervously. "Yes?"

He removed his glasses and pulled out a handkerchief to buff them clean. His dark blue eyes settled on her face. She squirmed under his scrutiny as her agitation steadily built.

We get it. You think I'm beneath you and your precious class. Can't we move on from that so I can prove you wrong already?

After replacing the black frames, he jotted something down on a yellow sticky note. He peeled it off and held out a finger with the little square sticking to the tip.

"Take this to the law library downstairs and ask someone at the front desk to help you find it. It isn't *Civil Procedure for Dummies*, but it is close enough that even *you* should be able to follow it."

Her eyes narrowed momentarily at the overt dig, hoping the tight smile hid her grinding teeth. "Thank you. This is exactly what I need to—"

"And get yourself a tutor," he cut in. "Don't be against paying for a good one either."

"Right. Thanks again."

No *you're welcome*, no smile, not even a little nod. Instead, Professor Clark looked back down to his papers, dismissing her with his silence.

Frankie clasped her hands together so as not to give in to the impulse to flip him the bird on her way out. Once in the hallway, she breathed a sigh of relief and headed downstairs in search of the library.

Another text buzzed in her pocket.

Oh my god, can't he tell I'm busy?

She crammed the phone deep into her bag and ignored the tug of shame in her chest. Avoidance wasn't her typical MO, but focusing on salvaging her educational career seemed to warrant the temporary personality shift.

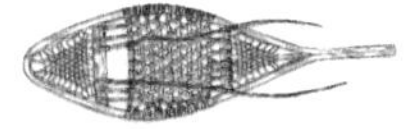

The law library was so silent that Frankie worried her slap-happy flip-flops would get her kicked out. Overcast light spread in through the windows, bathing the rows and rows of study tables in a subdued glow. Straight ahead, a glass-sided stairwell led further into the depths of the book basement. Glass half-walls rimmed the balcony overlooking the lower level as more of the frosted panes enclosed meeting rooms and small alcoves meant for studying. Everything, aside from the shelves and a few interior walls, was translucent, perhaps to welcome as much natural light as possible and detract from the library's subterranean location.

To the right stood the circulation desk. A young woman with teal hair and a pierced septum approached with a gleaming smile.

Finally, someone warm. She could use a pallet cleanser after being trapped in a classroom for the last two hours with nothing but an umbrella of pretension and her own panic.

"Hi. Can I help you with something?"

"I hope so." Frankie eyed her name tag. "Rayne, I'm Frankie. I'm looking for this book."

The library intern took the sticky note and read the scribble. She grimaced. "Family law with Clark, huh?"

Frankie nodded, trying to camouflage her wince with an excessive grin.

She failed.

"Don't worry. You'll get used to him."

"God, I hope so." She didn't anticipate becoming accustomed to the snobby dickhead, but she didn't need to. Developing enough of an understanding of the justice system to become a good advocate and social worker was all that mattered. Not some tall, scowling, navy-eyed professor who oozed toxic masculinity.

"Gimme a sec. I'll grab that book for ya," Rayne piped. Spinning on her toes, she and her shiny blue-green ponytail disappeared into the stacks.

In the depths of Frankie's bag, her phone buzzed again. She fished it out and read the notifications.

Sheriff Howards:

> I have an urgent matter to discuss with you.

> Please respond at your earliest convenience.

She rolled her eyes at the sheriff's message but grinned at the most recent text from her mother.

Mom:

> Good luck today, smarty pants!

Frankie

> Thanks. Love you!

She pocketed her phone as Rayne returned with a substantial

pile of books.

"Woah. I don't think I need"—she counted—"seven books."

"It seems like a lot, but based on the recommendation from Clark, I think these would be helpful too. This one in particular"—she tapped one entitled *Law for Non-Lawyers*—"will give you a solid orientation."

"Is it that obvious that I'm not a law student?"

Rayne waved her hand dismissively. "Pfft. Take it as a compliment."

Frankie left a few minutes later with textbooks in hand and a bonus list of third-year students offering tutoring services. Her new favorite librarian drew pink stars next to the ones she could vouch for personally. The exchange with Rayne had been her first positive interaction of the day, and it helped take the edge off her frustrated mood. Armed with enough books to start her own library, Frankie hurried home to drop off her loot and eat lunch before the start of her next class.

Chapter Three

Benjamin

Immediately following his final lecture of the day, Professor Benjamin Clark marched down the office hallway like a crazed warrior poised for battle. The furious pump of his arms propelled him past startled colleagues. Wrath radiated off of him in waves strong enough to part clusters of students awaiting meetings with teachers' assistants and advisors. His black-rimmed glasses crept down his nose with each stomp, and he winced slightly as he jammed them back in place with miscalculated force.

He was fuming.

He was pissed.

He was determined to figure out what the hell Dean McCaffery was playing at.

Approaching the closed door at the end of the hallway, Benjamin almost forgot himself and barged in without an invitation, but he stopped with his hand on the doorknob. He rapped two heavy knocks on the solid oak and swung its heavy weight open upon hearing his boss's welcome.

"Ah, Benjamin." The older man leaned back in his chair, propping one immaculately buffed loafer on his opposite knee. He beamed happily at the seething professor, deep crow's feet and laugh lines engaged, and a mischievous glimmer in his pale blue eyes. "To what do I owe the—"

"When were you going to tell me?"

"Tell you what, exactly?" Dean McCaffery's grin didn't falter as he ran one hand through a patch of thinning hair and gestured with the other to the two chairs opposite his desk.

"I'll stand," Benjamin barked. "And you know quite well what I'm referring to."

Benjamin registered a sharp glint in his boss's eyes, though that smile of his held firm.

"Watch yourself, Clark. You forget who you're talking to." The warning was level but had the intended cooling effect. "I insist you sit and calm down."

Begrudgingly, Benjamin obeyed and lowered into an old office chair. He sank into the lumpy, brown cushion but kept his back ramrod straight, gripping his knees to keep his hands from balling into fists. He sucked in a breath through flared nostrils and willed himself to settle down. McCaffery wouldn't be receptive to a tantrum, and Benjamin couldn't blame him. If a student had come barging into his office on a similar tirade, he'd have tossed him out the door by the scruff of his neck. He managed a few more lungfuls of air, noting the scent of dusty books and whatever garlicky dish had been on the menu for lunch that day.

"Very good," the dean gently praised. "Now, what is this you're going on about?"

"The interloper," he forced through gritted teeth.

"Ah."

"When were you going to tell me about her?"

"I wasn't aware I was under any obligation to tell you anything. I'm *your* superior, remember?"

While there was no refuting the sanctioned hierarchy, surely simple professional courtesy would dictate a warning of some kind—or at the very least, mutual academic respect should. But there stood the problem. Benjamin was certain his boss held very little respect for him—not as a professional, not as a peer. McCaffery approved of his hard-nosed methods and results as a professor, but what he got off on was the power he held over the younger man's head.

Even at half the dean's age, Benjamin had already succeeded in twice the career McCaffery ever could, and it clearly boiled the older man's pride. He was well past his prime yet continued to hang on to his position for the sheer joy of lording over the *lowly* family law professor.

"She's in the *MSW* program," Benjamin spat. He had nothing against the various graduate schools around campus—Northwest Washington University was at the top of its field in many disciplines—as long as they didn't disrupt his precisely orchestrated lectures.

"It doesn't matter what a student is studying, so long as she keeps up with the rest of the class. Wouldn't you agree?"

"She has no clue how a law class is structured. She showed up late and didn't come prepared to discuss the assigned cases. She didn't just waste my time; she wasted the time of every single one of my students."

"Let me be frank." Smirk fading away, McCaffery's face took on a pinched countenance. One Benjamin had become accustomed to during his time teaching at NWU. "This comes down from on high. The board wants to see interdisciplinary cooperation. They believe that lawyers and judges shouldn't be the gatekeepers to the justice system and want to see a mingling of programs to produce more well-rounded graduates."

"Wouldn't it make more sense for the professors in the MSW program to formulate their own family law class that's easier for their students to follow?" Benjamin sneered.

"Wouldn't it make more sense for law professors at the top of their game to teach their craft to those who will benefit most from their expertise?" McCaffery challenged with a sigh. Twisting a thick gold signet ring on his bony finger, the dean peered over the rim of his wire-framed glasses, leveling a heavy gaze on Benjamin. "I may disagree with it, but my hands are tied. Which means so are yours."

Benjamin's rage fizzled, leaving behind a mild headache and a bitter taste in his mouth. This wasn't the first time the board attempted to implement some flight of fancy into the curriculum. And it wouldn't be the last. He had to deal with it and let this particular train wreck run its course. But one thing niggled at the back of his mind.

"Why this girl? Why did you pick her to be a part of your little experiment?"

"If you must know, she gave a compelling argument in her proposal about why she would be an asset to the class and how connecting the two disciplines made logical sense. Not only that, but I saw her GRE scores, and they were fantastic—top five percent."

Benjamin was impressed. Mildly.

"I won't make things easier on her. I already told her that." Benjamin wagged his finger toward his boss, but the wind had already blown out of his sails. "She must keep up with everyone else."

"Of course. That was never at issue," Dean McCaffery stated.

"And if she's late or ill-prepared again, she's out."

"I would expect no less. However, after talking with her, Miss Miller doesn't appear to be the kind of woman who makes the same mistake twice. She is very intelligent and clearly a hard worker. She received the Thirty Over Thirty scholarship from the Gilcrest Foundation.

Benjamin was aware of how challenging it was to earn that honor. Only thirty people received the national scholarship each year, and of those selected, typically only five were from disciplines other than STEM. It wasn't an easy award to win, and one really had to be something to earn it.

"Nevertheless, Miss Miller is expected to meet the same bar as the rest of my students."

"And if she does not, I will personally apologize to you, admit I was completely wrong in my judgment, and never again place another rogue student in your classroom. Sound good?"

"Fine." Benjamin gave a curt nod.

"Splendid." McCaffery slapped both hands down on the mahogany desk. "Then, if you'll excuse me, I have much to do. You can see yourself out." One bony hand, palm facing up, gestured toward the door.

With considerably less fire in his belly, Benjamin left Dean McCaffery's office and proceeded to his own. While dazed from the exchange with his boss, an anxious frustration ricocheted around inside his chest, and he couldn't decide where to direct his agitation. Should he blame his boss for insisting on the cockamamie scheme or Miss Miller for summoning his ire by starting off on the absolute wrong foot this morning?

Regardless, while he had to play by McCaffery's rules, he didn't have to make things easy on the intruding MSW student. In fact, he was fully prepared to prove his boss wrong and watch with satisfaction as Francesca Miller crashed and burned.

Chapter Four

Frankie

The daze set in by six-thirty that evening as Frankie sat with blurry vision, trying desperately to comprehend the difference between appellate, appellant, and appellee. The terms she attempted to define and commit to memory felt like a foreign language—correction, lots of it *was* a foreign language (those judges sure loved their Latin). With a brain too full to go on, she dropped her face into the crease of the family law book sprawled open in front of her and groaned.

"Was it that bad?" a deeply sympathetic voice cooed.

"Worse," she grumbled against the crisp pages. Frankie lifted her head and watched as her roommate, Todd, shuffled into the kitchen, towel wrapped around his waist and well-loved slippers on his feet. The scent of cocoa butter and freshly washed skin followed him from the bathroom as he poured himself a cup of coffee and angled his phone in Frankie's direction. Her soon-to-be sister-in-law's smiling face filled the screen.

"*Uh-oh.*" Frankie couldn't miss the giggle in Lucy's voice despite the tinny quality of the speakerphone.

"Wanna tell us about it? I still have"—Todd glanced at the microwave clock—"an hour before I need to head to work."

Rising from her chair, Frankie grabbed a cup of the steaming brew for herself. She needed the pick-me-up if anything was going to stick the rest of the night.

"I don't want to relive it, so let's just say it was embarrassing."

"Embarrassing like something green stuck in your teeth or embarrassing like your duet partner broke an eight-inch heel on stage and accidentally ripped the dress off you on the way down?"

"Oof," Frankie cringed. "Did that happen to you?"

"I plead the fifth." He cleared his throat and took a sip.

"It happened," Lucy sang loudly. "I was there."

"Thanks, sweet pea," Todd drolled, reducing the volume by a few clicks and propping the phone against a stack of notebooks. Turning back to Frankie, he demanded, "Spill."

"The exposure scenario, definitely." She looked down at her mug, wishing it had a splash of whiskey to dull the mortification. "My professor scolded me publicly for being late to class, sat me front and center, riddled me with impossible questions, implied I was stupid, then threatened to kick me out if I was late or 'ill-prepared' again. He thinks I'm a joke. I'm not sure how to come back from it."

"Yikes," Lucy gasped. "What a prick."

"*Professor Prick*," Todd shouted through a hoot of laughter.

"Is that what we'll call him?" Frantic claps accompanied a shrill giggle.

"Works for me—"

"Uh, guys? Can you focus? You aren't exactly helping," Frankie moaned while secretly grateful that the chuckle twins were in her corner.

"You could always drop out and come help me plan the wedding," Lucy offered, shoulders shrugged and a grimacing smile pulled across her lips.

Frankie leveled a scowl on the tiny image of her almost sister.

"I know. Not helpful either. I just miss you—both of you."

Frankie softened, feeling a subtle ache in her chest. She and her brother's fiancée had become close over the last year, and after the day she'd had, Frankie would rather do the debrief in person over a couple beers. The quarter had only just started, and already she was wishing it was Thanksgiving break—or better yet, winter break so she could go home and celebrate her brother, Jonathan, and Lucy's wedding. The twelve weeks until then felt insurmountable.

Frankie sighed and said, "We miss you too."

"Back to business, ladies." Todd turned to Frankie. "Tell me your why."

"You already know my why."

"But I think you need to hear it out loud again."

"Fine." The sigh that accompanied Frankie's eye roll reached teenage-angst proportions. "I want to get my MSW so I can work with kids in the foster care system."

Her roommate waved his hand in a *give me more* gesture.

"Specifically, I want to open a non-profit that introduces at-risk youth to outdoor activities," she recited the meticulously crafted section from her grad school application. "I want to show them there are spaces where they belong and can achieve things they never thought possible. Nature is a place of healing, and exposure will help them cope with the challenges they experience at home."

"Beautiful." Todd grinned.

They both turned to the sniffles coming from the phone.

"Ignore me. Something's in my eye," Lucy said, dabbing at her nose with a tissue.

"Moving on. Let's dream big." Leaning back in his chair to reach into the fridge, Todd pulled out a protein shake and cracked the lid. "In your ultimate fantasy scenario, if you could snap your fingers to make it come true, what would happen at your next class?"

"Can't I just undo what already happened?"

"*Ehhh!* Wrong," he said, impersonating a gameshow buzzer.

"It's a waste of time to look back, love. Far better to dream big for the future."

"Fine," Frankie grumbled, knowing Todd was right. "If I could wish for anything, it would be that Professor Cl—"

"Professor Prick!" Lucy corrected with a shout.

Frankie shook her head. "It would be that *Professor Prick* took me seriously."

"And what would make him do that?" Todd asked.

A miracle.

"It would probably help if I showed up on time to class."

Todd snorted. "And?"

"And knew the material and how to answer the questions he'd ask."

"Good, anything else?"

Frankie shrugged. Wasn't magic of that proportion enough?

"How about you dress the part?" He waggled his eyebrows and grinned.

Leave it to a drag queen to suggest a costume for an occasion as mundane as class.

"I doubt he'd care what I wear one way or another. I already walked in wearing this," she said as she swiped her hands toward her outfit. "A blazer won't change his opinion."

"Probably not, but it wouldn't be for him." Todd tutted gently. "Do you know what happened to me the first time I wore full drag?"

"What?"

"I met the inner goddess who'd been dying to come out and perform. The more I tuck and pad and paint my face, the more emboldened I am to lean into the fantasy that is Dirty O'Feelya. Out of drag, I'm not her—even if she does lurk just under the surface. The right outfit might help you actualize your inner law school maven. It's worth a shot, isn't it?"

"He's got a point, chickie," FaceTime Lucy interjected.

It wasn't the wildest idea. If she felt professional—paired with punctuality and a solid grasp of the material—she might just survive Professor Clark's class.

"You're right," she said with a sigh. "I'll add clothes shopping to my list right after 'find a tutor' and 'understand the law.'"

"Haven't you already learned that I'm always right?" He winked, ignoring her sarcasm, and squeezed Frankie's shoulder. "I'll take you to the mall tomorrow after you treat me to brunch."

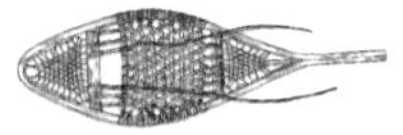

Exhausted from another few hours of studying, Frankie flopped on her bed and burritoed herself in her favorite quilt. The heft of the patchwork flannel and corduroy, along with the homey scent of lavender dryer sheets, quieted her mind. She turned off the lamp on the side table and tunneled further into the familiar comfort. But before drifting off, her phone lit up, emitting a low buzz.

She sighed, already knowing full well who it was.

Again.

Sheriff Howards:

You wouldn't be avoiding me, would you?

Leave it to a dude in law enforcement to finally put the clues together. She swallowed her guilt and typed out the lie anyway.

Frankie:

Of course not, Clint.

Sheriff Howards:

> Haven't heard from you since Thursday. Forget about me already?

Frankie:

> How could I possibly forget about you?

Sheriff Howards:

> Aw, shucks.

> When are you home next?

Frankie:

> Not sure, Thanksgiving?

Sheriff Howards:

> Yikes, that long? Will my rain check still be valid?

Sheriff Clint Howards, Chelan County's finest.

Frankie had met him the year before when Jonathan and Lucy had gone missing on Mount Stuart. She'd been a frazzled mess, and the good sheriff getting in her way didn't help matters. They'd exchanged numbers, at his request, to stay in better contact throughout the whole ordeal. It wasn't until after the hikers had been found that Clint's primary motivation became clear. And something about him laying the foundation for some kind of romantic interlude while Frankie was losing her mind worrying about her brother pissed her off.

It took him a while—unanswered phone calls, texts left on read, and one explosive run-in at a local bar—but eventually, the self-assured, presumptuous sheriff got the message.

Then, a few weeks before leaving for Seattle, Frankie ran into

Clint after finishing up a rafting job on the Wenatchee River. While her participants huddled together eating sack lunches and jabbering excitedly about the run, Frankie stood near the bank, assisting other rafting guides and kayakers as they slid ashore at the busy take-out spot.

While helping lug a massive raft ashore, a flash of teal and yellow caught her eye. She could barely keep hold of the slippery boat's handles as a shredded Hercules strode by, kayak hefted on one shoulder, neoprene wet suit unzipped and dangling off his hips. She hungrily perused the sheriff from his wet, wavy blond hair to his abs, which boasted an *eight-pack*. How was that even possible?

Once done lending a hand, she casually ambled over and stood beside him at his truck while he chugged water from an old, banged-up Nalgene.

"How does someone with a sheriff's salary afford a sixteen hundred dollar boat?" She tilted her head toward the flashy Gnarvana kayak perched in the truck bed.

Water ran off his chin, dribbling down his dinner plate-sized pecks and ridiculously wash-boarded belly. His cocked eyebrow and one-sided grin weakened Frankie's knees. "When you've been single for a year, you tend to save up a little pocket change."

"What? Your shuttle bunny doesn't expect dinner and drinks after carting you and your kayak around?"

"Is that your way of asking if I'm *currently* single?"

Frankie just snorted and shook her head. "Doesn't matter to me either way."

"Well, seeing as how my cousin Ian and I swap *shuttle bunny* duties, we tend to go Dutch. Except for tonight. He has to get back home to the wife, which means I'm free to take you to dinner."

She'd chewed on her lower lip, trying to decide if she was still upset with Sheriff Howards or if the year of space was enough to cool her irritation. "Pick me up at seven."

That warm summer day seemed so long ago.

Despite the current fall chill, Frankie was suddenly too warm in her cocoon. She flipped off the toasty quilt and gave a resigned sigh. Maybe it wasn't a bad idea to have a stress reliever on retainer when she returned for Thanksgiving break. Lord knows she could use a little therapeutic fun.

Frankie:

I suppose I could extend the expiration date just this once.

Sheriff Howards:

Awesome.

Frankie:

But for now, I need to get to bed. Long day.

Sheriff Howards:

Sleep sweet, princess.

Frankie cringed at the nickname and tried to ignore the pang of . . . something she couldn't quite put her finger on. It might have been guilt over stringing Clint along. He'd put in a valiant effort to woo her. By the time she left for Seattle, they'd gone on four dates and kayaked once together. He even helped her pack and load boxes for the move, never going further than a few kisses and a little groping.

But her education was too important to screw up. She knew how distracted she'd get after hooking up with the sexy sheriff, and she couldn't afford to focus that level of attention on a fuck buddy. So, she'd decided to make a temporary vow of celibacy until she got a handle on the whole grad school thing.

Unfortunately, she'd miscalculated. Intentional radio silence and a literal mountain range separating them hadn't managed to cool his advances. Instead, he texted her daily, really putting in the work to keep in touch. Frankie hadn't made any commitment to him before leaving, aside from a promise to get dinner once she was back in town, but perhaps in Clint Speak, that meant more than *just dinner*.

Maybe the pang she felt had nothing to do with guilt.

Maybe she was just horny. Plain and simple.

All the more reason to take sex off the table. If she could manage to satisfy her own needs, she'd have much more time for studying. And if she passed her classes, she'd indulge in a little reward while visiting Leavenworth for break.

Frankie stared up at the ceiling, willing herself to fall asleep, but agitation nagged at her with growing ferocity. Fortunately, her self-imposed celibacy didn't have to extend to solo activities. She located her favorite vibrator from one of the many boxes she'd yet to unpack and settled back into her cozy cocoon, grateful that her roommate worked at night. Twenty-eight minutes and two orgasms later, she finally relaxed and slept like a rock for the rest of the night.

Chapter Five

October, Seattle: Frankie

Over the next several weeks, Frankie put in the work. She focused all her time studying, apart from the sporadic quest to restock the fridge at the grocery store or take-out restaurant.

She'd even managed to find a third-year law student to work with once a week for a reasonable fee. Studying with a tutor was an absolute game-changer. The weekly session, paired with the library books Rayne had picked out, helped Frankie see the case law more clearly.

Even the book Professor Clark recommended was helpful when she studied solo. She was glad he'd suggested it, even if she was a little resentful of his comment that first day in class.

Even someone like you will be able to follow it.

Elitist bastard.

As promised, the few precious hours of study time she spent shopping for professional clothes with Todd boosted her confidence. She traded her favorite worn tank tops and distressed jeans for black leggings, conservative blouses and sweaters, and neutral flats. With her honey-colored hair pulled back in a neat bun and a subtle layer of makeup, playing the part of the studious academic was that much easier.

Maybe *easier* wasn't quite the right word.

Despite spending all of her free time buried in books, her fantasy of spouting off the correct answer in class remained just that—a fantasy. Because even though she'd stride into that classroom brimming with confidence, the moment Professor Prick leveled that condescending glare on her, all bets were off. His piercing midnight eyes and commanding presence inevitably left her tongue-tied. If anything came out of her mouth at all, it never made any sense. Inevitably, the garbled string of consciousness left her in an inferno of shame, with her ears burning and her skin itchy beneath her clothes.

Occasionally, her answers came out semi-cogent, and an initial warmth of pride would bloom in her chest. For once her cheeks would glow from success instead of embarrassment.

Until Clark, with eyes continuing to cut through her, opened his mouth and said something like, "Mr. Smith, please tell Miss Miller where she erred." Or, "Miss Kennedy, please explain to Miss Miller why her statement was incorrect." All while that stupid, smug smirk tugged at his ridiculously plump lips.

After each class session, Frankie would study that much harder. She knew she'd get it eventually. And finally, on one sunny Friday afternoon, something clicked. The light switch finally flicked on, and everything she'd been reading made perfect sense.

That next Monday morning crept back around, and she marched into class, allowing herself a sliver of optimism. She opened her laptop, laid out her notes, all highlighted in bright sunny yellow, and waited to be called on.

"Miss Miller," the haughty inquisitor boomed in the bored voice of a man who knew what to expect.

"Yes, Professor Clark." She could hear the class turn in their seats, ready to eat up the humiliating exchange and leave no crumbs behind.

"What are the key elements of *Obergefell v. Hodges*?"

Like a woman possessed—with legal knowledge—she spouted off the pertinent information in a clear and concise manner. She didn't leave any important bit out, nor did she provide too much information. She got the lingo correct. And more importantly, she made Professor Clark pause in his rapid-fire demand for information.

The man actually *paused*.

He blinked a few times, adjusted the glasses perched on his nose, and then looked down at his list. "And, Mr. Trenton, what triggered the court's ruling?"

Be cool. Be cool.

Frankie couldn't help the smile that spread uncontrollably across her face as she managed to hold back a celebratory *hell yeah!*

She'd finally done it. It took her a few weeks, but she'd cracked the code to successfully participate in the daunting class. She casually glanced around the room. A couple students gave her a little smile or a brief nod. One guy a little older than her even flashed a quick thumbs-up—hidden behind his computer of course—as if to say *way to go, kid.*

When class was dismissed, Frankie leisurely packed her belongings. She continued floating on cloud nine and for once wasn't in a mortified rush to exit the building. She hauled her computer bag over her shoulder and adjusted her sweater to lay correctly under the strap. She was nearly out the door, when a deep voice barked from the lectern.

"Miss Miller, a moment."

Frankie froze and cringed before she turned, wearing a calm mask. "Yes, Professor Clark."

"I see you took my advice."

"Oh, about the book and a tutor?"

He leveled a critical gaze on her.

"Have I given you any other advice?" he asked with humorless sarcasm.

Asshole must be his default setting.

She chose not to let it fluster her. "Thank you for recommending the book. It's been helpful. Along with a hefty stack recommended by Rayne in the—"

"Are you prepared for the midterm on Monday?" He studied her over the rim of his glasses, his expression a cocktail of scorn and boredom.

"I'm getting there." Fidgeting under his perusal, she forced herself to hold still. She'd done well in class, and deserved to be in that lecture hall just as much as the rest of the students. Professor Clark was intimidating, but his hostile tactics weren't going to beat her down anymore.

"Law exams are completely different than any soft, undergraduate tests you have taken in the past. I hope, for your sake, your tutor is adequately preparing you for the event."

"I believe I have it under control," she sniped back, shoulders squared.

"Because if you don't get a C or above, you will not be permitted to resume my class. Is that clear?"

Frankie flinched at his admonishing tone as tiny cracks formed in the veneer of her momentary confidence. "Of course, Professor Clark."

Once again, he didn't nod or make so much as a grunt before turning his attention back to the papers on his podium.

She'd been dismissed.

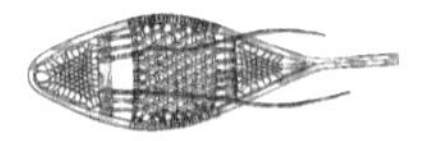

QUIET PLEASE
TESTING IN PROGRESS

The laminated notice, in all its caps lock glory, was anything but quiet. It screamed at Frankie, reminding her that the next three hours would dictate whether she'd be allowed to remain in Professor Clark's demanding family law class. No amount of preparation had been effective in shaking her nerves, and she remained anxious despite her tutor's assurances that she knew the material.

A tall, slender woman pushed through the door and propped it open with a stopper. "Family law midterm, Professor Clark. Fifteen minutes until the exam begins. The doors will lock at commencement. Do *not* be late."

Frankie filed in with the rest of her classmates. An unsettling hush emphasized the tension that rippled throughout the auditorium as everyone found a spot. She unloaded her allowed supplies: computer, pens, blank papers (to be left with the proctor following the midterm), refillable water bottle, and snacks. Many of the professors allowed their students to use notes and even casebooks in their exams. But not Clark. Nope. He wanted to test his students blind in order to, as he put it, "separate the weak from the strong and thin the herd."

She checked her watch and decided she had enough time to use the restroom and get water. At the fountain, as a steady stream of cold water filled her Nalgene, she felt a familiar chill creep up the back of her neck. Frankie turned and froze. Professor Clark stood at the end of the hallway, mid-stride, staring at her. Though he was some distance away, his frigid glare was unmistakable.

Frankie raised her hand, wiggling her fingers in a friendly—ok, fine—mocking wave. Was she poking the bear with her taunt? Sure. But she refused to allow his childish intimidation tactics to sabotage the countless hours she spent buried in her casebooks.

He huffed and then stomped away, probably off to blow

down some poor sap's house of straw. She found odd satisfaction in bothering him as much as he bothered her.

Imbued with a sudden rush of confidence, Frankie knew to her core that she was going to ace that test and take great pleasure rubbing Professor Prick's nose in it the rest of the quarter.

Chapter Six

Two weeks later, Seattle: Benjamin

Benjamin's long strides beat the icy pavement in time to his measured breaths. The late autumn air filled his lungs, emitting misty puffs with each exhale. His snug running beanie and gloves—which he'd pulled from his cold weather bin that morning—managed to ward off the chill of the shifting seasons. The Verve's "Bitter Sweet Symphony" piped through his earbuds as he let the familiar melody quiet his busy mind.

That morning, he felt lighter. Why he'd woken up on the right side of the bed after having been perpetually surly the last two months was beyond him. Nothing had changed. Miss Miller continued to sit in his class and Dean McCaffery continued to demand weekly updates on her progress. He was in an impossible situation, one he'd been fighting against daily. But when the clear, crisp morning greeted him, despite his ingrained hatred of cold weather, he felt strangely at peace.

Perhaps it had something to do with his upcoming trip to Leavenworth for his best friend's wedding. He and Johnny had met on the first day of macroeconomics their sophomore year, became roommates a week later, and best friends shortly after that. They remained inseparable until a year after graduation when Johnny got the call to return home to Leavenworth. His father had cancer and needed him to pick up the slack at Off the Beaten Adventures, the family guiding business. He eventually took over the guiding company once his father lost the battle and passed away. A few years later, tragedy struck again, claiming Johnny's wife in a white water rafting accident.

Benjamin wanted to head east countless times to support his friend, but between the chaos of law school, getting immediately hired by Hewitt, Moser, and Pratt upon passing the bar, and then making the switch to teaching, time simply slipped by. Well over a decade had passed, and he hadn't once made the two-and-a-half-hour drive to see how his friend was doing—not even for the funerals.

Some friend I turned out to be.

But next month would be different. Johnny was getting married again and—despite the distance and lapsed connection—he'd asked Benjamin to be his best man. He had no excuse not to attend the wedding. Not that he wanted an excuse. He missed his buddy and was happy to be there to support the happy couple.

Even if their marriage was doomed.

Something about spending six years as a divorce attorney and witnessing the absolute destruction of his own mother's world when he was twelve left him jaded where marriage was concerned.

Perhaps Johnny and his blushing bride would beat the odds. He hoped for his best friend's sake they would. And if the marriage failed, Benjamin would be first in line to help him handle the divorce.

It's the least he could do.

Benjamin's watch buzzed against his wrist, pulling him out of his hazy runner's high and wandering thoughts.

"Shoot." He'd lost track of time and forgot to backtrack sooner. He was about three miles off course and needed to hoof it in order to make it back to his condo in time to shower and stop by his office before class.

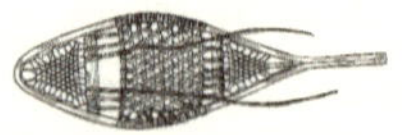

Benjamin made it to his office with just enough time to drop off his things and scan his email for anything critical. His computer took its sweet time booting up, so he snatched the spare protein shake from his desk drawer. Of all the things in his morning routine, skipping breakfast seemed the easiest to drop and save the maximum amount of time. What he hadn't accounted for was how hungry he'd be by accidentally extending his run that morning.

He shook the chocolatey breakfast in a carton and called up his email once he logged into the campus server. He twisted off the cap, but before taking a gulp, the subject line of a particular email jumped out and slapped him in the unshaved jaw (another thing he dropped in his routine courtesy of his accidental detour).

FAMILY LAW MIDTERM EXAM RESULTS

Yes.

Finally.

He'd be rid of that woman. Once he handed out Miss Miller's failing grade, she would no longer be in his class and would cease to be an unwelcome distraction.

He licked his lips and stared unblinking at the screen as he opened the spreadsheet listing the midterm scores.

Chapter Seven

Benjamin

B enjamin's day was ruined. Ruined!

He traced the lines of the Excel spreadsheet four times to make sure he'd read the right grade attached to Francesca Miller's student ID number. There was no mistaking it. She'd gotten a C. A score only slightly above dismal, but passing nonetheless.

Four more weeks.

He still had an entire month with that woman in his class, sitting in the front row with her hair—the color of golden honey—pulled into a sleek bun, sitting up straight with her shoulders back. Trying to look professional in her well-fitting blouses and painted-on leggings. A single eyebrow cocked, challenging him, *mocking* him, as she responded to his barrage of questions. She was such an unnecessary distraction and Benjamin had been so hopeful to be rid of her. Jesus, he'd even beefed up the midterm in hopes that it would be way over her head.

I blame the rest of the students. If they had done better, she would have been lower on the graded curve and out of my class.

He sat there grumpy, fully aware that his mood was childish. Why did he react like this when it came to that woman? She wasn't rude. Definitely wasn't stupid. He supposed her effort was commendable. Keeping up with the flow of each class didn't seem to be a problem for her anymore. She was attractive and in any other context, he would have happily flirted with her in a bar or some other gathering. She had a petite little body, except for her rear, which was full and swayed seductively when she walked. Benjamin closed his eyes and let out a slow breath. He imagined sliding his hands over her round, perky bottom and—

No.

NO!

He *wanted* her.

That was his problem. He wanted to get his hands on Francesca Miller. Well, not just his hands.

This is bad.

She's a student, and he's her professor. Never was there a more cliché scenario than him lusting over her. Or—god forbid—acting on that lust. Aside from being tacky, it would also be unprofessional. He could lose his job. She could lose her scholarship. And all for what? A tumble or two in the sheets? Not worth it. No, Benjamin had to nip this in the bud immediately.

But how was he supposed to do that? She wasn't going anywhere before the end of the quarter, so he was stuck with her for another four weeks. Benjamin's head flopped back as he let out a frustrated groan. Two classes per week—aside from Thanksgiving week—which meant only seven classes. Fourteen measly hours in total. Surely, he could behave like a grown man for *fourteen hours*. He was one hundred percent capable of resisting the urge to throw her over his shoulder and march down the hall to his office—

"Enough!" he roared at himself.

Hunger pangs scratched at his stomach. He shook the carton in his hand, forgetting it was already opened, and sloshed some of the chocolate drink onto his shirt and tie. He recoiled, looking down at the mess he'd made. His once immaculately white shirt displayed brown splatters, stains that would never (no matter how much bleach he used) ever come out. The plastic shake cap sat beside his keyboard, taunting him with its uselessness. He grumbled and momentarily contemplated chucking the carton across the small office but thought better of it, opting instead to down the necessary calories.

After depositing the empty into the waste bin, he sat with his elbows on the desk and forehead in his hands, grabbing fistfuls of his hair. This was ridiculous.

Two quick raps on the door startled him from his pathetic cesspool of annoyance. Before he could call out that whoever it was should go away, Dean McCaffery popped his head inside, looking surprisingly cheery considering his usual demeanor.

"Goooood morning, Benjamin. A moment." He didn't wait for a response but instead stepped into the office and closed the door behind him. Taking a couple steps forward, he bent slightly at the waist so he could lay both hands on the desk.

Benjamin was in no mood.

"What do you want, McCaffery?" he asked bluntly. *Come to gloat, I assume?*

"I wanted to see if you had a chance to look at Miss Miller's midterm score."

Bingo. Here to gloat.

"I saw it just now," he ground out around clenched teeth.

The older man wore a smug smile. "Then I believe we should applaud ourselves."

"And why is that?"

McCaffery rested a hip on Benjamin's desk and held up his arms in a grand gesture. "Because with my eagle eye selection and your magnificent ability to educate, we have pleased the powers that be." He meant the board members and wealthy donors who gave to the college. Usually, they were one and the same.

"That's great. Is there anything else?" Benjamin sighed,

suddenly feeling very exhausted.

"You do realize that if this all goes well, there is an almost guaranteed chance that your tenure will finally be approved. Think of the security. Think of the prestige." He leaned forward. "Think of the raise."

"Tenure," Benjamin muttered. "I submitted my application for consideration almost a year ago."

"Yes, and I am certain that Miss Miller's successful completion of your class will grease the wheels, so to speak."

Interesting.

Benjamin deserved tenure. He worked harder than any of his peers and his dedication to the university was unparalleled. He barely had a social life because he was practically married to his job. But for whatever reason, he hadn't been approved yet. And now he was starting to see why. Could it be possible that Dean McCaffery requested the tenure committee hold off on the approval so Benjamin could be under his thumb for a little longer? Just long enough for this hairbrained interdisciplinary nonsense to come to fruition? He could feel the heat rise in his chest.

"Well." The dean tapped an arthritic knuckle on the desk as he stood to leave. "If there is nothing else, I must be off. Reviews to complete. Funds to raise. You know, dean stuff."

McCaffery opened the door, but before exiting turned back to his subordinate. "Between the stains on your shirt and the hair"—he gestured to Benjamin's mussed appearance—"you may want to pay more attention to grooming. If tenure's still your goal, that is."

Before he could respond, his boss closed the door behind him, leaving Benjamin alone with his scorn and too many thoughts assaulting his brain.

In the span of a measly fifteen minutes, he'd realized his lustful feelings for one of his students and learned that his boss was using him as a puppet by withholding tenure.

He dragged his hands down his face. "I need to go for another run."

Looking at his watch, he groaned again. Three minutes until nine. His family law class was about to begin. Benjamin felt completely drained but pulled himself up anyway. He shrugged into his navy blazer, noticed it had taken the brunt of the chocolate shake incident, and tossed it back onto his chair. He snatched up his briefcase and hastily shoved fistfuls of papers through the zippered top then marched out of the office.

He was going to have to grin and bear it because, for the next four weeks, the dean of the law school owned him. So, like it or not, he was going to have to do what he could to ethically ensure Miss Miller's successful completion of family law.

His hopes of tenure depended on it.

His *career* depended on it.

Chapter Eight

Frankie

Frankie continued to ride the high of passing her family law midterm all the way to her assigned seat.

Earlier that morning, she'd shrieked and squealed so loudly that Todd had come thundering out of his room wielding a massive platform shoe. Upon hearing her fantastic news, he'd patted her head.

"We'll celebrate later," he'd groaned through a yawn and slogged back to bed.

The classroom buzzed uncharacteristically with chatter and excitement, most likely resulting from the receipt of exam results. She made her way to her seat, front and center, noticing there weren't as many students there as usual. She wondered if it had something to do with the exam scores. Perhaps some people took today off to celebrate. More likely, those who hadn't secured a passing grade made the decision not to show.

Settling in and glancing up to the front of the class, Frankie noticed that one person was most definitely missing. Professor Clark. He was always there when she arrived. It didn't matter if she was five or fifteen minutes early. He managed to beat her there every time. Mean mugging her as she walked to her seat. She typically felt it like a flame on her neck. And every class session his pointed glower made her tingle uneasily. But today . . . no glaring. No professor. Two minutes 'til class.

Hmm . . . curious.

Frankie skimmed through the highlighted sections of her notes.

Suddenly, the doors burst open, and Professor Clark strode into the lecture hall.

No, that wasn't quite accurate. He normally strode around with an air of contemptuous confidence. But not today. Today, he sort of scrambled to the lectern. His typically impeccable grooming not quite meeting its usual muster. He wasn't wearing a blazer, but instead only his white dress shirt with a few splatters of what looked like chocolate milk across his left shoulder. His top two buttons were undone, and his sleeves were rolled up to his elbows, revealing tanned, powerful forearms. His hair fell about his forehead like he had been running his hands through it all morning. And instead of his briefcase slung over a shoulder, he gripped it to his chest with both arms, a few pieces of paper sticking out of the unzipped top.

He looked caught off guard.

He looked stressed.

He looked like someone else completely.

As he did his best to settle at the head of the classroom, Frankie wondered what had happened to throw him off that morning. She bit her lip, fighting the prideful grin spreading across her face. Maybe he was upset that she'd passed. He clearly disliked her and would have rejoiced if she'd failed out. That was probably it. Ha! She sat up a little straighter and prepared herself. There was no doubt that he was going to come at her with all his might this session.

But she was ready.

"Bring it on, Professor Prick," she murmured under her breath.

Clark started class six minutes late. After offering a brief apology, he proceeded with his lecture. Soon, he began calling on students as he went. When he finally came to Frankie, she was shocked that the question he asked was a gimme—something so easily answered with a yes or no. After she successfully responded, he moved on to the next person. He didn't call on her again for the remainder of class.

Frankie felt torn. On the one hand, she should be relieved that she made it through another class without the wrath of Professor Clark coming down on her. But on the other hand, she almost felt snubbed. Excluded.

Once dismissed, she packed up her belongings and waited yet again for everyone to depart before she approached the abnormally disheveled Professor.

This is a bad idea. What am I doing? Just leave and count the class as a win.

"Excuse me, Professor Clark," Frankie said tentatively.

He sighed the sigh of an exasperated man. "Miss Miller?"

She didn't really know how to proceed. Did she ask about being skipped over in class? Did she ask if anything was wrong? Would that be crossing a boundary? She chewed on her lip for a moment, deciding what to do.

"Miss Miller, was there something you needed, or are you just trying to delay me for fun?" he asked, clenching his jaw, sapphire eyes aflame.

Her heart sped up, and she felt the heat climb from her neck to her cheeks. "Sorry, never mind."

He grunted and gave a curt nod before returning to his papers.

Frankie turned to scurry out of the classroom, but something stopped her. She faced him once again, now about ten feet away. "It's just . . ." She paused again. Why couldn't she get her mouth to work?

"What, *Francesca*?" Not quite a yell, her name boomed out

of his mouth, affecting Frankie low in her belly. Professor Clark must have recognized his dropping of typical formality because his eyes widened. He cleared his throat and neutralized his expression. "Apologies. What is it, Miss Miller?"

Taking a shallow breath, she was overcome with a wave of bravery. "I just wanted to make sure you were ok."

Professor Clark's mouth flopped open for a second before he remembered himself and snapped it shut. He stood a little taller and straightened his shoulders as he turned to face her. His hands settled on his hips, elbow jutting out to the sides. "I am sure I don't know what you are referring to. I'm perfectly fine."

Everything inside Frankie urged her to accept his words and leave. But something held her. He attempted to maintain his usual composure, but a flicker in his eyes belied his efforts.

"It's just that you're not quite yourself today. You showed up late and seemed a little stressed. Frazzled even. You also didn't call on me for anything other than one super easy question." She was undeterred by his scoff. "And you aren't dressed as you usually do. All signs point to there being something wrong, and I thought I would ask if you were all right."

His expression softened for a flickering instant before he donned his usual irritated-yet-bored professor mask.

"Your concern is unnecessary, Miss Miller. There is no need to play social worker with me. I assure you I can manage my own life perfectly fine without your *support*." His tone felt more brusque than usual, almost snide.

Frankie recoiled as though being punched. She was attempting to be a decent human, one who wasn't wrapped up in the celebration of making it through an easy class session. Her chosen career path had nothing to do with her concern. Though to him, all bleeding hearts probably looked alike.

"I wasn't trying to—"

"And worry not; since you found today's session so easy, I will be sure to increase the difficulty of my questions when you return from Thanksgiving break. Now, if you'll excuse me, I have another class starting shortly."

He gathered his briefcase and papers in his arms and brushed past her. As he strode from the room, he left Francesca wondering if she should have just kept her big mouth shut.

Chapter Nine

November, Seattle: Frankie

"Honey, you're running yourself ragged," Frankie's mother, Patty, sighed. "You've worked so hard all quarter. Isn't it time to come home and take a break? See your family?"

"I would love to, Mom, but I don't want to get behind," Francesca said, standing in the longest line that ever existed in a grocery store. She shifted her handbasket from one elbow to the other to balance its heft.

"What if you came home for a day or two? That wouldn't put you behind, would it?"

"You know as well as I do that if I came home at all, you would just convince me to stay until Sunday, and then where would I be?"

"You would be with people who love you. Eating my famous leftover turkey and stuffing sandwiches. Plus, I'm baking two pies this year so you have one to take back with you to school."

Frankie nearly drooled on herself. Her mom was an insanely good cook. And Thanksgiving was always the best meal of the year. Her ability to make a perfectly moist turkey was so award-worthy that Frankie didn't mind *using* the word moist to describe it. Her sausage and walnut stuffing was famous throughout the Leavenworth community. But the pumpkin pie. Her made-from-scratch pumpkin pie was like a dream. It was the essence of autumn baked into a buttery crust and topped with a cloud of perfectly sweetened whipped cream. She looked down at her selected groceries: a couple frozen lasagnas for one, bananas, and a case of off-brand diet cola.

Depressing.

"You. Are. Diabolical."

"I know, honey." Patty chuckled sweetly.

Maybe Frankie could go home tonight and leave first thing Friday morning. Then, she could have her pie and make it back to Seattle with plenty of time to study.

Unfortunately, Frankie knew herself, and that was most definitely not how things would play out. She'd wake up Friday morning and her mom would convince her to go Black Friday shopping in Wenatchee. *Just for a couple of hours,* she would say. *"Then you can head back to campus after lunch."* Lunch of leftover sandwiches would be amazing, and the toasty crackle in the fireplace and the smell of warm mulled wine on the stove would lull her to stay until Saturday morning. Then Lucy would take over Francesca's mom's task of waylaying her return. *"Let's go get a mani-pedi; you've worked so hard the last couple of months and deserve a relaxation day. My treat!"* she'd offer rather convincingly. And Francesca would agree. They would go out to eat after that and by the time they got back to her mom's house, Francesca would reason that it was safer to wait until morning to drive home. Especially because of the whiskey she'd have to warm up at the restaurant. By then, it would be Sunday, and she wouldn't have read a page.

Nope.

She had to stay strong.

"Mom, I love you and wish I could come home, but I think it's best for me to stick around here." She sighed longingly, setting her basket on the ground to give her arms a break. "I miss everyone, but it's the right call."

"Ok, sweetie." Patty crooned, "I'm proud of your dedication. It won't be the same without you, but you do what you have to do."

"Thanks for understanding."

"You're welcome, my little scholar."

"Plus, the next few weeks will fly by, and I'll be home for the wedding and winter break before you know it. But for now, I need to go."

"Don't study too hard."

"No promises. Love you."

"Love you too."

Frankie ended the call and shuffled her basket forward with her foot as the line progressed. Two customers stood between her and the cashier. First, a woman attempting to corral three kids as she feverishly stacked boxed stuffing, baking supplies, and a beastly turkey onto the conveyor belt. Behind her hunched a middle-aged man with strikingly similar contents to her own basket. He glanced back and down at Frankie's very un-Thanksgivingy selections and offered her a morose nod of solidarity.

I should have grabbed some wine.

Eyeing the rack full of impulse buys, she snagged a couple peppermint patties. Eating the minty treat from the freezer might give her the sensation of breathing in the icy air back home. It was a lackluster consolation prize, for sure, but she tossed a third into her basket anyway.

Finally, Frankie hit the front of the line. After taking her change back from the frazzled cashier, she smiled and made her way to the door. While struggling to retrieve her keys and balance the paper bag of food-for-singles in one arm, she dropped the fistful of bills and coins. She stopped, knelt down, and got plowed over by a set of legs wearing neatly polished dress shoes.

"What the fu—"

"Oh! I didn't see you down there," a smooth, deep voice crooned.

Frankie scoffed and collected her scattered items.

"Here, allow me to help you."

The man knelt, scooped up the frozen entrées, and deposited them into her paper bag.

His swift movements wafted his cologne, or shampoo, or whatever it was her way. He smelled divine, like warm spices and crisp autumn air. Everything Frankie loved about the season. She ventured a glance at the man's face then froze like a deer in headlights.

What were the fucking odds?

"Professor Clark!" she choked out as he placed a hand beneath her elbow to help her rise.

"Miss Miller." His face morphed into a pinched expression. "I should have guessed it was you."

"I see it's not enough for you to knock me down in class, now you're resorting to the same abuse in public." The bold sentiment rolled off her tongue before she could stop it. But instead of shame or regret, she felt liberated. She wasn't some meek, shy, easily embarrassed little coed. She was a thirty-two-year-old woman, damn it. And Professor Clark wasn't some almighty entity, especially outside of the classroom. He was a man. And Frankie had never been afraid of a man.

Well, not as an adult, anyway.

She suddenly felt very aware of his hand bracing her arm and shook out of his grasp.

Professor Clark cleared his throat and rubbed the back of his neck.

"Pardon," he mumbled.

"Really?" Frankie snorted. She dragged a slow appraisal from his polished shoes to his scowling face. "All that eloquence and fancy law degree, and that's the best apology you can come up with?"

"What?" he drawled incredulously. "Would you have me fall to my knees and beg for your forgiveness after what was very clearly an accident?"

"It'd be a delicious start," she purred. *Delicious?* Was she flirting with him now? The crotchety professor was absolutely beautiful, wearing an impeccably tailored outfit that showcased what Frankie assumed was a *re-donk-ulous* body, but he was also, without a doubt, unequivocally the last person she should be flirting with.

Stepping forward and well into her bubble, Clark scooped up one of Frankie's hands and held it close to his chest. The heat from his fingers bit through the white knit of her mittens while the icy chill of his sapphire eyes drilled into hers. Her heart raced, and she cursed the thumping organ along with her tongue as it unconsciously licked at her dry lips. The impulse to fling her panties at him was strong and she barely managed to keep them in place. Usually, the roles were reversed. She was always the one to play it cool while the menfolk fawned all over her, flexing like silly peacocks to get her attention.

It had to be the celibacy making her feel like a wanton ninny.

"Francesca," he said as he continued to look down at her. "Please accept my sincere apologies. To say I regret causing you to tumble beneath my oafish feet is the gravest of understatements. And though it may take weeks, years even, for you to forgive my callous response, I am willing to wait with bated breath for you to bestow mercy upon my wretched soul. I have never been so sorry." His words slid over her skin like hot honey, sweet and soothing.

It took a moment for his cocky smirk to break through the fog.

He was blatantly ridiculing her.

"Prick," she muttered, pulling from the warmth of his large hands and stepping back. The resulting chill had her hugging the bag of groceries tighter to herself.

"I've been called worse." Professor Clark shrugged.

Frankie clocked the large bouquet in his hand.

"Hot date?" She nodded toward the flowers.

"What? Oh no. I'm visiting my mother; it's her birthday." He shifted from one foot to the other, clearly done with the exchange.

"I'm surprised you have a mother." She was sure her eyes glinted as she smirked. "I would have guessed you were spawned in some fiery pit somewhere."

He recoiled, eyes widening momentarily, then schooled his expression.

"Right, well." He glanced at his watch. "I'd better get to it then."

"Fare thee well, professor."

"Miss Miller." He nodded then turned and strode out of the grocery store.

Chapter Ten

Benjamin

"The renowned Benjamin Matthew Clark, esquire, finally returns my call," Johnny crowed good-naturedly through the car speakers. "It's about damn time."

Benjamin grinned as Johnny's cheery tone eased his apprehension. The warm fondness for his friend resonated deep in his bones.

It was difficult for Benjamin to fathom that he hadn't spoken to his friend on the phone in years. Massive, pivotal life events came and went since he'd last heard Johnny's voice. Even the request to be his best man had come through as an out-of-the-blue text. Since then, Johnny had sent a barrage of messages and voicemails, insisting on hashing out the details of the coming nuptials. Unfortunately, the quarter had felt particularly challenging, what with a certain interloper front and center in his family law class, that he'd been preoccupied. But that wasn't all of it. If he was being honest, Benjamin was a little nervous about finally speaking with his friend.

"I know, I know. But you have my near undivided attention while I drive out of the city." He glanced at the estimated arrival time on his phone and cringed. "The next hour and forty-five minutes are all yours."

"All I need is five."

"Ha! That's what your fiancée said."

"Thanks," Johnny snickered. "I set myself up for that one,

didn't I?"

"Yep."

For whatever reason, Johnny still managed to bring out the playful side of Benjamin. Even after all that time apart, his stodgy, professional veneer quickly cracked and fell away. It was most likely because he trusted Johnny, and it felt natural—even after so much time had passed—to let his guard down. No matter what he said or did, Benjamin's friend accepted him completely.

"I wanted to make sure things were still a go for the wedding," Johnny continued.

"If by 'a go' you mean, will I be there? Then yes, that's a go," Benjamin reassured.

Johnny let out a breath as he said, "Good. It'll be great finally having you here."

"I wouldn't miss it."

"Be sure to pack enough winter clothes. We may or may not be doing some kind of outdoor activity. It all depends on if I can convince the old ball and chain to agree to it—ow!" Johnny cut off, chuckling and groaning. His voice sounded more echoey. "I've got you on speaker now so Lucy can say hi."

"Hi, Benji!" A melodic voice danced through the phone. He could hear the cheery grin in her words and smiled impulsively.

"Hello, Lucy."

"I'm excited to finally meet you. It'll be nice to put a face to the far-fetched stories my husband-to-be keeps telling me."

"She doesn't believe me about the scooter streaking incident," Johnny hollered at a volume unnecessary for speakerphone, reminding Benjamin of a middle-aged man and not the college kid who dared him to ride down University Way al la nude on a razor scooter.

"It's true," Benjamin offered.

"See? Told you," his friend gloated.

"I should never have doubted you," Lucy said.

"Since I won the bet, I'll be collecting my winnings this evening, sunshine," Johnny practically growled.

"Why wait 'til this evening?" her sultry giggle murmured through the phone.

Benjamin cringed as the sloppy sounds of kissing filled his car, along with groans and a little squeal.

"Still here!" he all but shouted, suppressing a gag.

"Sorry, brother. It's easy to get carried away with this one."

Lucy said her farewells and left the men to iron out their plans. "You got a room from the block we reserved at Wilhelm Haus Inn, right?"

"Yep, and I have my tux pressed and ready. Am I forgetting anything?" Benjamin flashed his blinker and pulled into the carpool lane just as a few snowflakes landed on his windshield. The lane choice was a futile one because it moved at the same pace as the rest of the gridlocked interstate.

"Doesn't sound like it."

"Great. How's the family?" Benjamin continued, not quite ready for the call to end. "Everyone excited for your big day?"

"My mom and Lucy have been a gale-level force to be reckoned with in planning this shindig. I've been staying out of the way and hoping they don't make me do anything too embarrassing."

Benjamin barked out a laugh. "Smart man."

"And my kid sister—you remember me talking about Frankie—anyways, she's great. Started her graduate program at our alma mater this fall."

"Is that so?" A prickle of recognition crept over his scalp. "What's she studying?"

"She wants to be a social worker, but she's taking family law, and apparently, her prof is a real dick."

Frankie.

Francesca . . . Miller.

Unbelievable.

How could he have missed that, not put it together? Sure, Miller is a common enough surname, and he had no idea she was going back to school. Really, he had no way of knowing. But now that he thought about it, the clues were there. In her thirties, that honey-colored hair, and amber eyes. She looked so much like her older brother now that he knew, and with that sharp little tongue to boot. He felt dense for not catching it. And then he felt a little queasy for lusting over the female version of Johnny. Or was that guilt from fantasizing about doing unspeakable things to his best friend's little sister?

Oh my god.

"You still there?" his friend called through the speaker.

"Yeah." He coughed to clear his throat and lowered his voice to the appropriate octave. "Yes, sorry, traffic distracted me for a minute."

"That's right, you're in your car. Shit. I'll let you go then so you can drive safely."

"Good plan." He needed the next hour and a half to work out the chaos in his mind. Or the next decade. "We can catch up in a few weeks."

"I plan on grilling you about how the practice has been going. I bet you've already made partner at your fancy-pants law firm. But don't tell me; I've got another bet going with Lucy."

"Yeah." Benjamin barely registered his friend's warm chuckle. "See you in a few."

"Bye."

The call disconnected, and a familiar '90s riff replaced the brief silence in the car. "Poison" by Bell Biv DeVoe thrummed through the speakers.

Francesca Miller—Frankie—had been stuck, rattling around inside his mind, consuming his thoughts and focus. For weeks his efforts had been focused on how to eject her from his class, never realizing her connection to one of the most important people in his life.

She was Johnny's family. Great. Not only did Benjamin have to stress over the cliché of being a professor who wants to nail his student, but he could also add a hefty scoop of guilt for lusting over his best friend's little sister.

He had to play this carefully or all manner of hell would rain down on him and the consequences would be catastrophic.

Losing out on tenure.

Continuing to be under the thumb of Dean McCaffery.

Straining the relationship between him and Johnny; his only true family.

He needed to censor his treatment of Miss Miller if he had any hope of maintaining his professional trajectory and personal relationships.

Easy enough.

What would prove trickier would be curtailing the lustful musings that slithered through his mind at an alarming rate. Miss Miller's image haunted his thoughts, and he struggled to dispel the curve of her body and that seductive lavender scent from his daydreams. And while he was determined to muscle through the next few weeks of class, their close proximity would extend through the wedding festivities.

Maintaining professionalism in a classroom was doable, but how would he fare off-campus with the alcohol, dancing, and formal wear?

He resolved to focus on the task at hand. Visiting his mother.

Benjamin's scowl deepened as he flicked on his wipers to sweep away the increasing flurry. He sneered at his GPS. The estimated arrival time to Tacoma jumped by another half hour. The trip would be a long walk for a short drink of water, but a necessary one nonetheless. He glanced at the two dozen pink roses in the passenger seat. Bailing wasn't an option, even though his mother wouldn't be holding him accountable. And by the looks of the gloomy layer of clouds above him, he and the rest of the commuters on Interstate 5 were in for a slippery drive.

Damned snow.

Chapter Eleven

Frankie

Later that evening, after too much studying and far more lasagna than any human should eat, Frankie rolled into bed and burritoed herself in for the night. While the apartment felt eerily quiet, the night-before-Thanksgiving-Day ruckus outside her window was in full swing. Hordes of excited students danced around the streets, rejoicing in the freedom of the long holiday weekend and the prospect of their mothers washing their accumulating mountain of laundry.

"Go home," she grumbled. "Don't you know it's"—she snatched up her phone and squinted at the time—"just after ten? What's happened to me? I used to be young." Flipping a forearm over her eyes, phone still clutched in her grip, Frankie sank back into her blankets to mourn her abandoned youth. She began to drift, only to be jolted awake by the buzz of a text message. Startled, she flung her cell halfway across the room.

She scurried out of bed, picked up the accidental projectile, and whispered an oath of thanks to her OtterBox case.

Sheriff Howards:

> Are you back tonight or waiting till tomorrow morning?

Shit, Clint.
She'd completely forgotten to tell him she wasn't going home for break. The realization that she'd be waiting another four

weeks to get laid sank in, and she considered throwing the phone again, this time on purpose.

Frankie:

> Change of plans. I need to stay here and study.

Sheriff Howards:

> Well, that's unfortunate. Anything I can say to change your mind?

Frankie:

> Sorry, but no. I need the extra time to work through this reading.

Sheriff Howards:

> Your teacher's a real ballbuster.

Frankie:

> You're telling me.

Sheriff Howards:

> Are we extending the rain check?

Frankie:

> Why not? :)

Sheriff Howards:

> All right then, princess. Get some rest.

Frankie's loins screamed in protest. She hadn't gotten any—not so much as a kiss—in eighty-one days. One hundred and six if she counted full-blown sex.

Damn her newfound scruples.

Flashes of rippling abs, veiny biceps, and a hard jawline flitted through her mind. Clint had a beautiful body, both in his uniform and half-bare in an unzipped wetsuit that exposed his dripping torso. Frankie swallowed thickly and reached for her side table drawer. Using her favorite vibrator, she conjured more images of the hunky sheriff. She imagined how the evening would go after he cashed in that drawn-out rain check. They'd probably be at his place, warm and cozy by a fire.

His large hands would skim the sides of her body. Playful, deep brown eyes gazing down at her as his lips poised to capture hers in a needy kiss. But he'd hold back, warm breath playing across her jaw, dancing to her ear. She'd slide her fingers through the loose blond curls that managed to give him that California surfer boy innocence. A true wolf in sheep's clothing.

Frankie trailed the tip of the sapphire blue toy around the perimeter of her panties, the slight hum muffled by the heavy blanket. She spread her knees and used her free hand to play with her nipples.

Clint would slide his palm down between her legs, exploring with his strong, calloused fingers as the first contact would pull a little gasp from the back of her throat. He'd whisper in her ear. What would he say? Would he say naughty things to her or just groan her name? Would he be into playing up his authoritative role? Insist on her calling him sheriff?

"Do you like this?"

She'd nod, unable to produce words.

He'd slide a finger, two fingers, into her before slowly pulling them out again.

Frankie feverishly increased her own motions, pinching and flicking as she pictured him hovering over her, his dark, coiffed hair pulling loose from its structured style.

A rumbling chuckle would reverberate up her neck as he

made his way to her lips. The five o'clock shadow that seemed to appear around ten every morning would deliciously abrade the sensitive skin at her jaw. He'd nibble gently on her plump lower lip, whispering filthy, commanding things, then remove his probing fingers and grip the head of his rigid arousal.

"*Is this what you want?*" he'd ask, a smirk in his deep voice.

Another nod.

"*Say it,*" he'd demand with a gruff voice at her collarbone, braced against her, ready to sink deep.

"*Yes.*"

"*Yes, what?*"

"*Yes, Professor Clark.*"

He'd let out a devious chuckle, his endless blue eyes connecting with hers, and push swiftly into her.

Frankie's orgasm engulfed her body from head to toe, back arching off the mattress. She pulsed hard against the vibrator, letting the sensation of fullness and release dance across her sensitive skin. The tension slowly retreated as her senses returned, and her breath gently returned to a normal rhythm. Only then did she register where her fantasy had swept her, ending with a completely different man than it had started.

"Shit," she murmured violently into her pillow.

Chapter Twelve

The day of the family law final exam,
Seattle: Frankie

Thanksgiving break came and went along with the next few weeks. Before she knew it, Frankie was sitting in another large auditorium, waiting breathlessly for her final exam to begin. Everyone was spread out in the usual fashion. Despite her intense preparation and extra sessions with her tutor, she remained nervous. The final determined two-thirds of her grade. If she screwed up, the past twelve weeks of toil and anxiety would have been for nothing.

The ensuing exam was her last school-related task before the break. Her other two classes required final papers, which she found surprisingly easy to write. After completing Clark's hellish course, the rest of her program would be a breeze. Had she learned a lot about family law? Absolutely. But she would be happy to move on to less intense class sessions and to say buh-bye to the Socratic method for good.

Eventually, the proctor walked to the front of the class. "If you are here for Professor Clark's family law final, you are in the right place. If not, please, find an exit." She paused. The silence was unnerving, but no one rose. "Good. You have three hours to complete the exam. Good luck. Your time starts now."

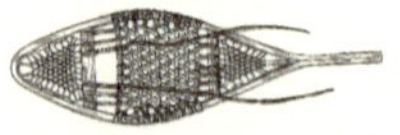

"Frankie, you home?" Todd's sing-song voice coaxed her awake.

"In here." She groaned, still half in a sleepy trance. After the final, she'd stumbled back to the apartment, dazed and exhausted, and passed out the moment she hit her bed.

Footsteps advanced down the short hall and to Frankie's open door. "It's so dark in here," Todd said, flipping the switch just inside the bedroom. She hissed as the flood of light slapped her across the face.

"Yeesh," he yelped, eyeing the fatigued mess lying on a drool-soaked pillow. He quickly flicked off the light, chuckling. "I see why you wanted it dark."

"Bite me." Her words scratched from her throat but held a considerable amount of affection for her sassy roommate even after he flipped the switch and blinded her again.

"Why are you wearing your shoes and coat in bed?" Todd laughed. Frankie couldn't have missed the judgment in his voice even if she'd still been sound asleep.

"I just laid down for a second and must have passed out." She sat up and took her hat off. Sweat lacquered her hair to her head. The distinct sensation of being boiled alive in wintery layers swept over her.

"How was the final?"

"I think it went well . . .?"

"That's . . . good?" He mimicked her ambiguous tone.

"Let's just say I'm happy it's behind me. Now all I have to do is sit and wait." Frankie peeled off her damp coat, silently cursing the way it trapped body heat so efficiently. "I need a shower."

"Now that you're done for the quarter, and since you just

had a four-hour power nap, you have zero excuses," Todd stated.

"To shower?"

"To come to the Tackle Boxx and watch me perform." He cringed. "And, yes, shower."

"I don't know. I am so wiped and—"

"Tut tut tut," he scolded her, holding up a hand to demand she stop. "You haven't come to a single one of my shows since you've been in town. I'm beginning to think you didn't *love* my performance like you claimed when you and Lucy drove over last Christmas. You don't want to hurt my poor little feelings, do you?"

"I'd be a monster if I said no now, wouldn't I?"

"Of the worst variety." His eyes glimmered with his mischievous grin.

"Ok, ok. I'd be happy to watch you perform." She attempted to run her fingers through her hair and frowned. "But, again, shower first."

"Fabulous. You have plenty of time, I don't go on 'til ten."

Frankie smiled and nodded. Climbing off the bed, she headed to the bathroom to wash off the nap sweat. She hummed as she went, feeling a little high after the stressful morning and impromptu four hours of sleep.

"What time do you want to leave tomorrow?" she called down the short hallway to her roommate. She and Todd had planned to carpool to Leavenworth for Johnny and Lucy's wedding.

"I refuse to do anything before noon," he called back.

"Twelve-fifteen it is, then."

A middle finger popped around Todd's door frame, and Frankie snickered as she moseyed into the bathroom. The water took a while to warm up, and she perched on the edge of the tub to wait until it was ready to climb in. Thoughts about winter break, the wedding, and the last quarter skated through her mind until it snagged on an unwelcome image.

Professor Clark.

Now *there* was a man she'd be glad to never see again. He made it perfectly clear that he didn't want her in his precious family law class and did what he could to intimidate her into dropping the course. But little did he know, Frankie was too stubborn to bow out and make life easier for him. Eventually, she was able to match her professor, question for question. Yet he remained stiff and unyielding like he couldn't accept her success. He was cold and grumpy and intimidated the hell out of her in that classroom.

She assumed it would take a while for him to slip from her thoughts, but she was determined to make it happen. By the start of the winter quarter, Frankie would return clearheaded and prepared to focus on the new set of classes. Professor Clark and his imposing nature would be a distant memory.

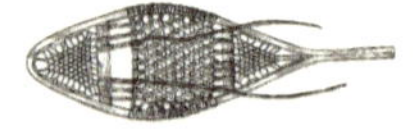

Climbing from her rideshare just outside the Tackle Boxx, Frankie reveled in the damp winter air slipping over her cheeks. The driver had the heat cranked all the way up, treating Frankie like she must be an icicle despite her knee-length red dress, tights, and black peacoat. He couldn't hear her requests to lower the temp over the loud thump of EDM blasting from his speakers. All that was missing from the "Prius Rave" were glowsticks and giant cans of energy drinks.

Frankie shut the back door and waved at the driver, who threw up a peace sign and darted seamlessly into traffic. She chuckled and dug into her purse to find her ID and cash for the cover. She scurried, head down, toward the front door—

—and slammed into a brick wall.

Frankie tumbled to the ground, landing hard on one hip, with feet sprawled out in front of her. Blessedly, she hadn't flashed anyone nearby because her flowy skirt stayed low around her thighs. Small miracles. The biting chill called attention to her point of impact. She rubbed her sore rump as a dull throb made itself known.

That's when a hand lowered into her field of view.

"This old trick again, Miss Miller?" A throaty chuckle curled around her like a warm blanket.

Frankie snapped her head up and caught a glimpse of absolute male perfection smirking down at her.

"Ah, Professor Clark." She slapped his hand away and ambled to her feet. "Do you take pleasure in mowing unassuming students down or are you really that unaware of your abnormal size?"

"It would seem you are my only victim," he assured—somewhat playfully?—with a hand placed across his heart. His blue eyes, almost black under the flickering streetlamp, perused her from head to toe until he pulled off his glasses and needlessly buffed them.

Frankie beamed, knowing full well how good she looked. If he was searching for judgmental satisfaction, he would find none of it there.

"I'm not sure if I should be flattered or offended."

"The interpretation is entirely up to you." When Frankie rolled her eyes—she so didn't have the strength to deal with his particular brand of banter just then—he switched directions. "Actually, there was something I wanted to discuss with you—"

"Sorry, teach." Frankie brushed past Professor Clark. She

marched toward the Tackle Boxx, its bright neon sign glowing like a lifesaving beacon. She threw a brief glance over her shoulder, hoping to catch the last scowl of his that she'd ever have to see. "But I'm not yours to torment anymore. Besides, I have someone waiting on me."

Chapter Thirteen

Saturday, 6 days until the wedding, Leavenworth: Frankie

*B*rrring. Brrring. Brrring.

Frankie sat bolt upright, gasping for air as the hotel room phone ripped her from a restorative slumber. She fumbled in the darkness for the offending relic, desperate to put an end to its obnoxiously shrill ring.

"What?" she rasped grumpily into the receiver.

"*Wakey, wakey, eggs and bakey*," Jonathan hollered in the usual upbeat tenor he reserved for irritating his little sister.

Frankie grunted in response to his cheery tone.

"It's four-thirty in the afternoon," he chuckled. "What are you doing asleep? The sun's bright as hell."

"They're called blackout curtains, my friend. And I'm still catching up from lack of sleep due to immense educational stress." She flipped on the bedside lamp and sat up, squinting at the flood of light.

"Educational stress," he mocked. "Aren't you on break for the rest of the month?"

"Yes, but the damage has already been done."

"Aw, poor baby," Jonathan teased pitifully. "Do you need your big bad brother to beat up the mean old professor?"

Frankie snorted. "You're the last person I'd call to kick someone's ass. But is your fiancée free? I'm sure she could handle the prick."

The laugh through her phone was so booming that Frankie had to pull it away to save her eardrums. "Any man who tussles with her would regret it."

"No doubt. Why didn't you call me on my cell? How'd you even know I was here?" Leavenworth was a small town, but she hadn't gone anywhere yet. Not even to grab a snack. And she knew for a fact that Todd was getting a little beauty rest before dinner too.

"I tried. Twice. It went to voicemail. Gunther ratted you out. I asked him to send me a text with your room number once you checked in."

Damn you, Gunther.

She should have known the jolly front desk manager at the Wilhelm Haus Inn was a snitch. His cheer seemed a little too manufactured.

"Ever the protective big brother." Frankie rolled her eyes, but really, the concern always comforted her.

"I gotta look out for the ladies in my life. It's my job to keep you all safe." From any other man, the sentiment would have been condescending, but Jonathan never meant it as such. He didn't have a macho-alpha-male bone in his body, but he was a natural-born protector when it came to anyone he loved. No matter what, Jon was always there in her corner, ready to throw down. Metaphorically of course. She never could recall a time when he'd ever been in a fistfight. He might dad-joke someone to death, but that was the extent of his attempted assaults.

"How are Lucy and Mom?" Frankie asked through a big yawn.

"A little stressed but managing. They've both been working so hard to make sure everything's all planned out. It doesn't help that Aunt Agnes and the twins are staying with Mom. Be glad you decided to stay at the inn. There's already *plenty* of hard-headed energy at the house without you there too.”

“Hey,” she said, trying to sound offended but knew full well he was right. Their mom and aunt butted heads like the alphas they were. Frankie getting involved would just add fuel to the flames. “How are you faring?”

“Fine. I’m trying to help where I can, but it proves safer to stay the hell out of their way, ya know?”

Francesca did know. “Smart man.”

“It took a little time, but I eventually got there.”

“Don’t take it too hard, most guys never grow up. Take Zac, for example . . . Man-child all the way. You’re among the rare specimens that actually managed to claw their way out of adolescence.”

Jonathan let out a little snort. “Awe, thanks, sis. Speaking of the devil, he seems pretty excited to see you. Is there something going on there that you’re not telling me?”

Zac Hartford. Now, *there* was a guy Frankie wouldn’t touch even with her enemies’ genitals. The perpetual playboy would happily bang anything that moves. And did. She wasn’t judging. What happens between two consenting adults is their business. Frankie was all about sex positivity, but her brother’s friend since elementary school was a little too active for her tastes. To top it off, they’d worked together at her family’s guiding company, which meant any funny business would have elevated an ill-advised decision to a downright bad idea. Countless times, he’d tried to initiate an encounter with Frankie, and every time, he’d struck out. No doubt he’d take another swing—or two—during the wedding festivities and find himself slinking away from the plate yet again.

“Absolutely not. There’s not enough penicillin in the world.”

“I feel compelled to say ‘ouch’ on his behalf,” Jonathan said through a giddy chuckle. "What are you up to now?"

"Getting ready," she lied as she snuggled back under the covers and wondered if she could fit a king-sized bed in her tiny room back in Seattle. "Just putting the finishing touches on before the party."

"Bullshit. I literally woke you up five minutes ago, remember? I bet twenty bucks you're wrapped in a robe and a comforter and about to fall back to sleep."

"Wrong," she lied again, doubling down. "As usual."

"Cool, then I have some free time before dinner. Meet me at The Rooftop in a half hour for a beer so we can catch up." Jonathan challenged his sister, knowing full well she needed every minute of the next two hours to get ready. An awkward ten seconds of silence crept by before Frankie finally caved.

"Fine. You win. I'm a cozy burrito with drool on my face, ok?" She groaned, finally accepting the end of her nap. "I'm just about to hop in the shower."

"I'll take my twenty bucks in small bills, thank you."

"I'll bring you a bag of nickels."

Jonathan let out a hearty laugh that reminded Frankie of their father's. Her heart pinched.

"It's good to have you back home, sis."

"I'm glad to be home. See you guys in a couple hours. Love you."

"Love you too. Don't be late. Bye."

"Bye." Frankie deposited the receiver back in its cradle. She rolled over, snuggled further under the covers, and shut her eyes before letting out a long, groaning sigh. She didn't want to let her brother down. Or her soon-to-be sister, Lucy. Or her mom. They were all working so hard on the wedding while she moved to Seattle for school and hadn't helped with a damned thing. The least she could do was be ready and on time.

It took all the mental and physical strength she could muster for Frankie to flip the covers off and let her feet touch the ground. The comforter seemed to beckon and whisper sweet nothings to entice her to stay. *I'm warm. I'm snuggly. I'm a cozy sleep tortilla.* Frankie jumped off the bed to distance herself from temptation and begrudgingly stomped to the bathroom. Hopefully, a warm shower would snap her into party mode.

An hour later, as she finished blow-drying her hair, her phone buzzed. She walked to the nightstand and picked it up.

Jonathan:

> Wake up! It's officially T-minus one hour until you are supposed to be here!

She took a quick photo of herself, complete with her tongue sticking out and middle finger brandished, to show off her freshly dried hair.

Frankie:

> Bite me! Now leave me alone, you big bully.

She tossed the phone into the mass of comforter and returned to the bathroom to continue primping. Soon, with a fresh face of carefully applied makeup and hair curled into Hollywood waves, Francesca shimmied into the hunter-green wrap dress she'd chosen for the night. Tugging the sleeves into place, she realized she filled the outfit more than when she'd bought it in August. The switch from rafting and climbing forty-plus hours per week to studying all the damn time added a little fluff to her typically firm form. Taking in the near-overflowing bust and rounder hips, she grinned, not minding the added curves one bit.

Gold pumps, dangly earrings, and a clutch completed the ensemble. She dug through the purse she'd used daily for the past few years and pulled out the necessities that would fit into the shiny little handbag: lip balm, lip gloss, ID, cash, aspirin, and her hotel room key card.

Where is my phone?

She dug through the covers to find it. Eventually, she picked up the fluffy white comforter and shook it until her phone landed with a thud on the ground.

She winced. "OtterBox two, gravity zero."

A glance at her phone showed she had a missed call and a text message from an unknown number.

Unknown:

> Francesca. It's Professor Clark. We should probably talk. Soon.

> It's rather important.

> Please, Francesca.

Whaaaaaaat?

Frankie couldn't think for a moment. Static crackled in her skull, mimicking the sensation of a head stuffed with Pop Rocks. So many questions buzzed together in a jumble of chaos.

Why the hell is Professor Clark calling and texting me?

Was whatever he needed to talk to me about last night outside the Tackle Boxx really that important?

Is it about my exam?

Isn't it against the university's policy to talk to me about my exam before it's graded?

How did he get my freaking number?

She nearly dropped her phone again as her fifteen-minute warning alarm chimed aggressively. She had to get ahold of herself, and the only way to do that was to silence her phone and ignore the persistent professor until after the party. Stuffing it in her purse, she blew out a breath, feeling grateful that a full bar awaited her. She shrugged into her cream wool coat and left her hotel room. Whatever Professor Prick needed was going to have to wait.

Chapter Fourteen

Benjamin

Benjamin was running late and it grated his nerves. He scrambled around the hotel room to collect his wallet, key card, and navy blue peacoat. Phone in hand, he scowled down at the silent device and cursed a certain someone for ignoring his attempts at contact. He'd wanted to give her the heads-up. Informing Miss Miller of his presence ahead of time, instead of sauntering into the Bella Notte banquet room unannounced, seemed like the merciful thing to do. He desperately wanted to avoid drama; he owed Johnny that much.

Despite his friend's marriage being doomed from the get-go, he could at least play along and do his part to ensure a happy wedding week.

But a certain stubborn little sister refused to respond, which threw a rather imposing wrench into his plan. Francesca was the wild card in this whole affair, and while he doubted she'd do anything to intentionally disrupt the nuptials, he wasn't so confident in her ability to play nice. He scolded himself for his behavior in class. Had he behaved like . . . well . . . an impartial adult, he wouldn't have found himself in the current state.

It was too late for all of that, and while he could play *shoulda, coulda, woulda* until the end of time, the useless musings would fix nothing. All that remained was damage control.

If only Miss Miller would answer the blasted phone.

Benjamin reached up to run a hand through his hair but

remembered it was pomaded into place, and he didn't feel like arriving looking disheveled. It was bad enough that he hadn't shaved. Snoqualmie Pass was more congested than he'd planned and ate up an extra half hour of his time on the trip over. Fortunately, he doubted his friend would mind the stubble; Benjamin just preferred a certain level of grooming, and going into a potentially tenuous situation less than immaculate left him feeling half-cocked.

Agitation pricked over his already tense shoulders. He needed to calm down, and fast. The cold air would mellow him out—maybe a scotch as well.

He pulled the door shut behind him and adjusted the tan cashmere scarf looped around his neck. The chill swirled around, managing to locate every square centimeter of exposed skin and tunnel into his bloodstream. Gritting his teeth to distract from the sting of winter, he glanced down at his phone.

Still no response, not that he expected one.

In a final attempt, before catching her off guard at the restaurant, he tapped out another message. He took a few assured strides from his door and propelled squarely into some barrier he hadn't noticed.

"*Oof.*" He grunted.

His hard chest plowed into a petite form. She made a breathy gasp, and he flung his arms around her, letting his phone fly from his hands. The scent of lavender and eucalyptus struck him first, followed quickly by the sensation of warm, soft curves pressing against his tense body. Wisps of silky hair stuck to his stubble as he inhaled the heady fragrance before a tickle of recognition stopped him cold.

"What the fucking fuck?" came the sputtering words from the woman in his stabilizing embrace.

No. Oh no, oh no. It can't be.

He looked down into amber eyes, rimmed by impossibly thick lashes, wide with shock.

It was.

"Jesus, Clark!" Miss Miller spat. She reached up and braced her hands against his chest, pushing him away like he'd tried to grope her against her will.

He supposed he accidentally, sort of did. His cheeks flushed—from the cold, certainly not embarrassment.

"Miss Miller," he said, straightening his black-rimmed glasses and clearing his throat with what he hoped passed for a friendly chuckle. "It appears we are doomed to repeat history."

"What the hell are you doing here?!" Her shock morphed into fury. "Are you following me? Did you come all the way to Leavenworth to torment me?"

Her outrage was almost cute. Scratch that, no. Not cute. Benjamin tried to open his mouth and speak, but the whirlwind of her ire stopped him cold.

"What? Did I fail the final and you decided it would be a super fun Christmas present to see the look on my face when you told me in person?" She took a tentative step back. He couldn't blame her; from her vantage point, he had followed her home for the holidays without her ever divulging where she lived. In the hotel room directly adjacent to hers, no less.

"I can explain," Benjamin began, holding up both hands.

"You'd better, pal." She fumbled in her little golden purse and pulled out her phone. "You've got three and a half seconds to state your case before I call the cops. And there's not much for them to do around here, so they'll love fucking up a creepy, pretty-boy stalker like you." She took another step back, eyes feral.

"I'm here for your brother's wedding," he blurted, not daring to move for fear of bloodshed.

"What?"

"Johnny and I went to school together." He let out the breath he'd been holding as she lowered her phone from her ear. "At NWU. I'm Benjamin, er . . . Benji."

"His friend Benji is a lawyer, *not* a professor." Her face dripped with skepticism.

"I was a divorce attorney but switched to teaching a few years ago." He glanced around for his fallen phone. "Here, let me show you proof." He knelt, flinching at the crack that webbed down the center of his screen. Serves him right for not putting it in a case. He scrolled through his photos and pulled up a shot of the two men—much younger versions, of course—standing with arms flung over each other's shoulders. He flipped the phone around and held it so she could see.

Her mouth gaped.

"Well, I'll be fucked down the road and halfway 'til Tuesday." She looked back up at Benjamin. Shock once again beginning to morph into something more volatile. "Wait. Was this some sick joke between you and Jon?" She stepped forward, jabbing a pointy finger against his chest. The lingering daylight caught the gold of her earrings, glimmering in a way that matched the wrath flashing in her amber eyes. This fiery version of Miss Miller was rather intriguing, and Benjamin felt a peculiar ripple of curiosity at the back of his brain. The outlandish urge to get a closer look at her gilded gaze nagged momentarily, until he shook the notion away.

"No, no," he urged. "Of course not. I only just put the pieces together during Thanksgiving break when he and I spoke on the phone. But he doesn't know who we are to each other."

"Who we are to each other?" she sneered. "You mean how you tormented me for twelve weeks? Did your best to make me feel unwelcome and . . . and stupid twice a week for an entire quarter?"

Benjamin cringed. He had done that, hadn't he? But that was

before he knew who she was, which didn't really seem to make it any better.

"Perhaps I was overly harsh," he began but quickly rerouted as her nostrils began to flare. "All right, all right, I was horrid. But you held your own. You did surprisingly well considering your experiential shortcomings."

She huffed and turned away, marching through the external hallway and down the steps at the end of the building.

He had to fix this. For Johnny. Benjamin had been a terrible friend for so many years, promising to come out and visit, not being there when Johnny's first wife, Cynthia, died nor when his father passed before that. It was his mission to do everything in his power to make things right. Carrying on a needless rivalry with his sister wouldn't help matters. He jogged after the angry woman.

"Wait, Miss Miller." She dismissed him with a swat over her shoulder and continued along the snow-plowed sidewalk. "Francesca. Please." He didn't know why she halted her steps, but he assumed it was the desperation in his voice. She turned and crossed her arms.

Oh wow, she was stunning. Under the residual twilight of the setting sun, her hair glistened like silk and flowed like rich honey in lustrous waves. The pink on her cheeks and scrunch of her nose proclaimed her anger. It wasn't that he hadn't found her attractive in his classroom, but with rage pulsing off her, she seemed particularly powerful.

Her ferocity stirred something in his chest. Something he hadn't felt in some time. Something that bordered on carnal.

Woah, maybe I should unpack that later.

She had every right to be pissed at him. He was a little pissed at himself. Benjamin's hands itched to fix the mess he'd made.

"I'm waiting." She tapped her foot. Flashes of cherry red toenails peeked out from the keyhole at the tip of her golden shoes.

The same red that shone on her manicured fingertips. Would they also match the lingerie she wore beneath?

Focus, man.

"Look. I was awful. A monster. My behavior was completely reprehensible." He held out his hand, palms up in supplication. "But we must suppress whatever disdain we hold for one another for your brother's sake. This is his wedding. We need to ensure it goes well instead of selfishly ruining it because of our precarious history."

She chewed on the inside of her cheek rather aggressively but released her arms and nodded.

"Fine. Under two conditions." She pulled her coat snuggly around her waist.

"Name them."

"First," she said as she held up a finger. "Stop calling me Miss Miller. I'm not your student anymore, and I sure as shit won't be calling you Professor Clark ever again. You can call me Frankie."

"Of course, Francesca." he crooned, struggling to quell a grin.

She rolled her eyes. "Close enough. Number two." She held up a second finger. "Keep your distance. I know there will be times when we have to interact, but I want them kept to a minimum. We are not friends. We are not colleagues. We are acquaintances who tolerate each other *at best*."

"Your terms are agreeable."

Francesca nodded and began to turn toward the restaurant.

"One clarifying question," he braved.

"What?" She glared over her shoulder. A puff of condensation released from her glossy, parted lips. Her frustration was palpable, and for some reason, he wanted nothing more than to continue egging her on just to see what might happen.

That wasn't right.

He wanted even more to ensure his friend's happiness as best he could, especially after all he'd done for Benajmin.

"What are we going to tell Johnny?"

"The truth. I don't lie to my family. But I will downplay how dickish you really were. I would hate for my brother to stain his rented tux with your bloody nose."

Benjamin's pulse spiked at her smirk as she turned and marched away.

Chapter Fifteen

Frankie

"A-ma-zing," Frankie whistled as she walked into the banquet hall at Bella Notte, the only Italian restaurant in downtown Leavenworth. Strings of white lights twinkled between the rustic beams holding up the low ceiling. Iridescent white balloons clustered around the perimeter of the room, camouflaging the bulk of the dark, outdated wood paneling. Mellow jazz drifted from speakers in all four corners at a volume that couldn't be more pleasant. To one side stood a long table covered end to end in food-warming trays. The waft of Parmesan cheese and garlic permeated the room. The scent was so delicious that Frankie half expected a cartoon hand made of mist to escape a lid and lure her over to the fettuccine Alfredo.

The transformation from musty restaurant basement to elegant banquet setting was so remarkable that Frankie didn't protest—or notice at all—when Benjamin helped her remove her coat.

She scanned the crowd and laid eyes on Jonathan first. He stood toward the middle of the room, arm securely wrapped around Lucy's shoulders, beaming like a fool in love.

"Think we should go say hello?" The velvety voice tickled her neck and she shuddered before she realized it was Benjamin conferring with her like they were some kind of co-conspirators.

Instead of responding, she marched over to her brother and soon-to-be sister-in-law. Lucy spotted her first and squealed with delight. She detangled herself from her fiancée and practically skipped over to wrap Frankie in a disproportionately tight hug. How that woman could squeeze so tightly was a mystery.

"I'm so happy you're here," she gushed, gliding her hand along the sleek waves framing Frankie's face. "You look beautiful. Now that I think about it, I don't think I've ever seen you all gussied up before."

"Probably not. Jeans with a sweater is about as fancy as I usually get."

Lucy smiled warmly and flitted her eyes back and forth between Frankie and whoever stood just behind her. The bride-to-be leaned in a little, wiggled her eyebrows, and asked, "Aren't you going to introduce me to your hunky date?"

Frankie's eyes widened in alarm before she steadied her features. "He's not my date. This is—"

"Benji!" Jonathan bellowed. He rushed over and wrapped his arms around his friend.

"*This* is Benji?" Lucy leaned over and murmured behind her hand, "What a dish?"

"I'm sorry you mean *dick*, right?"

Lucy peeled her gaze away from the two men embracing and produced a cheeky grin. "Is there history I'm unaware of? Jonathan said you two hadn't met."

"Oh, we've met all right," she snorted. In a louder voice, she announced, "Lucy, allow me to introduce you to Professor Benjamin Clark. He happens to teach family law at Northwest Washington University."

"No, that's not right. He's a divorce attorney in Seattle," Jonathan corrected then paused and turned a curious expression to his friend. "Is . . . is that true?"

Frankie thought she spotted a blush flash up Benjamin's stubbled face, but it dissipated just as abruptly.

"Yes, it is. I left the practice a few years back and started lecturing full time." He shifted on his feet and gestured to the scowling blonde at his left. "Francesca was one of my students this last quarter."

Lucy and Jonathan's jaws dropped.

"Shut up. You're Professor Prick?" Lucy didn't even try to contain her shock. Frankie elbowed her in the ribs.

"It appears I'm one and the same, and you must be Lucy." Benjamin held out his hand and she took it with hesitation. After a moment, she tightened her grip and intensified her eye contact.

"You'd better behave this week, buster," she warned then flashed a radiant smile.

Jonathan clapped Benjamin firmly on the back. "Now that I know who Frankie was bitching about, I can only assume she exaggerated a few things."

"Hey!" Frankie complained. "Whose side are you on anyway?"

"My fealty is strictly reserved for my beautiful bride." He stepped past Benjamin, wrapped his arms around Lucy's waist and lifted her so they faced one another eye to eye. He abandoned all decorum and kissed her passionately as though no one else was around.

"That went better than I'd expected," Benjamin murmured closer to Frankie's ear than she'd liked. The cloying scent of warm cinnamon and autumn leaves surrounded her as his hot breath tickled her neck. She stepped away, adding some distance between herself and the aromatically delicious man.

"For you, perhaps. But the night's still young." She eyed him over her shoulder. "I'd watch your back."

His endless blue eyes held hers and he arched a thick brow as though to say *let the games begin.*

"Let's eat. Everyone, help yourselves and sit wherever you'd like," Jonathan called out, disrupting the tingly staring contest and pulling Frankie back to the event. "After a bit, we'll talk game plan."

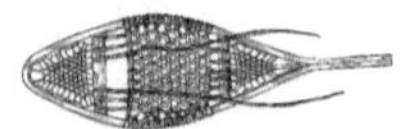

With a belly full of rich, garlicky goodness as well as a heaping scoop of dread, Frankie peered down at the paper in front of her. Jon and Lucy had created an itinerary for the next week, complete with everyone's responsibilities and tasks. Nothing on the list was overly taxing (perhaps the snowshoeing would be physically so, but she lived for that kind of challenge), yet seeing her name partnered with the best man washed her in trepidation.

The plan was for Benjamin to keep his distance, but how was that possible when she was the maid of honor and he was her groom's side equivalent?

"The schedule may seem a bit dense," Lucy continued, "but it's all meant to be fun."

"Is everything mandatory?" Todd asked. It was well known that Lucy's best friend and the couple's officiant was not a nature fan. "Specifically, the snowshoeing?"

"Yes, Todd." Lucy placed her hands on her hips and narrowed her eyes at her impeccably dressed friend. "If I have to clomp through hell frozen over, then so do you. I'll need all the emotional support I can get."

Frankie snorted into her mulled wine. The excursion must have been her brother's idea because Lucy, who hated the snow, was a fair-weather adventurer all the way. Snowshoeing was a special activity that Jon and Frankie used to do with their dad and likely Jon had insisted on going as a way to honor the beloved man.

Lucy would never say no to something so important and being the bride, she'd decided that the rest of them couldn't either.

Frankie's phone buzzed in her lap.

Sheriff Howards:

> Hey, princess! What are you up to after Jonathan and Lucy's dinner?

Oh, Clint. She didn't have the energy to deal with one more bullet point on her itinerary. No matter how chiseled and sexy that bullet point may be.

"Princess, huh?"

Frankie clutched the phone to her chest and scowled at the raven-haired pain in her ass sitting directly to her left. How—or why—Benjamin ended up sitting beside her through dinner was a mystery.

"This is private. *Shoo.*"

"Why isn't your boyfriend here making merry with the rest of your friends and family?" Benjamin whispered.

"Clint's not my boyfriend, he's just—" She clamped her mouth closed. *Shut up, Frankie. You don't owe him an explanation for anything.*

"Oh." Benjamin cleared his throat and sat up straight. A flicker of something skittered across his features before he set his expression to his recent default: mild amusement. "He's just a 'friend' right? Someone to scratch an itch, perhaps?"

His quiet, suggestive drawl heated her insides. For the briefest of moments, she felt embarrassed. Then the anger took over.

"Who do you think you are?" Her voice was harsh yet low so as not to disrupt the . . . announcement? Meeting? Whatever the hell you'd call it. But the lava in her chest was gradually rising to the surface, and she struggled to manage her volume. "You agreed to give me some distance, and yet here you are," she gestured, "glued to my side and reading my texts over my shoulder."

"Uh, Francesca—" he tried to interject.

"*No*," she continued, allowing the wrath to take hold. "My life, my family, my messages are not your business. So, butt the fuck out, Clark."

"*Francesca Miller*," a deeply maternal voice scolded. No matter how old she got, her mother's "I mean business" voice always managed to stop her in her tracks.

The room went silent except for a few snickers and the gentle clinking of flatware. Frankie could feel her cheeks flush red. Everyone stared at her and Benjamin with curiosity.

"Should we separate those two?" Lucy asked Jonathan, who chuckled behind his hand.

"Nah, I like that there's someone giving her grief in my place. It's comforting."

"Apologies," Benjamin began. "The disruption is my fault. Please continue, Lucy."

Frankie mouthed a silent *sorry* to her mother, who pursed her lips, though it almost looked like the older woman was stifling a giggle.

Great, yet another person enjoying my misery.

Lucy nodded and wrapped up her final thoughts. Frankie suddenly felt exhausted. What should have been a fun, enjoyable week was quickly turning out to be nearly as draining as her family law class. Ironically, she'd been stoked to leave Seattle and get some space from the dreaded Professor Clark, but what she got instead was more face time with him than she could tolerate. She needed another glass of spiced wine and the comfort of her cozy bed.

She flipped over her phone, angling it away from certain prying eyes, and responded to Clint.

Frankie:

I'm sorry, but I'm exhausted from the drive and have an early start tomorrow. I'd better conserve my energy for snowshoeing with the group.

How about tomorrow evening? Dinner?

Sheriff Howards:

Sure, sounds good.

Chapter Sixteen

Sunday, 5 days until the wedding, Stevens Pass: Benjamin

Benjamin sat in the back of Johnny's Subaru strapping snowshoes to his winter boots. He triple-checked the buckles to ensure a snug fit and prayed they would stay on during this god-forsaken "adventure."

He peered out through the open hatchback, taking in the trailhead and excited hikers bustling about. The conditions were perfect for the excursion, according to his best friend anyway. Thick cloud cover, paired with the utter lack of wind, kept the temperature at Stevens Pass at a *balmy* fourteen degrees. The night before, the skies had opened wide and dumped a fresh twelve inches of powder along the Pass—which Johnny assured him would make the late morning trek more fun.

Benjamin had to admit the view was spectacular. Blankets of snow on the surrounding peaks melded with the dense cloud cover, creating the feeling of being under a wintery dome. The sensation should have been suffocating, yet Benjamin found the illusion of confinement rather cozy. The base layer and puffer jacket he'd borrowed from his friend no doubt helped matters since the chill had yet to reach his skin.

Like many western Washingtonians, Benjamin was not a fan of snow. Aside from preferring milder conditions in general, dealing with anxious and unskilled sixvers on the notoriously steep Seattle hills raised his blood pressure. The second a couple flakes drifted into view, the commute around the city went to hell. Simple drives could quickly become treacherous.

After a final check that his snowshoes were secure, Benjamin hopped from the back of the SUV. He baby-stepped carefully back and pulled the hatch shut.

"They're on the wrong feet."

The smokey voice sent shivers down his toasty spine. The lilting melody of her cursory tease burrowed deep beneath the down and insulation, zapping straight into his veins. Hypnotized, he watched Francesca smirk as she passed without giving him a second look.

The thick, cream-colored waffle knit henley and fitted slate snow bibs failed to camouflage her shapely little body. Twin honeyed braids tailed one on each shoulder, and a soft lavender beanie was pulled snugly over her ears. He caught a glimpse of her glittering amber eyes and cheeks, pink from the cold. Boots securely—and correctly—fastened into her snowshoes, she glided gracefully along, navigating around others in the wedding party like she'd been born wearing the clunky footwear.

Speaking of treacherous.

Benjamin was doing a horrible job of keeping his distance from Francesca. He'd agreed to give her space and, in the very next breath, remained glued to her side, periodically picking on her like a fifth grader at recess. There was something about the way her cheeks flushed with equal parts rage and embarrassment. The combination was better than any opioid.

Riling her up was pleasurable, but Benjamin had to continually remind himself why he was in Leavenworth in the first place.

Johnny and Lucy's wedding.

His presence was meant to add to the joy, not amp up the drama by harassing the maid of honor. He had to figure out a way to stifle his mutinous inner teenager and act like the mature adult he was.

"Need a hand, my friend?" A solid clap on his back snapped him out of his trance and sent his glasses flying into the packed snow at his feet.

Benjamin removed his glove and scooped up the eyewear. The left lens must have landed just right on a rock beneath the snow. The resulting twin scratches were small but dead center in his line of vision.

Fantastic.

He buffed the specs as best he could and deposited them back on his chilly nose.

"Oh, hey. Zac, right?" he asked through a gritted smile.

"In the flesh." The other man grinned, clasping Benjamin's outstretched hand for a quick shake. He gestured down to Benjamin's feet. "You've got your snowshoes switched. First timer?"

"What gave it away?" Benjamin sighed and set to work unbuckling the straps and making the swap.

"Pretty much everything about you," Zac barked with laughter and slammed another playful slap on the crouched man's back, nearly toppling him over. Fortunately, his glasses stayed on, barely.

This guy is getting old real quick.

"Want a little advice?"

"One foot in front of the other?" Benjamin drawled, attempting to hide his irritation.

"Nah. About Frankie."

"Why would I need advice about—"

"Come on, man, we all have eyes." A broad grin and flash of dimples popping through his russet beard amped up the condescension in his voice. "You were up her ass all night at dinner, and you can't hide that dopey expression you get on your face when you look at her."

Dopey?

"Thanks, but I'm good—"

"She's a wildcat—from what I hear. I don't know firsthand. Not for lack of trying, though. I've been trying to nail her for years."

Heat strummed in Benjamin's gut, and his pulse thundered in his ears. The way this guy was talking about Francesca rankled him. He finished securing his snowshoes—fastened on the correct feet this time—and stood, hiding his balled fists in his pockets.

"I'm not trying to start anything with Francesca," he ground through clenched teeth.

"*Francesca*, huh?" Zac's dense eyebrows danced.

"Yes." *What is this guy's malfunction?*

"If you say so, man." One more hard hit to Benjamin's shoulder and Zac made his way to where the group congregated.

He watched the smug little jerk go and counted down from ten to cool his temper. Great. Not only did he have to pretend to believe in the façade of marriage and manage to keep the schoolyard shenanigans with Francesca to a minimum, but there was one more bullet point to add to his to-do list.

More of a to-don't, really.

Don't punch Zac.

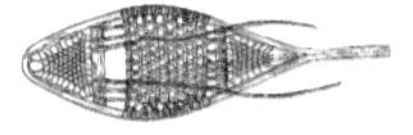

Thanks to Johnny's obsession with hyper-preparedness and safety, Benajmin once again found himself failing to keep his distance from a certain Miss Miller. The groom instated the buddy system, but it was the bride who determined each pair.

"Wouldn't it be great if everyone snowshoed with their aisle buddy?" Lucy beamed gleefully like she'd just decided they should ride unicorns to the top of the mountain.

"What the hell are 'aisle buddies'?" Scorn and suspicion battled for top spot in Francesca's tone. She ran her tongue over her teeth and flicked her narrowed eyes to Benjamin. He quirked a brow in return.

"You know," Lucy drawled, twirling her hand around the group. "The person you're going to walk down the aisle with during the wedding."

"Um." Todd raised his hand and threw a thumb back toward the cars. "I'm the officiant. Don't have an aisle buddy, so does that mean—"

"Nice try," Lucy scolded with syrupy sweetness. "You'll be with Jonathan and me."

"Touché." Todd's shoulders slumped, emphasized by numerous bulky layers.

"Buck up. I'll get you a Monte Cristo when we're done," Jonathan consoled, taking his own scarf off and looping it snuggly over Todd's other two. "The Rooftop makes a good one."

"Thanks, Buster."

"I got you."

"How set in stone are we with the pairings?" Francesca argued.

"Like dry cement," Johnny barked. "You'll survive. We head out in five."

Benajmin sidled up beside his aisle buddy as everyone paired off.

"You'd better not slow me down," she grumbled, tugging her gloves in place and looping the trekking pole straps on her wrists.

Benjamin copied her motions, taking particular pleasure in

how it raised her hackles. "I'm sure I'll get the hang of it," he assured her.

"You'd better. This is the first real physical activity that I've been able to do since school started because of someone's aggressive classroom expectations. If you screw it up, you'll regret it."

"I doubt I'll have any trouble keeping up with you," he purred, stepping a bit closer. Her scowl deepened.

The group left the trailhead two by two in a neat little line. Francesca lasted all of ninety seconds before she bolted out of that line and blew to the front. Benjamin bumbled his way behind her, trying frantically to get the hang of the cumbersome process.

"Hey, Frankie!" Johnny called, hands cupped around his mouth. "Eyes on your buddy. You know the rules."

She lifted a hand in the air, thick gloves prominently displaying her middle finger, but slowed her pace ever so slightly.

Most of the group had already managed to find their stride. Todd, in all his fluffy layers, was the only other person struggling as much as Benjamin.

"Fuck. This. Fuck. This. Fuck. Fuck. Fuck. This," he chanted, trying to maintain the same pace with the rest of his hiking triad. Benjamin caught his eye and gave Todd an empathetic shrug.

Soon, Benjamin figured out the mechanics and found his rhythm. He closed the gap between him and Francesca without falling. The rest of the group chattered with their partners while he and his surly companion marched onward in silence. The lack of chitchat magnified the crunch of fresh powder underfoot. Sweat collected and dripped down his back, and his lungs burned satisfyingly from the cold. He hadn't had a chance to run since Thursday morning, and because of the constricting itinerary for the next week, he doubted he'd find the time to get any miles in before returning to Seattle. Running kept his mind clear, and missing out on the daily exercise typically left him feeling antsy, which probably explained why he was finding such joy in harassing his former student.

Benjamin had hoped agreeing to a temporary ceasefire would ease Francesca's ire toward him. Perhaps they could even be cordial toward one another for Johnny and Lucy's sake. He glanced at his snowshoe companion—perhaps *companion* was a little too amicable of a term . . . *combatant* was more accurate. She pushed on, scanning their surroundings, overtly ignoring Benjamin.

Fine. Two can play that game.

He redirected his focus to the journey. The wintry scene of the snow-covered trail was incredible. Slowly, beams of sunlight peeked through the dense clouds, scattering glitter over the frozen landscape. Tall evergreens stood mightily, flocked in heavy white coats yet too strong to bend under the enormous weight. There was a certain silence that hung densely in the air, shrouding the voices of the rest of the group. The quiet was so big that Benajmin could feel it. It had texture. It had power.

The effect was serene, and he decided he quite liked how the combination of exertion and group seclusion made him feel—excited yet oddly at peace.

Benjamin hazarded another glance over to his partner. Francesca seemed to have genuinely forgotten all about him. Because she surveyed the trail and surrounding scenery with a sort of reverence. A calm smile formed gently on her lips, and joy glimmered in her eyes. She sighed lightly, dissolving the tension she'd been holding in her shoulders since the first day of class. The relaxation that swept over her was so palpable that Benjamin felt like a movie villain for having made the last twelve weeks so unbearable for her.

And yet he hadn't dimmed her light.

One thing was certain regarding Francesca Miller: She was just as stubborn as he was.

Chapter Seventeen

Frankie

"You're freaking me out, *Benji*."

Frankie glanced sideways, not faltering in her pace, and scowled at her trail buddy. He'd visibly startled then looked away with an exaggerated display of distraction that almost made her laugh.

Almost.

"Sorry," he said with a self-effacing chuckle. "I was lost in thought. It's beautiful here."

She fought to maintain a neutral expression even as her lips pulled up at the corners. She hadn't realized how much she'd missed doing something—anything—outside until she reached the trailhead. Since climbing out of her car, she'd been greedily filling her lungs with drag after drag of the fresh, chilly air. Playful gusts toyed with the ends of her braids and caressed the frustrated warmth of her cheeks. Being out in the expanse of Stevens Pass calmed the lingering irritation from the evening before when Benjamin had tried his hardest to drive her nuts. He seemed to be searching for any excuse to jab at her sanity, and she'd be damned if she gave him any more ammunition.

"No place like it," she said, matter-of-fact, refusing to allow him to witness the unfettered joy bursting from her chest.

"Indeed."

The ascent up to Skyline Lake had Frankie so enthralled that she'd nearly forgotten all about the terrifying Professor Clark.

Terrifying. Ha.

Since leaving NWU for winter break, Benjamin had morphed into nothing but a nuisance. And while her family law grade still hung in the balance, her former professor no longer held the same intimidation as before. In class, he had been a gatekeeper to a solid GPA, but out here in the snow, on *her* turf . . . he was just a man.

And Frankie feared no man.

Not since her last foster home all those years ago.

"So, you normally engage in these types of activities?" Benjamin asked through labored breaths and slight wheezes.

"Yes," Frankie scoffed. "I guide for Off the Beaten."

"And you enjoy this?"

"You don't?"

She noted his pause, assuming he was giving thoughtful consideration to something that should be a pretty simple answer. In her experience, the customers she guided either loved snowshoeing or hated it with a fiery passion. For Frankie, doing anything outside was like medicine. No matter what ailed her—stress or lingering trauma—getting back to nature soothed her troubles like a mystical balm.

After being adopted by the Millers—her destined family—most of her free time was spent exploring the area. Her mom and dad took her and Jonathan on every trail, down every river, up every mountain as though they were helping her search for peace. It didn't take long before she found it. The outdoors tamed the once-feral spirit inside of her by quieting the urge to constantly prepare for a fight. She found safety. Freedom.

Purpose.

"I suppose it has its merits," Benjamin began. "For instance, physical activity is good for the lungs and endurance. And the peace is rather soothing. Being cut off from the pressures of the everyday is proving to be—"

"Ohmygod stop," Frankie growled.

Benjamin huffed indignantly. "You asked me—"

"I know what I asked." She whirled around. "But you're turning it into some categorical analysis that you can lump into a pros and cons list. Not everything has to be so sterile or rigid. I don't give a rat's ass about the 'merits' of snowshoeing."

"But you *asked*—"

"I asked if you liked it." She sighed. "Not for a dissertation."

Benjamin chewed on his lip, and Frankie could practically feel him swallowing the rest of his bullet points. "I guess if I have to give a gut reaction . . ."

"Yes. Do exactly that."

"Then I hate it." His scowl gave way to a broad smile. Relief washed over his body, and he tilted his head back. The air was dense and foretold of snow. "I truly hate it. I will never snowshoe again."

The genuineness of his response shocked Frankie. She'd expected something a little more politically correct: *I can see why others enjoy this particular activity, but perhaps it isn't quite for me. Pip pip, blah blah.* She hadn't counted on an unedited expression of loathing. But it was his grin that startled her the most. Or perhaps it was how his deep dimples and the crinkled lines at the corner of his eyes awakened hibernating butterflies in her stomach.

"Well." She cleared her throat loudly to scare away the annoying bugs. "Isn't that better? Going with your gut instead of some empirical system?"

"Yes," he said with straight white teeth still exposed.

She ignored his indigo eyes as they scanned her face, lingering on the lip she worried.

"Let's go."

"If we must," he said with a sigh, an edge of mirth dancing on each syllable.

Frankie took off, ascending the trail at the same speed she'd been hauling since the start.

"Hey, slow down. Dang it," he mumbled, catching the front of his right snowshoe on the back of his left heel.

Dang it? Was this the Hallmark Channel or something?

"Do you ever swear?" Frankie did her best to keep any hint of humor out of her tone. She refused to warm to him; he didn't deserve it.

"Everyone swears sometimes, Francesca."

"I've never heard you do it." She shrugged, really thinking back, and, nope, he'd never dropped so much as a *damn* or *hell* in her presence.

"Of *course* you wouldn't," he said as though the reasoning should be obvious.

"Because it would be uncouth? Unseemly? Unprofessional?" She knew excessive cursing was frowned upon at the college, but it wasn't unheard of for a few choice words to get flung around during especially heated discussions. Her child and family inequalities professor loved a certain four-letter word and had zero qualms about using it.

He chuckled. It was a smooth and rich sound, like decadent hot chocolate for the ears, and made her shiver.

"No." He shook his head and looked at her, claiming her eyes with the frozen ocean depths of his. "But there are only two very specific times when I do, and you haven't been privy to either. *Princess.*"

His implication was crystal clear . . . at least with regard to one of the situations.

Sex.

If her cheeks weren't already flaming from physical exertion and the nip in the air, Frankie would have to admit she blushed. She never blushed, except this wasn't the first time he managed to make her do so. What was his problem? Hadn't he agreed to keep his distance this week? Yet here he was, weaseling in on her outside time, ruining her communion with nature. Prick.

She steeled her face and shrugged.

"And it appears I never will." She smiled sweetly before rolling her eyes.

His buoyant laughter floated across the glistening drifts on either side of the trail. It did things to Frankie that she refused to acknowledge.

They lumbered their way up a set of switchbacks. The elevation gain was minimal yet exponentially more challenging in snowshoes and the extra foot of untouched powder. Frankie pushed through, relishing the burn of her glutes and thighs as she sped her way up the winding route. She had to hand it to the professor; for a first-timer, he was holding his own despite her ambitious speed.

And it pissed her off.

She wasn't trying to lose him, not completely. She just wanted a gap between them so she wouldn't have to hear his voice. Or smell his warm cinnamony scent, which seemed to grow stronger the more he pushed to match her speed. A wafting breeze added to her frustration as it swirled the heady, befuddling aroma around her.

Eventually, Frankie couldn't see or hear any of the others in their group.

"Do you suppose we should pause and wait for the others to catch up? It might be the safe thing to do," Benjamin said. He hid his elevated exertion well, yet Frankie could still make out the ragged drag of his heavy breath.

"There's no need." She didn't slow. "Buddy system, remember?"

"I highly doubt Johnny's reasoning for pairing us off was so you could blast up the trail like an out-of-control rocket."

She stopped and peered over her shoulder.

"And how could you possibly know anything about my brother? It's not like you've been there for him since college."

She caught him flinch. She'd hit a nerve.

Good.

Her brother never uttered anything but the highest praise about his best man, and yet he hadn't shown up when Jon needed him—not when their father had passed away or following Cynthia's accident. He didn't even know Jon and Lucy had gone missing on Mount Stuart for several days last summer. What kind of "friend" checks out of someone's life like that?

Benji was merely an acquaintance her brother hadn't had the heart to cut loose.

He remained silent. Rolling back his shoulders, he resumed his pace, staring ahead of Frankie's position on the trail. She continued forward as they passed a large green structure on their left. The ski resort's utility tower marked the halfway point of the ascent.

"Feel free to stop and catch your breath," she drolled over her shoulder. "I understand if you can't handle it. Someone should be along shortly."

"Not a chance," he said, using his stern professor tone. "We have to stay together, Francesca."

"Then keep up."

Chapter Eighteen

Frankie

They continued in silence as the wind whipped a few wayward strands of hair around Frankie's face. She ignored everything besides maintaining her breakneck pace. Nothing broke through her impenetrable focus and for the first time ever, the view of Stevens Pass ski resort didn't take her breath away. The few lingering sunbeams glinting off the crystalline snow were only an obnoxious glare, making her long for a pair of shades.

They were up the next set of switchbacks in a flash. Sweat dripped down Frankie's back and between her breasts. She knew she should slow down and remove a few layers. Staying cool and dry in freezing conditions was important. The moment she'd stop, her body heat would plummet, and the perspiration would remain damp against her skin—not exactly the ideal scenario for cold-weather hiking.

She desperately wanted to remove her coat and hat and stow them in her backpack then take a drink of water, but all of that would mean stopping. No doubt Benjamin would coast right past her and take the lead. She wasn't racing him—that would be childish. She just didn't want him to get to the lake before her. So, she continued, huffing through the steps and the sweat and the fire in her lungs.

Nearing an abrupt edge, they halted simultaneously, though Frankie would swear she got there a snowshoe or two first.

"Goddammit!" she spat, curling her fingers into fists and

wishing she could throw something.

"Whoa." Benjamin wisely took a little step back and held up his hands. "What's wrong?"

"We missed the fucking turnoff," Frankie grumbled and pulled off her hat, allowing her head to cool in the wisps of chilly air. She snatched the water bottle from her side pouch and drank half of it. "There was a fork in the trail about a quarter mile back that we blew past because *you* were distracting me."

"I'm not sure if I should be amused or offended by your blame." He drank from his insulated thermos and removed his scarf. A few snowflakes drifted around them, creating a soft speckle pattern on Benjamin's coat and hat. One landed on Frankie's nose, and she angrily swiped it away.

"If you'd given me space like I asked, then we wouldn't have overshot the fork." Fully aware that she might be—slightly—overreacting, Frankie couldn't help but feel embarrassed that she'd gone off the planned route. She was a seasoned guide who had snowshoed this trail at least two dozen times, not some inexperienced rookie. Oh-ho, her brother was going to have a heyday making fun of her for the detour.

Awesome.

Frankie brushed past Benjamin, clipping his shoulder with hers, and started to backtrack.

"I think you might be overdramatizing the situation. Is it really that big of a deal?" He set his hiking poles aside and removed his gloves, placing them neatly on top.

That condescending tone.

Because of course the professor knew best.

Frankie shook with frustration. To be honest, the error probably wouldn't have been that big of a deal if she'd been partnered with Lucy or one of the other bridesmaids, or hell, even with Zac sniffing around her like he does. But for some reason, the fact that Professor Clark led her astray . . . sidetracked her from a task she could have done blindfolded, seemed to flip just the right rage switch.

She stopped and swung around.

"Listen here, you pompous windbag. You have no right to tell me how I should feel in any given situation. Am I overreacting? Maybe. But it's better than being a soulless"—she poked him with a gloved finger in the chest, shuffling closer—"uptight"—another jab—"sadist who gets off on his students' misery."

Benjamin stood there, accepting the verbal onslaught, his eyes darkening as she advanced. Her puffy coat brushed against his until her chest came up against solid resistance. The heady scent of cinnamon, sandalwood, and fresh sweat radiated off him, along with his overwhelming body heat. She felt lightheaded, nearly hypnotized, as his eyes tunneled into hers.

Compulsively, she pressed up.

His lips met hers halfway with ferocity.

One strong hand splayed across her lower back, fingers pressing divots into her skin through her warm layers. The other hand slid up her neck into the base of one loose braid and gripped. She gasped as he tilted her head to gain truer access to her mouth and plunged his tongue inside. Devoid of gentleness, the kiss was consuming, though Frankie didn't know who was to blame. She'd short-circuited, and her brain zeroed in on the sensations of his touch. She gripped the collar of his coat, clinging tightly to him, desperate to release all the frustration she'd been feeling toward him into the kiss.

The way his prickly stubble scraped at her lips and his fingers tugged at her thick hair drove her mad. He tasted like hot apple cider. Sweet, spicy, sinful.

The falling snow did little to chill the heat between them. A needy moan slipped from her parted lips as Benjamin trailed his teeth and tongue along her jaw and down her neck. He pulled her hips toward his, nearly lifting her feet from the ground to compensate for their difference in height. A deep ache bloomed low in her belly as she felt his rigidity press against her through thick snow pants. A glimmer of rational thought niggled at her consciousness.

What am I doing?

"Francesca," he rasped against her collarbone. The single word held so much depth, so many layers to peel away and study. She wanted her name on his lips again.

"Frankie." The static of her walkie-talkie crackled at her shoulder. The abrupt blast jarred her, snapping her back to her senses. She pushed herself back and out of Benjamin's reach, instantly feeling the icy sting where his lips had just been. *"Frankie, where the heck are you?"*

She watched his chest heave desperate breath as rapidly as her own, not daring to tear her eyes from his as she reached up with one hand.

"We . . ." She released the button and cleared the residual lust from her throat. "We overshot the fork and hit the end of the alternate trail."

Crackling laughter boomed through the device because of course her brother would hold down the push-to-talk button for that important message.

"How is that even possible?" he asked after a hearty bout of giggles.

Benjamin stepped forward, crowding Frankie's space with his size and wafting testosterone. The heat and spice of his breath puffed beside her as he leaned down and engaged the PTT.

"It was my fault, Johnny. She was too busy helping me figure out this whole snowshoeing thing." He turned, breath hot and sweet on her chin. "I distracted her."

He released the button, and the knuckle of his thumb grazed her neck, just above her thundering pulse. Goosebumps splashed over her despite the flames licking at her core. She shivered from his nearness and the lingering sensations of his lips on her skin.

"We're just about to backtrack," Frankie explained, taking a wise step back and shaking her head. "See you in ten."

Space. She needed space.

She couldn't think straight with him so close. It had been so long since she'd had any physical contact with a man. No wonder she'd reacted the way she did. She wanted to blame him, claim he took advantage of her self-imposed celibacy, but the accusation wouldn't hold up because how would he have known? And if she was being honest with herself, she was the one who inclined her chin and leaned into him, subtly offering.

He took her up on that offer. So easily.

Simmer down, woman.

"Get your stuff." She took another step back, increasing the necessary distance between them. "We need to rejoin the group."

"Francesca, I—"

"Forget it." Another retreating step. "We got caught up."

Frankie touched the crown of her head then scanned the ground for her beanie. She'd taken it off once they neared the drop-off and lost track of it when Benjamin had—

He knelt, picked up the lavender knit hat that lay abandoned in the snow and took a step forward, holding it out to her. Impulsively, she took another stride backward.

"Wait," Benjamin gasped.

Frankie didn't remember much after that, aside from the feeling of snow breaking away like loose sand under bare feet. She watched Benjamin's eyes widen in horror as he lunged forward. But she quickly descended, sinking, sliding, then somersaulting down a slope. Trees, snow, peaks, and cloudy gray sky spun round and round, causing a dizzying fear to rise in her chest.

Then the world went dark.

Chapter Nineteen

Benjamin

Benjamin watched, frozen in terror, as Francesca careened down that snowy embankment. Her body cartwheeled, wholly consumed by gravity's greedy pull. Arms and legs jerking in all directions like some abused ragdoll in the hands of a four-year-old tyrant. Her descent was endless, until her wild, helpless grunts and gasps halted with a sickening thud. Her body struck a boulder at the base of the ravine. Silence followed—thick and ominous.

The same silence that had, only moments before, filled Benjamin with peace now ignited and sizzled like a thousand lit fuses looped around his torso.

"Shit! Shit shit shit!"

The moment of impact played over and over in his ears as he slid off the trail, displacing sheets of snow with each plunging step. He could barely pull his broad shoes to the surface before more of the powdery stuff broke out from under him. There was nothing solid to cling to and he lacked the skill to maneuver down to where Francesca lay limp at the base of a snow-coated rock.

"Oh, god. Oh, shit."

Unable to steer with any real accuracy, he prayed he'd end up somewhere stable enough to gather his bearings and get to Francesca's side. Landing about fifteen feet from her, Benjamin managed to slow his rapid descent as he approached a cluster of small evergreens. The flowing snow piled up against it, giving him a stable landing spot.

The only problem was that as he stopped, the snow above him continued to slide, and by the time it calmed, he was buried waist-deep. At that same moment, the clouds seemingly cracked open and released an aggressive flurry.

"Goddammit!"

He ferociously clawed at his icy constraints, scooping chunks of powder away from his body while continuing to watch Francesca's motionless body. The rapidly accumulating flakes glimmered against her golden braids, swiftly blotted out the flaxen strands, which had once played with the twinkle of her amber eyes.

"Francesca!" he shouted. Fear contorted his voice into one he didn't recognize. It bounced from one side of the valley to the other and back in a mocking echo. "Francesca, can you hear me?"

Nothing.

Not a shift. Not even a little twitch.

"Help!" he shrieked as he continued to shovel and push the snow that pinned him in place. The cold stuck like tiny blades jabbing into his gloveless palms. He ignored the pain. All that mattered was getting to her. Someone had to be coming along soon. Surely, Johnny would notice they hadn't joined the group and come looking. "Help!"

Benjamin heard a soft noise—a whimper—coming from Francesca as she finally began to stir.

"I'm coming. Stay there," he rushed out through the haze of panic. "Francesca, hold still. I don't know how badly you're hurt."

Benjamin had cleared enough snow from his hips and legs that he should have been able to pull free, yet the massive snowshoes kept him anchored in the frigid heft. He pulled, yanked, engaged every muscle he had to pry himself loose. Rumbles of frustration erupted from his mouth in a string of sharp expletives as he strained. The snowshoes weren't going to give, not unless he spent another ten minutes clearing the packed snow from around them.

The broad metal frames had to go.

He tunneled his bare hands into the snow, no longer feeling the cold. His fingertips felt thick with numbness as he fumbled them blindly over the clips that strapped over his winter boots.

"Come on," he bellowed, thumb slipping against the plastic that remained firmly clamped. "Come *the fuck* on!"

The click of the bindings giving way nearly brought tears to Benjamin's eyes. The second followed suit as he hooked his short nails on the edge and pulled. He wiggled his boots out and soon climbed clear of the snow well he'd been stuck in.

His eyes flew to Francesca as he crawled across the plush snow. He sank with every shift, limbs screaming in protest as he ambled to her. She was still laying on her side, mumbling and moaning lightly under her breath. The closer he got, the more he could see the damage from the hit she'd taken. Blood speckled the snow. A red smear glistened where she'd collided with the solid granite, and a stream trickled down her forehead and along her cheekbone. Gone was the rosy wash of exertion and surprised arousal from their kiss. Left behind was a startlingly pallid hue.

"Ouch," she groaned, lifting a hand to her forehead. She pulled back her fingers and spied the blood then groaned once more, letting her eyes fall shut.

"Francesca." Her name ripped from Benjamin's throat as though he were being tortured. He scanned the recesses of his memories for what to do. In years past, he'd hardly found it necessary to keep up with his first aid certification and cursed himself for the egregious error. She would know what to do if the roles were reversed. If she were anything like her brother, she'd be up on all the latest wilderness survival methods. "Francesca? Can you talk?"

"Benjamin?" she croaked through dry lips. "Dafuck happened?"

She was cursing, that's good!

"You fell and hit your head on a rock. Can you move? Wait! *Should* you move? Shit, I don't remember how any of this works."

"Don't you know first aid?" Her groan miraculously contained a hint of scorn amidst her tight words.

"I haven't taken it since college with Johnny," he rushed out. *What a fool.* How could he have been so shortsighted?

"Fantastic." She tried to push up to a sitting position but could barely lift herself without sinking elbow-deep into the snow. She settled on her side, arms curled in front of her chest.

Benjamin was useless.

What was he supposed to do? She was bleeding from a gash on her head, but he'd heard that head wounds tended to bleed more profusely than the rest of the body, even if they were minor. But wouldn't that mean she was losing blood faster despite the potentially minimal severity of the wound? Should he ensure she stays still? Should he be putting pressure on her cut? Should he even touch her at all? He looked up to where they had been hiking minutes before. She tumbled nearly fifty feet. The snow that had broken off in sheets during both descents revealed just how steep of an embankment they'd have to climb to get back out. It would be impossible in even the most ideal circumstances.

One thing at a time.

"Francesca," he huffed through a wave of nausea. "Sweetheart, you have to tell me what to do."

She cracked her eyes and peered over at him.

"Weird. I liked it better when you were calling me Miss Miller," she grumbled then cursed softly and raised a hand to her head.

"Shall we keep the snark to a minimum until we're back on solid ground?" His efforts to add humor to his words took everything he had. "Tell me how to help you."

"Remove my pack."

"Right." She unclipped the chest buckle, and he carefully removed the straps from her shoulders. Soon, the pack was separated from her body and sitting in his lap. "Now what?"

"There's a first aid kit. You need gauze, tape, scissors."

He pulled the red canvas bag from the main compartment and located the necessary items.

"Don't forget gloves," she scolded.

"Why are there condoms in here?"

"How else are we supposed to smuggle the heroine?"

Her sarcasm injected him with an instant rush of calm. She wouldn't be so impertinent if she were in any real trouble. He glanced around and clocked the increasing snowfall. It wasn't time to celebrate, not yet.

Miles to go . . .

He opened a pack of sterile latex gloves and pulled them in place.

"Ok, what's next, *Miss Miller*?"

"Better." The corner of her mouth quirked up. "Rip open the gauze packets and stack a few sheets together. Press the wad to the wound and tape it in place. I can help apply pressure as you cut strips of tape."

Benjamin nodded. With wobbly hands, he followed her directions precisely. After a couple minutes, she was bandaged up with his beanie pulled snuggly over her head to apply added pressure to the dressing.

Francesca shivered, the body heat she'd accumulated from their excursion all but faded.

"Can I move you? You're freezing." Benjamin wanted to get

her settled in his lap so she wasn't making as much contact with the snow. Who knows how long they'd be stuck down there. The group had to find them shortly, but it wasn't a straightforward walk back up to the trail. He peered up to where they stood a few minutes ago. It wasn't as though Johnny could scurry down, scoop them both up, and fireman carry them out of there. "Is it safe to move you?"

"I'm pretty sure. Nothing feels broken. My head's pounding." Her chattering teeth jittered her words as she wrapped her arms tighter around her body.

Benjamin unzipped and removed his jacket then laid it across Francesca's torso. He took great care as he slid one arm under her knees and the other under her shoulders. Moving slowly, he gently scooped her up and settled her onto his lap. She didn't fight him, didn't protest.

Instead, she sighed and curled into the warmth of his chest.

Benjamin should have been freezing, with his coat, hat, and gloves removed, but holding Francesca so closely, knowing that she was all right, gave him added warmth from the inside. He felt a pang of guilt for finding enjoyment in their proximity and scolded himself silently.

Chapter Twenty

Frankie

"My radio," Frankie croaked, looking up into Benjamin's once panic-stricken face. He'd calmed somewhat, reducing his earlier overt terror to a humming anxiety. "We need to call Jon."

"Let me." He reached for her pack and unhooked the carabiner holding the walkie-talkie to the arm strap. Fortunately, her tumble hadn't destroyed the handheld device—they likely had the soft snow to thank for that. And her brother's renewed obsession with survival gear after his own wilderness mishap with Lucy the year before. Benjamin pressed the button, about to say something, then stopped. "Is there a specific distress code for something like this?"

Was this guy for real?

"Yeah," Frankie said as she rolled her eyes. "You need to do a series of Morse code clicks and pauses or else Jon will ignore the fact that we fell down the side of a *fucking mountain*."

His cheeks flushed with embarrassment.

"Right." Benjamin cleared his throat. "Johnny. Are you there, Johnny?"

The ensuing silence added to Frankie's unease as she watched more powder fall silently around them. It wasn't supposed to snow until later that evening. *Freaking meteorologists.* And yet here they were, lounging at the bottom of a valley, flakes flitting around them like they were in a damn Christmas snow globe.

Benjamin attempted another call with no response.

Last year, Jonathan had gone on a personal protection tirade, swapping old gear with the highest safety-rated equivalent. That included the new, super rugged GMRS walkies that were supposed to transmit further and through more obstacles than their FRS counterparts, but so far, his purchase had left a lot to be desired.

Frankie snatched the radio from Benjamin and scolded into the mic.

"Jonathan Stanley Miller. So help me god, if you don't answer, I'll include the Valhalla incident of 2018 in my wedding toast."

"Is his middle name really Stanley?"

She snorted. "No, it's Andrew. I use Stanley when I'm pissed or want to mess with him."

A crackle of static played through the radio, words indiscernible. Her heart leapt into her chest.

"Jon? Come on, Jon," she begged, thinly veiled panic stringing through her words.

"*Frankie?*" Still muffled, but better than nothing.

"Yes," she almost screeched. Looking up at Benjamin, she noted the tentative hope adding color to his pale features. He shivered slightly and held her close, likely as much for his warmth as hers. "By the drop-off. We fell down a ravine. I hit my head." She said each word with slow clarity to break through the grainy sound Jon would likely be hearing.

"*Sit tight.*"

"Oh, thank god," Benjamin breathed out, dropping his head to rest on Frankie's shoulder. His head snapped up as if he suddenly remembered something, then he unclasped his pack. He reached for his thermos and opened the screw top. "Here, drink this."

The heavenly scent of hot apple cider swirled up from the large container like a healing elixir. Testing a sip for temperature, Frankie moaned in delight then took a couple more gulps. Benjamin followed suit before he sealed the canister and replaced it in his pack.

"Thank you," she said with a sigh, snuggling further into his warmth.

"You're welcome. So, what do we do now? Just sit here?"

Frankie shrugged, partially to shimmy the accumulation of snow off the jacket draped over her. The clouds needed to stop dumping on them. More snow meant harder rescue efforts.

"That's all we can do." She gestured to the steep embankment. "There's no chance in hell we can climb that thing. Stay safe, stay dry, stay put. We don't want to make the evacuation harder for SAR than it already will be."

"What's the Valhalla incident of 2018?"

Frankie snorted. "If you don't already know, I doubt you and my brother are that tight."

She glanced up just in time to notice Benjamin flinch. The shame she saw in his eyes just before he turned to survey their surroundings tugged gently at her heart. As far as Frankie was concerned, he didn't deserve her sympathy, but she felt it anyway.

"I shouldn't be telling you, but seeing as you're keeping me warm and dry, this will make us even."

Benjamin leveled his sapphire eyes on Frankie's face, enveloping her with his undivided attention. The intensity stole her breath for a moment before she reminded herself it had everything to do with the gossip she was about to share.

"In July 2018, Jon and I decided to hike Valhalla on our day off. He'd just gotten over food poisoning—or so we thought. We reached the lake, and he . . . had an emergency." Benjamin cringed as she continued. "He found a semi-secluded spot, but while he was . . . you know . . . a family of four popped out of the woods nearby and scared the crap out of him . . . oof . . . pun not intended. Anyways, in his haste to finish up, he grabbed a fistful of poison oak instead of practically *any other* plant available. It was, all around, a very, *very* bad day for him."

Frankie watched as Benjamin bit his lips closed to hold back a laugh despite how much his shoulders shook. "Poor guy."

"I warned him. First, about the gas station sushi the morning before and again just before we left for the hike." She chuckled and shook her head. "Always been a slow learner, my brother."

By the time Jon's voice crackled through the walkie-talkie again, the snow was falling so heavily that it was nearly impossible to see clearly to the top of the embankment.

"*Frankie, Benji. Do you copy?*"

"Loud and sorta clear," she responded.

"*I'm trying to get eyes on you, but we can't tell where you went off trail. The new snowfall is obscuring things. Can you both yell out? Might help.*"

"Roger."

Together they hollered as loudly as they could. Benjamin waved his arms in the air to give Jon some movement to spot. Through the growing clumps of snowflakes, they could just make out the outline of a person peering carefully over the edge.

"*I see you. I'm going to hand you over to Miguel.*"

"*Hey, kiddo, ya hanging in there?*" Not even a decade older than Frankie, the head of the local search and rescue team was like another brother. He had four younger sisters himself and regularly said it made no difference claiming her as his fifth.

Hearing his voice imbued Frankie with an extra boost of faith as she pushed the button to respond.

"We're ok. Trying to stay warm and dry. Though the new snowfall isn't helping."

"I've sent Jon back to my truck to radio the team. It's going to be a while before we can get you out of there. What I need you to do for me is to describe your surroundings. We need to figure out a safe place for you two to hunker down and wait."

Benjamin helped her sit up and get a better look. Outside of the situation, Frankie would have described the setting as a magical, wintery paradise. Large boulders meandered along where they sat on the valley floor. Covered in glistening snow, they reminded her of icing-topped gumdrops bordering a winding path to a gingerbread house. A few trees stood mightily between them, mostly keeping to the steep hills on either side. The snow fell rapidly, swiftly covering the tracks that their clumsy descents carved into the embankments a short time ago. It was breathtaking. Frankie was so captivated that she imagined the tinkling of tiny bells to cap off the seasonal ambiance.

Scratch that. Not bells.

"Oh no," Frankie gasped. She carefully reached down beside Benjamin, hastily scooping the snow aside. After removing a glove, she sank her bare hand into the snow.

"What is it? Francesca, stop. You'll get frostbite!"

She shrugged off his concerns, reaching farther down until her fingers reached something cold, hard, and slick.

"Ice." She retracted her hand and jammed it back into her glove. "Miguel? Fuck. I think we're on a creek. I felt ice beneath the snow, there's a pretty open winding path through the valley, and I hear moving water."

Benjamin's eyes widened. She laid her hand on his chest in an effort to calm him, but the thundering pulse that beat against her palm caused her own heart to accelerate.

"Listen carefully. You need to get off the ice. There's no telling how long it will hold. The water probably isn't deep, but if you break through and get wet, the risk of hypothermia increases. Drastically."

"Got it." Frankie hooked the walkie back to her pack. "Help me slide this on, then I'm going to crawl off of you and climb through those boulders." She pointed to the stack of rocks a few feet beside them.

"But shouldn't we cross over and stay on *that* bank?" Benjamin's words linked together as they flowed from his chattering teeth. His icy blue eyes, wide with fear, collided with hers. "We'd be closer when they rescue—"

"We can't risk the crossing. You heard Miguel. Stay out of the water. Follow me but move carefully." She used every ounce of her authoritative guide voice, and it seemed to have the desired effect. Benjamin nodded, took back his coat, and helped her shimmy into her pack.

With great care, Frankie slid off his lap and onto the snow beside him. She moved with purpose, thinking light thoughts all the way. After a moment, she scurried between the two rocks and landed on solid ground.

A heavy breath escaped her, but she knew they weren't in the clear just yet. Benjamin was much larger than her. She'd felt so small and comfy nestled against his warm chest. Laying in his lap. Long legs curled up to act as a barrier between her and the snow. *Focus, Frankie.* The point was, the guy outweighed her by . . . well, by a lot. Any wrong move could spell disaster. There was no telling how thick the ice was in any given spot.

"You're next, *professor*. Move slowly, got it?"

Benjamin's eyes glinted at Frankie's tease. But he nodded anyway.

He gracefully shifted and pushed to a stand. Without his snowshoes, his feet sank all the way down to the ice. He appeared more and more comfortable with each lumbering stride.

"Like a walk in the pa—"

A fragile crack resounded from beneath his boot and echoed

throughout the valley.

Frankie captured Benjamin's eyes in a panicked flinch.

"Fuck," they mumbled in unison.

Chapter Twenty-One

Benjamin

The delicate cracking beneath Benjamin's feet sounded more like removing a shell from a hard-boiled egg than ice giving way. Yet just as he settled his hands on the rocks separating him from Francesca, his hiking boot dropped through the glassy surface and plunged into the icy creek below. The other followed immediately after.

Miguel had been right, at least; the water wasn't deep, only reaching him at the middle of his shins. There was also zero risk of getting swept downstream because the current was weak.

But as Benjamin's boot filled with the coldest water he'd ever felt, even an adventuring newcomer like him knew the severity of the situation. He looked up at Francesca, whose eyes were wide with shock.

"Fuck." The husky curse jettisoned from his snowshoe buddy's mouth. The single word carried the same level of anxiety that Benjamin felt down to his frigid feet.

He didn't linger. Instead, he used all his strength to muscle his way up and through the boulders. Francesca pulled at his shoulders the whole way. Sliding over the top of the icy rocks, his trajectory continued. He grunted and landed on top of her, squashing her into the fresh snow. He caged her with his forearms as a surprised gasp puffed from her lips. The spicy, hot apple cider had remained on her breath, melding with the soothing scent of lavender and eucalyptus.

A flood of pink washed over her cheeks. Benjamin wondered how she would respond if he dipped down for a kiss and brushed his lips against hers to regain some of the warmth he'd lost stomping onto that creek.

"Do you mind?" she finally murmured, gaze flitting from his eyes to his lips and back. "This isn't exactly the best time to hit on me."

"Right." He fumbled his way up to his feet and reached down to take her outstretched hand. "Now what?"

"Did you get water in your boots?" she asked, her voice quivering.

"Yes."

"*Great.*" Francesca blew out an aggressive breath. She grabbed the walkie-talkie from her shoulder. "Miguel? Hey, Miguel?"

"*I'm here,*" came the crackle scrambling through the speaker.

"Benjamin stepped through the ice. His feet are wet."

"*Did either of you pack extra socks?*"

He shook his head as Francesca raised her eyebrows in question.

"No," she huffed. Then her face lit up. "I can give him my dry socks; my boots have an extra fuzzy lining."

"*Yes. Do that.*"

"Francesca, be reasonable," Benjamin practically scolded. He wasn't going to take her socks and leave her at an increased risk of frostbite or hypothermia or whatever could happen. Did he have cold feet? Sure. The pins and needles were rapidly becoming more aggressive, but it wasn't unbearable. Yet.

"I'm not the one being unreasonable here," she harped, laces already untied. "Now sit your ass down and do as you're told." He could see her determination in the set of her brow and fire swirling in her amber eyes. She wasn't going to accept no for an answer.

Benjamin huffed but sat down and fumbled with the triple knot he'd fashioned earlier that morning to ensure his boots would stay on. His fingers were frigid and battled clumsily with the knot. Impatience won out and Francesca scootched closer. But when she swatted his icy hands away, she gasped.

"What happened to your gloves?" She admonished, already tugging hers from her small hands.

"I didn't think to put them back on before following you into this frozen void of misery."

Francesca rolled her eyes as she thrust his hands into her warm gloves. They barely extended past his knuckles, but at least his fingers had some reprieve. Nimbly, she managed to reverse the chaotic entanglement and loosen his laces. She then dug into her backpack and pulled out two gallon-sized food storage bags filled with snacks. She emptied the contents in the main compartment and thrust the empty clear baggies at Benajmin.

"After you put the dry socks on, put one of these on each foot. Otherwise, the water in your boots will immediately soak into the wool."

"Thank you," he conceded, accepting the dry socks and plastic bags from her. He slipped the frozen shoes back on, and then Frankie secured a more reasonable double knot.

"Pride won't do either of us any good if we freeze to death," she chided lightly. "Zip up your coat. And drink some more cider."

"I don't remember you being so demanding back in Seattle," Benjamin joked, shivering from the wind picking up around them. The snow came down in buckets and managed to fully obscure their line of sight to the top of the ravine.

"That's because a certain Professor Prick used up the bossy allotment all on his own." Her perturbed scowl was cloyingly adorable with her tattered golden braids and pink nose. She'd regained a bit of color since her fall, and Benjamin rejoiced in her improved state.

He hated that he'd been such a hard-ass to her throughout the quarter.

He hated that he'd intentionally tried to get her to drop the class.

He hated that she was so startled by his advancements up on the trail that she felt compelled to retreat from his reach and fell down the valley and hit her head.

Benjamin glanced at her forehead, noting that the gauze seemed to be holding beneath his navy blue beanie. Blood hadn't seeped through, but a few dried, rusty bits remained along her temple and cheekbone. Unease and nausea crept up his spine and clung to his shoulders like an over-cinched backpack.

"Jeeze, relax." Francesca huffed. She laid a hand on his arm and squeezed. "You just went white as a sheet. Are you feeling all right?"

"A little lightheaded, but that's probably the adrenaline."

"You're probably starving too." She rummaged in her pack and pulled out a fistful of snacks. "I've got energy gels, jerky, GORP, stroopwafel. Pick your poison."

His sweet tooth perked up and nearly barked like a dog.

"Definitely a stroopwafel." His stomach growled, reminding him of his manners. "Please."

She fished out a couple packets, handing one to him, then stuffed her goodies back into her backpack.

They sat in companionable silence, devouring the thin caramel-filled cookies and sipping the last of the still-warm cider. He could feel the life creep back in as the sugar hit his bloodstream, despite the niggling dread that accumulated as quickly as the snow around them.

The icy wind graduated to sharp gusts that scratched at

Benjamin's exposed face. Turning to face downwind proved futile because the frigid blasts seemed to bounce off the surrounding boulders straight back at him. He glanced over at Francesca, who sat huddled in a ball. She shivered continually no matter how small she made herself.

He swept his arm impulsively around her waist and pulled her astride his lap, chest to chest. He unzipped his coat and pulled her against his base layers before she could protest.

"What the hell?"

"Relax into me," he soothed breathlessly.

She remained tense, back rigid.

"It's smart to share body heat, right?" Benjamin asked abashedly. He'd seen it in countless shows and movies and read it in books but never really questioned whether it was a device to create proximity or something that would actually help matters. "You seemed warmer in my lap after I bandaged you up."

Francesca finally relaxed a little then sunk fully against him and grumbled.

"Yeah," she conceded. "It's true."

She rested her head beneath his chin and his stubble dragged across the wet knit of her hat. She hesitated until finally sliding her arms around his middle and burying her hands beneath his shirt to rest on his bare back.

Benjamin sucked in a breath at her little rebellion.

Her giggle was quiet and evil. "Are they cold?"

"Only if you consider a bag of frozen peas cold," he hissed.

"Or a witch's tits?"

"An abominable snowman's balls."

Her snort caused heat to bloom in his chest. Her content little sigh sent it lower.

"*Fr . . . you there—?*" The garbled static sent a jolt of hope through Benjamin.

Francesca scrambled for the radio, struggling to work the PTT button with her freezing hands.

"Y-yesss, w-we're here."

He pulled her even tighter at the warbled sound of her voice.

"*I have . . . and bad news. A snow . . . picking up . . . can't . . . safely.*"

Francesca locked eyes with Benjamin. While the staticky connection cutting in and out was difficult to translate, her panicked thoughts read loud and clear across her stricken face.

They were stuck.

"You can't get us out?" The shrill alarm in her voice gave Benjamin goosebumps.

"*No . . . but . . . about . . . half . . .*"

Francesca's narrow shoulders heaved, sharp and rapid, as she struggled to control her anxiety. Her fear nearly broke him as it registered that they'd be stuck overnight in the elements—snowing, freezing, potentially deadly elements.

"Miguel. Miguel! I can't understand you. Slow. Down," she urged.

"*Cabin. About half . . . north . . . hope . . .*"

Chapter Twenty-Two

Frankie

"A cabin," Frankie whispered.

"Out here?"

That's what Miguel was saying. Probably either a ranger station or a rental nearby. Her eyes widened, and she looked up at Benjamin, who scowled skeptically.

"Yes. There must be," she blurted at him then turned back to her radio. "Miguel! Where?"

"*Half. Mile. North.*"

"Roger. Leaving. Now." She reattached the walkie and pulled open a small side pouch to retrieve her compass. She scrambled off Benjamin and nearly whimpered as the cold struck her. Would it be unreasonable to stay huddled up against his warmth? Her hands playing over his smooth skin and solid muscle?

She knew the answer to that.

A half mile. All they had to do was head north for a half mile. It shouldn't be too hard, especially if the cabin was close to the creek. Sure, she lost her snowshoes as she yard sailed down the embankment, and the professor didn't have his either, but they didn't have too far to go. An hour or two at the most, and they'd be out of the elements.

Safe and warm for the night.

Alone.

Together.

One challenge at a time.

On her feet, with the pack settled on her back, she was ready and raring to move out, but a firm grip on her wrist halted her launch.

"Can you please slow down a minute?" Benjamin pulled her closer as he stood.

"No, we have to move." She shook off his hold and turned. "Get your bag on. You lost your snowshoes too. That's fine, we'll go slow and steady."

"Francesca, *stop*."

She scanned Benjamin's face. His dark, heavy brows furrowed hard over wild, fearful eyes. He breathed heavily in and out of flared nostrils. His full lips—lips she'd kissed earlier that day—pulled tight in a rigid line. Worry radiated off him in palpable waves as he looked around, frantically scanning the valley then back to her face.

His composure hadn't just slipped—it had bolted.

"Look," she squared off. "I know this isn't . . . ideal."

"Isn't *ideal*?"

"But we have limited daylight. We need to make it to the cabin before things get too dire."

"I'd say we're well past dire, Francesca."

She took another step closer, pressing her chest against his. She settled her bare hand on his cheek and was shocked by how cool his skin was beneath her icy fingers. Priority one was getting him somewhere warm. The cabin would probably have a fireplace or wood-burning stove. Worst case, they'd at least be out of the snow and wind, which whipped around them now like they were doing seventy in a top-down convertible. Either way, the outcome would be better than staying out in the elements overnight without warmth or shelter.

His jaw flexed under her touch, but he took a deep breath anyway. His eyelids relaxed, lowering to half-mast. Reaching up on tiptoes, she leaned into him. She let her warm breath play across his parted lips. Flashes of their fevered kiss from before played on a loop in her mind.

A swift gust of bitter cold pulled at Frankie's consciousness.

"Benjamin," she murmured. The ocean depths of his eyes captivated her, and she almost couldn't speak. Swallowing hard, she continued, "I know it's scary, but this is our only hope. Trust me?"

He scanned her face, lingering on her lips in good measure, then nodded. "I trust you."

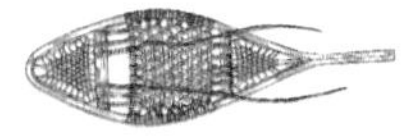

Frankie longed for the warmth of summer as the increasing snowstorm slammed into her hunched form. Thoughts of tank tops, sun-kissed shoulders, and the smell of SPF lotion flitted through her mind. The farther she walked, the more she curled in on herself. Perhaps the smaller she got, the less heat the blustering wind would be capable of stealing.

She snorted at her own delusion.

"Did you s-say s-s-something?" The wobbly timber of Benjamin's voice cut through the windy howl.

"You sound like a snake," she shouted over her shoulder, pressing farther into the headwind.

"What?"

"The cold is m-making your s's sound s-snakey. Like you should be t-teaching the dark arts or something instead of law."

"I don't f-follow."

"Forget it." She had neither the will nor the energy reserve to explain her joke. They'd been slowly dragging through the snow for the past hour, and it felt as though they'd barely made any progress. Everything around them looked the same under the whitewash of flakes.

Boulder.

Boulder.

Tree.

Curve in the creek.

Boulder.

They couldn't be far. Miguel had said the cabin was a half mile north along the valley, and she doggedly consulted her compass to ensure they didn't get turned around.

"Not to sound like a five-year-old, but are we almost there?" Benjamin's teeth chattered as loudly as his words.

"Yes?"

"Your confidence is ins-s-spiring," he sneered softly.

Frankie stopped and spun around, maybe not swiftly enough to launch the full weight of her frustration, but sufficiently enough to stop him in his tracks. How dare he? Of the two of them, she had far and away more experience in these sorts of situations. It wasn't her fault that the damned weather was kicking their asses. She thrust the compass at him.

Benjamin held up both hands. "What are you doing?"

"If you have an issue with my navigation, then by all means"—she pushed the disc against his chest—"you lead the way, *Columbus*."

One perk of the anger growing in her belly was the illusion of heat it created. Her ears burned—though more likely from the biting cold than actual warmth—and she almost expected smoke to plume from each.

After a beat, he nodded and took the compass from her,

brushing past so he could lead the way. Benjamin took a moment to get his bearings and then continued in the direction they'd been moving over the last hellish hour.

Frankie crossed her arms and allowed a smug grin to pull at her lips. *Let's see how well this chump does in these conditions.*

"I see something."

No way.

She pushed with all her remaining strength and overtook his sluggish pace.

"Where?" she demanded, following the direction in which he pointed.

Though barely visible in the whiteout, the shadowy outline of something large enough to be a building stood among a cluster of trees.

"Not too sh-shabby for a newbie, wouldn't you agree, Miss M-Miller?"

Frankie's face scrunched from the snow that peppered her sore skin like airsoft pellets. So many retorts came to mind, each telling him exactly where he could go. But all she could do was shrug.

"What are you waiting for?"

Chapter Twenty-Three

Benjamin

Benjamin prepared himself for the inevitable struggle to gain access to the building as they approached. He lacked the strength to bust down the door, and the thought of getting enough speed to hurtle himself shoulder-first into it seemed laughable. He plodded around the perimeter of the house, scanning each window for a point of ingress. The best plan would be to break a window that was low enough to crawl into but far enough from the main room that the gaping hole in the wall wouldn't affect the heat too much. Traversing the cabin seemed to take forever, but he wanted to be certain he was selecting just the right entrance. Along the way, he spotted two small outbuildings. He'd investigate those later. First order of business: Get inside, get warm.

Finally, he made his way back to the front of the building and stopped dead.

"Francesca?" he called, the shrill holler propelled outward as he pivoted around, scanning for his snowshoe companion. She couldn't have gotten far.

"You coming in?"

He jumped when she popped her head through the entrance. Chattering teeth did little to hide her mocking expression.

"How did you . . . ?" Stepping onto the porch, he knocked the snow off his boots and pants as best he could. The vibration stung his freezing feet. Pins and needles pierced his toes and heel with each thud. He couldn't hide the hiss sliding between his teeth.

She winced knowingly.

"They tend to keep these cabins unlocked to prevent broken windows. They're expensive to replace, especially since they try to keep the exterior as authentic to the original designs as possible." She shut the door behind him.

A puff of breath swirled around Benjamin's head as he let out a low whistle. Made of actual trees, the cabin had a life-size Lincoln Log vibe, reminding him of the set he played with as a kid. While the cabin provided much relief from the near-blizzard conditions outside, the internal temperature wasn't much better. They stood in the quaint living room.

"What the hell were you doing anyways?"

"I was . . ." he trailed off, feeling foolish for attempting to strategize a breach before checking to see if the building was even locked in the first place. He'd make a piss-poor spy. Seven-year-old Benji would have been ashamed. "Never mind."

"Was there anything of note out there?"

"Two small buildings. Sheds, maybe?"

She nodded, gears churning. "Probably a pit toilet and some kind of utility shed or something. We can investigate them once we've warmed up a little."

Francesca knelt in front of a large, ancient wood-burning stove that stood proudly in one corner with a stack of cut wood beside it. A loud, groaning creak resounded in the chilly room as she tugged open the sooty glass door. Benjamin watched as she used a small hatchet to chop kindling and arranged the dry wood in a neat stack.

He'd never cataloged wilderness survivalist skills among his list of desirable attributes in a woman until the crackle of flames snapped to life in the old cast iron box. The firelight flickered and glimmered in her amber eyes as she grinned over her shoulder. She was a vision in winter wear and pride.

Benjamin swallowed thickly and gave her what he hoped was a grateful smile.

"Impressed?" Her honeyed tone curled leisurely to his ears.

"Yes." Oh yes, he was absolutely impressed.

Her grin turned smug. "This old girl should warm things up quickly. They don't make wood-burning stoves like this anymore. In an hour or two, we'll be baking like a couple of potatoes."

An approving growl roared from somewhere deep inside of Benjamin.

"Hungry?" Francesca giggled, rising to her feet.

You have no idea.

Another rolling rumble boomed unmistakably from his stomach.

"It would appear so." He shrugged, only now recognizing how famished he truly was. It was well into the afternoon, and neither of them had taken the time to eat anything substantial since breakfast.

"Grab whatever you want from my bag; I tend to overpack on snacks. I'll check to see if there are any dried goods stocked away in the cabinets."

Benjamin found some jerky and followed her to a small cupboard across the room. He held out the bag and she grabbed a fistful. The top cabinet housed plates, mugs, and cutlery. She crouched and opened the bottom doors.

"Merry *fucking* Christmas." Her breathy sigh caused his stomach to clench. The sound was musical, alluring.

He knelt beside her as she pulled out a square five-gallon bucket. She wrenched the lid off and whooped gleefully. One by one, she pulled out glass jars containing various dry goods. Oats, rice, beans, flour, brown sugar, raisins, nuts, packets of instant yeast, even a small tub of shortening, freeze-dried veggies, and tea bags. Four gallon-sized jugs of sealed water sat in the small cupboard next to where the storage container had been.

"Wait. Should we be eating this?" Benjamin asked wearily.

"Absolutely. Why wouldn't we?"

"Because someone clearly lives here."

Francesca shook her head, laughing. "I appreciate the morality, but it's totally allowed in this scenario. In the early 1900s the U.S. Forest Service offered up thousands of cabins for people to buy and live in. Some are used as rentals, some are seasonal homes. My assumption is this is only accessible in the warmer months when the risk of being snowed in is minimal, but they leave food stores behind and the doors unlocked in case some needy traveler comes by."

"Are you feeding me a story to satisfy my sense of integrity?"

"Maybe. Maybe not. You're just going to have to trust me." She stood and lifted the bucket.

"Let me help." Benjamin shot up and took it from her.

Francesca snagged two jugs, both of which were frozen solid, and lugged them over to thaw beside the stove. "For now, we can make some rice and beans with the leftover water in our water bottles. There should be enough in them."

While she set to work, Benjamin surveyed the rest of the cabin. Two large wooden chairs with cushioned seats and backs faced the fireplace. A small table sat between them, large enough to share a meager meal. The small set of cabinets where they'd found the food stood just behind the chairs. Opposite the front door were two interior doors. He cracked one open and found a small bedroom with a double bed, side table, and window. An old woven rug covered most of the scuffed hardwood floor. He left the door open to allow the warm air to circulate.

Through the other door, he found what looked to be a tiled closet with a drain in the middle of the floor. A thick metal hook hung from the ceiling. He tried to make out what the room could be but came up blank.

"It's a kill room."

"*Aaahh!*" The shriek popped out of his mouth as he whirled around. He hadn't heard Francesca approach. How had she moved so quietly? He looked down and noticed she'd taken off her bib overalls and boots. What remained were a snug pair of black leggings and her cream thermal shirt. Honey waves tumbled wildly about her now that they'd been freed from her haphazard braids. Sweat dripped down his back as he took in the cozy sight of her. Mouth dry, he swallowed a few times to search for words.

What had she said?

"Wait? A *what* room?" Benjamin's eyes widened and then promptly narrowed as she bent over at the waist, laughing so hard she had to brace her hands on her knees. "Cute."

Her mischievous grin sucked all the oxygen from the room and pummeled his chest with heat. Suddenly, he needed all unnecessary layers removed or he'd sweat to death. He unzipped his coat and toed off his boots. She hadn't exaggerated; that stove had quickly filled the room with delicious dry heat. He stubbornly assured himself that was the cause of his flush, not her smile.

"Best guess, it's a shower." She pushed past him and surveyed the little closet. "That's where you hang the solar shower once it's warm and the water goes down the drain. Pretty genius when you don't want to strip out in the woods."

Flashes of the two of them squeezed into the tiny space flooded Benjamin's mind. He imagined washing the sweat from her body then carrying her naked and dripping across the hall. He shook his head to dislodge the problematic thoughts.

"There's one bedroom," he muttered.

"Oh?"

"It's yours. I wouldn't dream of invading your space like

that." Best to set the boundaries now before the sun set and exhaustion muddled their decision-making.

Was that disappointment scrolling across her face?

"Sounds good." She nibbled her lip, crossing her arms across her chest. "You should put your wet layers by the stove to dry. Food will be ready in half an hour."

Chapter Twenty-Four

Frankie

Frankie prepared a basic dinner of rice and beans while Benjamin made his best effort to give her space. He'd explored every inch of the cabin, even finding the solar shower in a chest in the little bedroom, along with a few card games and extra quilts and sheets. Then he took his investigation outside. Upon his return, he was happy to report that one of the outbuildings was a pit toilet, and the other was a woodshed stuffed full of dry, split wood.

Frankie was grateful for the armload of firewood he stacked beside the stove, but it was the outhouse that had her full bladder breathing a sign of relief. She practically leapt into her snow gear and sprinted to the little building. A few minutes later, she was back, tending to dinner once more.

Making it to this cabin—especially one so well stocked and cared for—was a literal lifesaver, and she couldn't be more grateful to whoever loved and cared for this little home away from home. It had everything they needed. Food, drinking water, stove, a bed.

It's yours. I wouldn't dream of invading your space like that.

Except that he already had. Three times now.

First, at the welcome dinner in Leavenworth, he hovered within arm's reach, peering over her shoulder to snoop on her texts and teasing her about them.

Then, when he kissed her on the trail while they argued. She'd been royally pissed that he'd distracted her enough to throw her off course. It made her feel like such a rookie.

Lastly, when he held her in his lap, cradling her tightly to his chest. Sure, that last one was a necessity, but the pattern still stood.

The professor inserted himself into her bubble repeatedly.

Why did the idea of him crowding her space in that cozy little bed sound amazing? Curled up all warm and comfortable beside him, smelling his spicy, autumn scent, listening to his heavy breath. That damned kiss was to blame. It had to be.

Frankie had tried to radio Miguel and Jon a few times during their trek, but the whiteout conditions jacked with the transmission. Search and rescue wouldn't be coming for them until the storm cleared, so Frankie and Benjamin were stranded—together—for the foreseeable future.

Once the meal was ready, Frankie dished up two bowls and deposited them on the table. Neither traveler said a word; they were too busy shoveling boiling hot spoonfuls into their mouths.

Frankie surreptitiously watched Benjamin as he plowed through a second helping of the bland concoction. His face was inches from his bowl, knuckles white from the death grip on his utensil. The steam from the hot food fogged his scratched glasses. Which seemed to have taken a few extra hits in his efforts to join her in the ravine.

"Can I help you?" he murmured, glancing up through his lashes and furrowed brow.

Suddenly transported back to the family law classroom, Frankie had a flash of Professor Clark analyzing her in a familiar way. She stiffened for a moment then remembered he no longer held the power he once had. It was she who'd navigated them to the cabin, started the fire, and fed them.

She was the authority in this scenario.

So, why did the way he looked at her make her feel . . . vulnerable?

"What grade did I get?" she blurted.

"Miss Miller," he rested his spoon in his bowl and raised his chin. "You know I can't tell you the results of your final exam until they are reported through the proper channels." Did she spot a twinkle of humor in his eye?

"I was referring to dinner," she said, batting her eyes and feigning innocence.

"Well, in that case," he took a thoughtful bite, closing his eyes to focus on the flavors and textures. His thick black brows came together in concentration. Frankie followed the proud line of his aristocratic nose and landed on his full lips just as the tip of his tongue slid along the corner. His jaw muscle flexed beneath a few days' worth of dark stubble with each chew until, finally, his Adam's apple bobbed as he swallowed.

Jesus. Frankie was hulled up in the middle of nowhere with an absolute Adonis.

Benjamin opened his ocean eyes and leveled them on hers.

"C-plus," he declared.

Frankie sputtered. "A C-plus? Really? You're telling me after the day we've had and how hungry you are that this isn't even worthy of something in the B range?"

"It's prudent to be objective when grading one's work. It would be unethical to take into account situational markers that might temporarily sway my opinion." He regulated his facial expression like a pro, aside from a tiny quirk of his left cheek, flashing a barely noticeable dimple.

"Well then." Frankie snatched his bowl and scraped the remaining rice and beans into hers then slid the empty dish back. "I won't subject you to any more of this objectively mediocre slop."

Benjamin barked out a hearty laugh as he rose from the table and proceeded to dish up another helping from the pot on the stove. "Just because it's not worthy of a gourmet restaurant doesn't mean that I turn my nose up at it. This is hitting the spot after a brutal day. Thank you, Francesca."

The way he settled his eyes on hers and rumbled her name deep in his throat was so satisfying that Frankie felt three beers deep. She was transfixed, as though she were drowning in the ocean whirlpools of his irises but didn't have sense enough to try to escape. Frankie was the first to blink, but then Benjamin removed his battered glasses and set them aside.

Cheater.

"You're welcome," Frankie offered stiffly.

"Besides, I've never been a picky eater," he mentioned, plowing back into his bowl.

"I bet your mom loved that. I was the same way. I ate anything my mom put in front of me."

"That's because your mother has the culinary prowess of Martha Stewart, according to Johnny anyway. I remember one year, she sent him a care package, and he shared some of those lemon triangle things with me. *Delicious.*"

"Her iced lemon shortbread. They're even better straight from the oven. What about your mom? Is she a good cook?" Frankie settled back after finishing the last bite and sighed with comfort. Warm room, warm belly—she felt comfortable for the first time all day.

Until she noticed Benjamin's shoulders stiffen and eyes darken. He didn't respond right away, and she replayed her last question, scanning it for whatever had caused the atmospheric shift.

"She . . ." He looked hard at Frankie. "She did the best that she could."

His tone sounded briskly academic and did not invite additional questions. Gone was the aggravating man who seemed to take great pleasure in ruffling her feathers. Frankie was—once again—sharing a meal with her cold professor.

Suddenly, she felt the urge to give him space. Continuing with the same line of questioning wouldn't lead anywhere good.

She rose, gathering the two practically licked clean dishes, and slid them into the blue enamel washbasin she'd been melting snow in by the stove. She fetched a towel and some biodegradable soap from the cabinet, when a large hand grazed the small of her back. Flames seeped through her thermal shirt and licked at her skin.

"You cooked. Let me do the dishes," came his voice, thick with apology without actually uttering one.

"Suit yourself." She sidestepped and handed over the towel, more to dislodge his large hand and the fever it caused than to concede to the help.

After handing off the responsibility to Benjamin, Frankie milled about the cabin, snooping in every container and cabinet. She grinned at what she found in the hope chest nestled in the corner of the bedroom. She scurried into the main room, wearing a broad grin.

Benjamin hadn't heard her, which gave her a moment to watch the muscles bunch and flex under the knit of his black base layer. With a dish towel slung casually over one shoulder, he sang quietly, swaying gently as though he were somewhere else entirely. She couldn't make out the words; however, she thought she heard him say something about a big butt and smile.

She slunk closer, trying to hear better.

Just above a whisper, he crooned "Poison" by Bell Biv DeVoe.

No.

That couldn't be right.

Her stodgy professor wouldn't recite a song so crass. And yet there he was, bobbing his head and subtly shimmying a shoulder to one of Frankie's all-time favorite R&B 90s hits.

Chapter Twenty-Five

Benjamin

The bowl Benjamin dried slipped from his fingers and slapped into the washbasin on the counter. He yelped, jumping back as a splash of water drenched the front of his shirt. He turned to the off-key caterwauling behind him.

Francesca twirled and swerved her hips as she sang the chorus from "Poison", the song he'd been murmuring while he washed. A laughing grin pulled hard at her rosy cheeks. He watched, mesmerized, as she lifted her arms languidly above her head and let her eyes drift closed while she swayed. Transfixed by her apparent witchcraft, his feet danced him forward until their hips met in a rhythmic cadence. He slid his hands down her ribcage and settled them on her rocking hips. Lavender and eucalyptus invaded his senses as her hair tumbled around her shoulders, shimmying with each wiggle.

More lyrics popped out of his mouth to match hers as they dueted and danced like fools. The performance wouldn't have won them any awards. But something about letting go—completely abandoning his give-a-damn—swept Benjamin up in a heady thrill. He leaned into it until the last few lyrics echoed off the cabin walls.

Breath heavy, chests rising and falling in unison, the song faded from their lips. Benjamin squeezed, thumbs pressing divots into the silky flesh just below Francesca's shirt. The light in her liquid gold eyes dimmed, becoming darker, more intoxicating.

The soft femininity of her molded seamlessly against the hard masculinity of his tense body. He'd lost all rationality when he'd sauntered over, began dancing with her, and refused to allow sensibility to return—not yet, anyway.

Instead, he leaned down, and the moment his lips touched hers, she melted against him. She emitted a tiny groan and entangled her fingers in his shirt, pulling him closer. He ran the tip of his tongue along her bottom lip, and she opened to him. Submitting, offering. He happily accepted, plunging his tongue into her hot little mouth. He gripped a fistful of wild hair, positioning her just so to gain the exquisite access he'd been craving for months.

She was perfection. He could have devoured her until the sun set and rose again on them the next morning had she not pressed a hand gently to his chest.

"Wait," she managed to say as he untangled his lips from hers. "This is . . . we should . . . just give me a minute to think."

"Of course." Her palm remained against his sternum as his heart continued to wail against it. Loosening his grip on her hair, he toyed with a strand at the base of her scalp. She shivered in response. Oh, the delight he could inflict on her.

"A mistake," she sighed. "We . . . we're in this wild and dangerous situation and . . . and it's only natural that we are at a heightened state of . . . of . . ."

"Arousal," he offered huskily.

Francesca swallowed hard and nodded. "Yes. It's just like what Jon and Lucy went through. Shared trauma leads to attraction and then comes the bad decisions."

"I highly doubt they view their decisions as bad. They're getting married this weekend after all." He chuckled, eyes flitting across her swollen lips and flushed cheeks.

"Is that a proposal?" she snorted.

"Ha!" He choked a little as a tightness clenched in his chest. "Not if we were the last two people on Earth."

"Ouch." She stepped back. His arms fell to his sides. "I was joking. You didn't have to sound so disgusted."

"It's not personal, Francesca," he huffed. He rammed a hand through his messy hair. "Marriage is the most asinine institution ever created. It has the capability to *destroy* people. I refuse to enter into that kind of arrangement with anyone, let alone with *you*."

"Woah. First of all," she began, ticking off each finger, "there's so much in that box to unpack that I won't be touching it with a ten-foot pole. Second of all, I'm a damn catch, you snobby elitist. Thirdly, can we calm the fuck down for a minute and reset? I was making a *joke*. You've heard of those, right? Something silly you say for the fun of it. Fourth—"

"You're going to run out of fingers soon." See, he could joke too.

If she heard him, she didn't let on that she had. "We got carried away—understatement of the century—and the day got to us. All the stress bubbled over and caused us to make out a little. No biggie. Water under the bridge, or whatever."

Benjamin scrubbed a hand down his face, suddenly feeling very tired. With growing shadows in the tiny cabin, he could barely read Francesca's face, but he knew he'd hurt her feelings. That was the last thing he wanted, but the idea of marriage was a sore subject, especially with how things turned out for his mother when she divorced his father.

He'd let loose and the moment got away from him. If he'd been paying more attention and practiced a little self-control, it never would have happened.

He also never would have learned how well her curves molded against him, like they were built from the same lump of clay.

He shook his head.

"You're right. I apologize if I was rude. Let's move past it." He held out his hand. *Why was he trying to give her a handshake? What* was *that?* But he held firm, arm remaining extended.

Her scowly smirk announced loudly that she also thought the gesture foolish and slapped her palm against his in a low-five. "It's been decided."

"Good," he replied gruffly, turning to finish his earlier chore. His damp shirt stuck uncomfortably to his belly. He pinched the fabric away from his skin only to have it slap back and cling. Wet clothes were the worst. He considered removing it to dry by the stove then dissolved the notion as quickly as it appeared. He'd hate to add more to the awkwardness he'd already created by playing along with Francesca's little dance party. The shirt would dry on its own.

"Do you play cribbage?" A warm light illuminated from where Francesca struck a match and ignited a hurricane oil lantern.

"I know how to play."

But haven't played since my father left my mother to rot in her own destitution.

"Great," she chirped. "I play muggins, so you'd better prepare yourself."

"Francesca," he began, drying the last dish and replacing the stack in the cabinet. He turned and spotted her glowing, hopeful smile. It had to have been one of the few genuine display of joy that he'd ever seen on her. The reconciliation of that—especially since they'd known each other for months—twisted the guilt dial up to eleven.

"Don't say no. Please? I need something to do that'll shut my brain off. Usually, I reread your posted lectures. They're so boring that they power me down like a robot with an off switch."

The guilt dial reversed to a solid eight.

"My lectures aren't meant to be riveting. Their purpose is to inform." He scowled. "And I'll have you know—"

"Chill, professor. I'm only teasing." She removed the playing cards from the pack and shuffled them expertly. "About the lectures, I mean. I'd never *choose* to read them. I meant what I said about needing something to turn my brain off at night."

"Well, what do you normally do to wind down at the end of a day?"

Benjamin thought he spied a flush creep up her neck and his brain went wild at the implication.

"Fine." Perhaps he could use a distraction as well. He settled into the chair opposite her and arched a brow as she dealt. "Shouldn't we cut to see who goes first?"

"I found the game, so I get the privilege." She winked gamely and all Benjamin could do was shrug. "Ready to get spanked?"

"Oh, Francesca," he crooned as he picked up his cards and deposited two in her crib. "You'll soon learn that I'm always the one doing the spanking."

Chapter Twenty-Six

Frankie

"Fifteen-two, fifteen-four, fifteen-six, and a triple run of three makes twenty-one." Benjamin's silky voice twisted the blade of defeat in Frankie's chest. "Oh, and nobs makes twenty-two. I believe that's game, and look . . . I skunked you *again*."

"Best four out of seven." Frankie swallowed the urge to flip the table and toss the damned board into the fireplace. She hadn't been this badly beaten in cribbage since the summer vacation before her junior year in high school when Jon had been on a lucky streak a mile long. She hadn't won a single game against Benjamin, and the accumulated losses started to sting.

"Three massacres in a row is enough, don't you think? I'd hate to get you too down." He leaned forward, gently taking the deck from her hands, long fingers grazing across hers as he went.

The contact zapped an electric bolt up her arm and down to her core. She'd thought a few rounds of the card game would make her drowsy; instead, the teasing and smug expression accompanying Benjamin's wins revved her up even more.

"Fine. I was about to hit my stride, but whatever."

His gritty chuckle scraped down her spine, and she squirmed in her seat. "Don't you think it would be wise to get some rest?"

"I suppose." Frankie sighed and rose from the table. "Thanks for playing with me."

"You're welcome, Francesca."

After tucking a few more logs into the stove, she made her way to the small bedroom and shut the door behind her. Now what? Wide awake, she paced across the threadbare rug. Her body was exhausted despite the cogs and gears cranking furiously in her brain.

Frankie removed her bra and flipped back the covers with a huff. She should be having dinner with Clint, not dancing and playing cards with Benjamin. If she was going to make out with anyone, it should have been with that massive surfer boy in a uniform, not her former professor.

But, holy hell, that man could kiss. Had he been anyone else—and still able to make her melt into a puddle of lust—she would have happily bought a ticket to ride that ride. Her self-imposed celibacy had been brutal, even if it was necessary for her studies, and she was ready to kiss it goodbye. Or, rather, fuck it goodbye.

She crawled into bed and fluffed one of the pillows, accidentally knocking the other off the edge and onto the floor. With a grumble, she leaned over and blindly reached. Snagging a fistful of the flannel case, she considered giving it to Benjamin to use tonight. He'd already offered up the bed and sequestered himself to the hard cabin floor. Fortunately, they'd found extra quilts for him to lay on, but the likelihood that the pile of blankets would be as comfortable as the small mattress was slim. Giving him a pillow would be a show of goodwill or . . . or camaraderie or—screw it, it would be nice.

She stepped through the bedroom door, clutching the pillow to her chest, and stopped dead as she entered the living room.

Laying on his back on a makeshift pallet of quilts, wearing nothing but boxer briefs and a relaxed expression, was the most perfect specimen of the male species she'd ever witnessed in person. His head, with a swirl of rumpled black tresses, settled onto one arm with an elbow splayed out to the side. The other rested on an ice cube tray of abs sporting a trail of matching hair that Frankie would have happily followed down beneath his waistband. She watched him as he gazed at the glass pane of the stove, staring into the flames that flickered across his olive skin. Perhaps she imagined it, but she could have sworn she smelled the heady scent of cinnamon and sandalwood from where she gawked like a creep across the room.

Shame prickled her neck, and she cleared her throat to either make her presence known or will words from her throat. Benjamin snapped his head in her direction and propped himself up on both elbows.

"Is everything all right?" he asked, sounding gruff and slightly . . . hopeful?

"I-I." *Words, Frankie. Say words.* "I have an extra pillow. I thought . . ." She swallowed the lustful lump in her throat. "Maybe you might want it."

He stood, put on the glasses that had been resting beside him, and stalked the half-dozen steps it took to reach her. Her eyes raked down the line of his chest. A black and gray tattoo spanned the entire left side of his ribcage. The woman in a gossamer robe, blindfolded and holding a sword and set of scales, looked real enough to jump off of his skin and saunter around. Of course he'd have a massive tattoo of Lady Justice. Anything else would be out of place on his sculpted core.

Benjamin reached out, and Frankie noted that when accepting the offering, he was careful not to touch his hand to hers. The pillow dangled from his fingertips until he tossed it onto the nearby chair.

"Thank you." Why did those words sound like a warning? "Goodnight."

"Goodnight," she croaked but stood frozen to the floor.

His eyes dragged as heavily over the front of her thermal shirt as if he'd used his hands. Even in the dim cabin, illuminated only by firelight, Frankie clocked the dilation of his pupils.

No bra.

She'd forgotten about taking it off a few minutes before. Her nipples beaded in response to his awareness of her exposure. Closing his eyelids tightly, he shook his head and looked back up to Frankie's face.

"Go to bed," he rumbled low in his throat, taking a step forward.

Instinctively, she took a step back, but only one to match his. He advanced another, and she retreated in kind. A few more, and they reached the open door of the bedroom. Benjamin raised a hand to either side of the doorframe. Her own curiosity and desire stood heavily at her back, caging her into the threshold just inches from his nearly naked body.

She licked her lips; he tracked the swipe of her tongue like a cat following its next kill. She worked up the nerve and said, "What if we . . ."

"Francesca." Another warning, but this one held indecision.

Benjamin lowered his hands, reaching one out to delicately trace her collarbone from shoulder to neck, where her pulse bashed violently through her veins. He settled his palm at the point in the center and urged her back toward the bed. Two steps. Three. The back of her knees hit the mattress, and she sat, unwilling to tear her gaze from his darkened face. He twirled a lock of her hair between his thumb and forefinger as she sat transfixed. Memorizing his outline, backlit from the roasting fire flickering in the next room. She squeezed her knees tightly together in an effort to satisfy the ache growing between them.

"Go to bed." He wrestled the words out, but Frankie was

convinced of their absolution.

Before releasing her hair, he gently tugged, coaxing a tiny whimper from her lips. He groaned in response but turned and left the room, closing the door without a backward look.

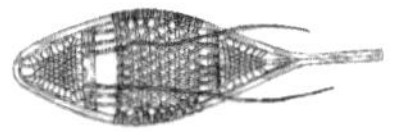

A thousand hours later, Frankie still hadn't managed to drift off to sleep. How could she after that . . . that . . .

What the fuck was that?

She thought she was horny before, but now her meter hovered squarely between blazing inferno and all-out combustion. The mattress spring squawked as she flopped around to get comfortable and squirmed from overstimulation.

Images of the bronzed man edging her toward the very bed she laid in was slowly—ok, fine, quickly—driving her mad. There was only one way that she'd be able to finally drift off, and counting sheep wasn't it. Reaching down, she slipped her fingers beneath her panties, stroking purposefully to quell the fever that lingered there. It didn't take long for her to summit the pinnacle and slide down the other side, a quiet whine slipping from her lips as she reveled in ripples of pleasure.

Two point four seconds later, she passed out, drooling on her pillow.

Chapter Twenty-Seven

Monday, 4 days until the wedding: Benjamin

"**O**uch!" Benjamin hissed, sucking on his pinkie to relieve the sting of accidentally touching the stove. He shook his hand out beside him as he labored over breakfast, adding enough water and powdered milk to the oats to get just the right consistency. He scowled at the thick paste and added more liquid.

He'd woken up in a miserable mood with a back nearly as stiff as the erection he'd tried to ignore all night. After returning Francesca to bed untouched—well, nearly untouched—featuring an admirable display of self-control, he might add, Benjamin had struggled to fall asleep. Eventually, he managed to relax his mind enough to reverse the blood flow pulsing below his waistband. That is until he heard the telltale wobble of bedsprings and a satisfied little whine seeping through the bedroom walls. At that point, all progress was lost.

As he continued with the oatmeal, pondering the injustice of masturbatory double standards, the bedroom door cracked open.

"Morning," came the husky, sleep-addled greeting.

"Mm-hm," he murmured.

"Sleep all right?"

"Fine."

She sniffed the air and grinned. "You're making me breakfast?"

"What makes you think I'm sharing?" He glowered down at

the pot he stirred.

She tugged on her snow bibs.

"It's a rough trek to the pit toilet this morning. It snowed eighteen inches and counting by my estimation, and the wind is brutal." As if on cue, an ominous howl whipped around the little cabin, rattling the shutters. "Blew the glasses right off of me when I went earlier." Benjamin adjusted the black frames as they slipped down his nose.

Francesca moved to stand beside him. He glanced over his shoulder and caught her just as she clocked the state of his eyewear.

"What happened?" She choked on a hiccupy giggle.

"I stepped on them." He grumbled, remembering how the wailing wind had drowned out his enraged roar. Fortunately, it had only been one of the arms and not the already scuffed lenses. A small twig and a bit of first aid tape made them wearable.

Francesca leaned in and evaluated his patch job.

"Not too bad," she murmured, reaching up to touch the tiny splint. She sucked in a breath as Benjamin encircled her wrist.

"My point is"—he released her and turned back to the oatmeal—"that it's rough out there. Do you want an escort?"

"Breakfast and security detail. Be still my heart."

"I'm also making tea."

"The trifecta. You're going to make a Mrs. Professor Clark one happy lady someday."

He grunted.

"Teasing." She moaned, rolling her eyes in judgment. "Thanks for the offer, but I can manage the out and back on my own. If I don't return in five, come find me." She stepped into her boots and out the door.

Through the night, the storm had seemed to settle yet awoke in the early morning with renewed fervor, guaranteeing an extension to their stranding. Perhaps they'd get lucky and the squall would die down enough for them to make their way out of the valley. Though Benjamin rarely found himself to be that fortunate.

He dished up two bowls and carried them, along with the brown sugar and raisins, to the little table. As he poured boiling water over the teabags in each mug, the front door burst open.

Shivering and splatted like a Jackson Pollock on all sides with snow, Francesca hustled into the cabin. She pressed her weight against the door to latch it shut then made a beeline for the stove.

"Holy fuckery of fucks, it's c-cold out there," she said as she peeled off her coat and bibs and shook the flakes from her hair.

"Like I said," Benjamin drolled. He gestured to the spread. "Breakfast is ready."

Francesca's grin lit up the small, shadowy room as she settled into one of the chairs and topped her oatmeal with two heaping spoonfuls of brown sugar. She picked up a raisin, popped it into her mouth and cringed.

He eyed the dried fruit he'd already tossed into his bowl with concern. "Have they gone bad?"

"Nope." She mixed her breakfast, blowing on it to cool it down. "I hate raisins."

"Then why did you eat one?"

"What if I liked them today?"

Benjamin felt his face contort in confusion. "If you hate them, what would one day make?"

Francesca leveled a scowl on him that was so exasperated he questioned his own sense of logic for a moment. "Tastes can change, professor."

"Sure, but in a day?"

"Why not?"

She scooped into her bowl and took a big bite. She smiled

cheerfully, cheeks full of oatmeal.

"Sometimes you confuse me, Miss Miller."

"That's because you're stuck in your ways," she said, wiggling her spoon at him. "A creature of habit."

She had him pegged.

He did have a tendency to set up his days methodically. Perhaps to an outside observer, they were mundane, but to him, it was a measure of adulthood. Long gone were the random flights of fancy that accompanied youth. At twelve, responsibility had rolled in like a thunderhead. He could either whine about it or grab an umbrella. He chose the latter. Since then, he'd organized his world to follow a carefully curated trajectory. The day-to-day schedule was what kept him on track and allowed him to survive. Even better, it allowed him to find success.

"There's nothing wrong with routine," Benajmin scolded.

"To an extent. But you'll miss out on so much if you're *too* rigid."

"Like eating my version of a raisin?"

"Something like that," she chuckled through a mouthful. "Thank you for breakfast."

"My pleasure."

He found satisfaction in providing something that might ease the burden of their situation. The only thing he'd managed thus far was bandaging her wound and washing a few measly dishes. He tended to be the expert in most of the situations he found himself in, and this adventure made him face his discomfort with feeling helpless. He wanted to contribute. Craved the knowledge that he was pulling his own weight.

"Did you sleep all right?" Francesca scrunched up her face like she already knew the answer.

Benjamin shrugged. "Eventually."

"I doubt you were comfortable," she began, scanning his eyes and furrowing her brows. "If we can't get out of here by tonight, you can have the bed."

He warmed momentarily from her generosity then immediately scowled. He wasn't going to take the bed from her; he'd feel like an absolute rat if he did. The floor was fine. Once he finally calmed his boiling blood last night, he drifted off and slept like the dead, which was probably why he woke up with a crick in his back.

"Thanks, but I'd rather focus on getting out of here before then," he stated, finally digging into his meal.

"I get that. However,"—Francesca paused, glancing out the window of the rustic log cabin—"we may need to accept that this could go on for a while."

Benjamin followed her gaze and swallowed a clump of oats, cringing at what he saw.

A whiteout.

Zero visibility.

It would be suicide going out there, and who knew if search and rescue would even be around to collect them? For all he knew, Highway 2 was closed, and if that were the case, where would they be? Stuck in the elements with no shelter.

He sighed, conceding to their mutual fate.

"Then how do you suggest we spend our time?"

She grinned. "I have a few ideas."

Chapter Twenty-Eight

Frankie

"Where'd you learn to do that?" Frankie purred as the warm, yeasty scent bloomed throughout the cabin.

"Didn't everyone learn how to make bread from scratch a few years ago when we were all stuck at home with nothing to do?" Benjamin tapped on the crusty shell of the loaf. Nodding with satisfaction at the hollow tone, he removed it from the Dutch oven and set it on the table to cool.

"Some of us tried and failed miserably." She stood beside him, sniffing up all the fresh carb smell her nose could hold.

"Perhaps I'm gifted."

"Resorting to stroking your own ego these days, are we, professor?" She pinched his side and gulped at the feel of solid muscle beneath his shirt. He swatted at her with the flour-dusted towel, and she yelped when it cracked just below her rump. "Ouch, watch it!"

"I have exceptional aim too." He waggled his eyebrows as a gleaming white smile split wide across his handsome features. The stubble he'd grown over the last few days, paired with his rumpled hair, softened him in a way that made him more approachable. It had Frankie thinking that if she'd come across him at The Rooftop Tavern in Leavenworth, she might've considered chatting him up. He gave off a softer vibe, in a ruggedly handsome way of course. Not that he wasn't sexy as hell in a suit with his hair immaculately styled and a fresh shave, but she liked him better this way.

She'd spent the better part of the day creeping on her cabin mate as they did whatever random things they could think of to pass the time.

Especially when he did his little workout routine.

Benjamin had mentioned running every day and complained that he felt antsy because he hadn't been able to in a while or something like that. Honestly, Frankie wasn't really listening because she was too busy drooling. Hiding behind an ancient issue of *National Geographic*, she kept sneaking peeks. The magazine fell from her hands completely when he started doing lunges.

Following breakfast, they'd clawed their way through the storm to the little woodshed out back and gathered a few more logs. Frankie collected and boiled snow to replenish their drinking water then switched to a desperate insistence on filling the solar shower to bathe later. Benjamin had laughed at the "unnecessary" task. But no amount of scoffing from him would deter her from her mission.

Midday, as Benjamin lumbered around the main room, practically swaying on his feet, Frankie insisted he take a nap on the bed. It took some convincing and a little shoving, but he finally agreed, waking up two hours later in a seriously improved mood. They played a couple dozen rounds of cribbage—in which each win earned the victor a point that could be added up and cashed out from a list of "prizes" they'd agreed upon in advance. Frankie had eventually hit that stride she'd been blabbering on about and led the final point tally sixteen to eight.

All the while, the snow dumped around them, the wind practically vibrating the little cabin off its weathered foundation. One thing was clear as ice: They were staying another night.

In the cabin.

Still alone.

Together.

And for whatever sadomasochistic reason, Frankie wasn't really bothered by it.

She rubbed her ass cheek that still stung from where Benjamin had snapped her with the towel and glared as he set about finishing dinner. Sitting in one of the chairs with a cup of warm tea in her hands, a beautifully sculpted man at the stove, and the lingering scent of fresh bread swirling around her, Frankie secretly hoped this fantasy could last a little longer.

Is this what Stockholm syndrome feels like?

She shook herself, appalled at her misguided musings. They weren't playing house. And while Benjamin was beautiful, and an incredible kisser, he had treated her horribly with zero remorse while she was his student. Why did she continually have to remind herself of that? Getting along with him enough to make it through this ordeal was all that was required of her.

So why did she want more than to merely *survive* with him?

"Bon appétit," he sang, setting a bowl in front of her and retrieving the still-warm loaf of bread. He ripped off a chunk and handed the rest to Frankie, who followed suit. She sank her teeth into the soft, chewy center and used a piece of the flaky crust to scoop up a bite of rice and beans similar to the dinner she'd prepared the night before.

"Ohhh yeahhh." The meal was perfection, and she frowned at that fact. "How did . . . what? I made the exact same thing last night. Why is yours so much tastier?"

"It's called salt." He smirked through ravenous bites.

Frankie considered flicking a spoonful in his direction but decided it'd be a crime to waste any of the delicious dish. Instead, she rolled her eyes and ripped off another hunk of bread.

"Did you camp much as a kid?" she asked, chewing thoughtfully.

"No," Benjamin clipped, shaking his head. "We weren't the camping type of family."

"What type of family were you?"

"The broken type." He hadn't meant to let that sentiment pop out; his expression made that little fact obvious. But he relaxed his shocked eyes and shrugged.

"Divorce?"

"Just like half of the U.S." His sigh was resigned.

"How old were you?"

"Twelve."

"That must have been hard."

"Divorce is never easy, Francesca." His hard stare froze her in place. Sweeps of sadness and shame rippled over his stern features, and Frankie found herself desperate to know the layers beneath his comment. Then she remembered what he had done for work before teaching at Northwest Washington University.

"At the welcome banquet, Jon mentioned you were a divorce attorney?"

"Are you asking or stating fact?"

"Don't 'professor' me with your Socratic bullshit, *Benji*. We're equals now that the quarter's done." She smiled sweetly, happily making *him* squirm for once.

"But you haven't received your final grade yet." He leaned back, arms crossed.

"And when were you going to get around to handling that?" She shoveled in another bite, brows raised.

"I don't," he conceded. "I already gave my TAs the rubric that they use to score the finals."

"Like I said," she chirped, scooping stray flakes of bread and crumbs into her palms and dusting them off into her empty bowl. "Equals."

"There are some things I'd like to move on from. Rehashing

the past leads to nothing good."

"You mean besides closure?"

He said nothing, only bored his eyes deeper into hers.

But she was immovable.

"Five cribbage wins."

"You can't be serious—"

"As a heart attack. I'm cashing in. We agreed that five wins could get an answer to one question. My question is: What was it like being a divorce attorney?"

Benjamin released his crossed arms and raked his fingers down his face.

"Soul-sucking, guilt-inducing, made me feel like the scum of the earth." He appeared suddenly tired, almost older in his exhaustion—all the cheery effects of his earlier nap gone.

"Why?"

"I answered your question."

"Five more points, then," she responded to the emphatic shake of his head and downward gaze. "Why?"

"Because it made me feel like my father." His ocean eyes darkened into tumultuous swells, hinting at the squall that never quite quieted inside of him.

"Five more points." His shoulders tensed, jaw flexed. She saw it and still pressed further. "What did your father do that makes you so disgusted to be like him?"

She thought she saw a glistening of moisture in his tormented eyes. The rise and fall of his chest morphed from slow and steady to labored and jagged, like he'd just finished another set of lunges in the middle of the small cabin. The urge to retract her question was strong, but she had to know. Curiosity won over in her quest to understand the depths of the man who had once been her terrifying professor.

"Benjamin."

"He's the reason my mother is dead."

Chapter Twenty-Nine

Benjamin

Francesca's mouth hung open, and Benjamin watched as her cheeks quickly flamed from a cozy pink to an embarrassed, regretful red. She'd pushed. Used the silly point system to get him to talk. He could have denied her. Could have said that he refused to answer such personal questions. Yet why did it feel critical to be candid with her? He'd tried to fight it, but after blurting out the truth, he felt the dam give way.

"My father dropped my mother and me for a woman twenty years his junior. If that wasn't bad enough, he hired a team of divorce attorneys to ensure we wouldn't get a penny beyond the laughable child support he paid every month. We went from living in luxury—literally having every whim fulfilled—to barely getting by in a one-bedroom apartment in South Tacoma. I adapted. Quickly became familiar with food banks in the area and churches that provided shoes and clothes for teens. I figured out how to survive, but she . . ."

The beautiful, jovial, statuesque woman who'd raised Benjamin flashed through his mind. Images of her in cocktail dresses as the family hosted annual Christmas parties. Sweeping wayward strands of black hair off her face as they sailed on their boat on Lake Washington. Smiling warmly at him when she'd lightly kiss his forehead before bed each night. *I love you to the moon and back,* she'd say as he climbed the stairs to his room. *Until tomorrow, my love.*

"My mother wilted. Drank to drown her sorrow over the fabulous life she'd lost. Her parents wouldn't help us either. Said she'd made her bed, and if she couldn't keep her husband in it, then it must have been her fault. For whatever sick, self-torturous reason, I became a divorce attorney and a damned good one. I managed high-profile cases, earning buckets of money off vulnerable, powerless people. I helped countless rich pricks do to their spouses what my father did to my mother. All the while, I justified the cyclical behavior because I'd suffered too. Like it was my turn to be the powerful one. I worked hard, kept my nose clean, cared for my mom when she was too broken to care for me, and so I figured I was owed."

At some point during his blabbering, he'd stood and started pacing. Francesca said nothing. She just sat there with tears rolling down her face. He turned, couldn't watch the salty trails left on her cheeks, feeling torn between wiping hers away and crying his own.

He'd allowed himself to weep for his mother on the day of her funeral. Surprisingly, his father had shown up, landing a heavy hand on his shoulder.

"She wasn't like us," his father had said.

Benjamin had turned and looked at the man beside him, an older version of himself, but kept his mouth shut.

"We're strong. Resilient." Benjamin felt nauseated under the squeeze of his father's fingers. *"I'm proud of you for making something of yourself. Just like your old man."*

The next day, Benjamin had marched into his boss's office and resigned. He left without a backward glance, determined to make amends in some way for the rich dirtbags he'd helped in his years at the firm. He spent every day at the university trying to churn quality, socially responsible lawyers out into the world to rebalance the chaos he'd unleashed. His efforts hadn't quelled the regret. But being so busy distracted him from the pain and anger that remained locked up in his chest.

Out of sight but ever-present.

Dormant.

That is until Francesca decided to waltz in and open the Pandora's box of his repressed memories.

"Anyways." He cleared his throat. "She died of liver failure just before I started teaching, and ever since, I've been doing everything in my power to be the opposite of him."

"So, last month? When you told me you were on your way to visit her?"

"I take flowers to her grave every year on her birthday. Pink roses were her favorite."

"I'm so sorry," Francesca gulped out on a sob. "I was such an ass. I made comments about your mom not *existing* and you being spawned instead. And I've been so mean to you since we arrived. Had I known—"

"You couldn't have. I haven't even told your brother about half of this. He knows about my youth and everything leading up to graduation and me joining the law firm. Since then, he's shared with me, but I've held back everything from him."

"Why?"

Benjamin dropped his head into his hands, struggling even to contemplate weighing someone else down with his issues, like how he was at that moment with Francesca. This was wrong. He shouldn't be sharing this with his best friend's little sister. He shouldn't be seeking out understanding and comfort from someone he'd been judgmental and unyielding with the last few months. A sharp woman with a bright future, intentionally sabotaged by a professor who couldn't see past his own conflicting feelings.

His actions were unforgivable.

"I didn't want to burden him with my problems, not after his father—your father . . . and then Cynthia. It would be selfish."

Francesca sniffled and wiped her nose. "I can empathize. We had a rough start, but it got so much better once we were adopted. Others have it so much worse. I have no room to complain, seeing as I got my happy ending, and so many others don't."

He'd always forgotten that Johnny and his sister were adopted. His friend was so solid, forever talking about his amazing family, that it was easy to forget they weren't biologically linked.

Francesca released a slow, wobbly exhale, and reached over to lay a hand on Benjamin's forearm. She squeezed.

"It's good that you want to be better than your father, but don't punish yourself for following his lead in the past. You switched gears and now you do something positive with your gifts. You might be a hard-ass in the process, but I guess I can see why."

"I was unnecessarily hard on you."

"Yes, you were," she said with the hint of a smile. "But I'll survive. Water under the bridge or whatever cheesy euphemism you want to use."

"What can I do to make amends?"

She rolled her eyes. "Saying you're sorry is a good start."

"I am sorry, Francesca."

"I forgive you," she stated simply.

"Just like that?" It couldn't be that simple. He really had been unbearably cruel to her, holding her to an impossible standard, intentionally trying to edge her out of his classroom. There's no way those few little words did anything. Yet any animosity she'd been harboring seemed to drift away as she sat opposite him wearing a calm, if sympathetic, expression.

"Do you mean it? Are you actually sorry?"

She couldn't imagine how much Benjamin's poor treatment

of her weighed on him. He felt like he'd reverted to his heartless days as a high-powered attorney. He'd spent months cutting Francesca down, attempting to reduce her to a dog that had been beaten down enough times that there was no fight left. He was disgusted by his actions. He did not deserve her forgiveness, but the apology wasn't about him.

"More than you can fathom."

She chuckled softly and nodded. "Then I forgive you. Just like that."

Something pricked at his heart. He hadn't learned how to forgive. In his experience, forgiveness wasn't something freely given. Ever. Following his parents' divorce, his mother held onto her hurt and anger, allowing its intoxicating venom to poison her heart. In turn, she added alcohol to the mix and poisoned her body along with it. She allowed herself to rot from the inside because she refused to let go and create a new life for herself.

For her son.

Francesca drummed her fingers on the table. "Especially if you clean up from dinner so I can test out that shower I've been working so hard on."

"You call melting a little snow hard?"

"Hey. I've melted a whole damned igloo all right? Either way, I'm doing philanthropic work by washing the stink off. You should be thanking me." She stepped close, leaning down and taking an exaggerated sniff of Benjamin, then moseyed across the room. "And do the same."

"That all depends on how things shake out for you." He shrugged. "And if you leave me any hot water of course."

"No promises," she grunted as she lifted the five-gallon sack of water she'd left warming behind the stove.

"Allow me." Benjamin rose from his seat and took the hefty container from her. Following her to the closet-turned-shower—necessity really was the mother of invention—he lifted and hung the water jug from the metal hook. Slowly releasing his hold, they both stepped cautiously out of the way to see if the contraption would, in fact, hold. Miraculously, it did. Francesca wiggled with glee and then disappeared into the bedroom next door.

Returning to the main room to clean up from dinner, Benjamin wondered how he felt both heavier and lighter. Something had felt—not quite comforting, but perhaps cathartic to confide in Francesca about his fear of becoming just like his father. She listened, empathized. Selflessly. It was like she snatched the ache from his chest and stuffed it into hers so she could help him process it.

A flicker of warmth invaded his heart.

Which became enveloped by an all-out inferno at the sound of her showering. She squeaked with the first hit of water, groaned after a few minutes when she'd likely gotten the majority of her delectable body clean, and sang a couple of his favorite 90s songs. She was off-key, but still. He imagined scooping her up after she finished and making her filthy all over again.

Did he want to take advantage of their time stranded together in the cabin? Yes. Was it a smart idea to sport fuck his best friend's little sister? While Johnny was a great man—solid, loyal, joyful—he probably wouldn't take too kindly to the overstep.

"No peeking." Her words startled him out of the problematic fantasy.

"I would never." Benjamin scoffed a little too adamantly. Because while he would do just about anything to see Francesca wrapped in terry cloth, water dripping from the ends of her hair, nipples straining hard through the threadbare weave of the towels he found in the hope chest, he also had some honor. Perhaps not enough to boast about, but enough to where he didn't feel like a complete creep.

"Ha! Don't sound so disgusted."

"The only person I'm disgusted with is myself," he murmured.

"What was that?"

"Nothing."

"Fine." She cleared her throat. "There's still half the bag left. If you want."

"Thanks, I think I will." It was probably wise to wash the desperation off with lukewarm water before the day was out.

He waited for the bedroom door to click shut before he stripped his shirt and pants off and strode to the shower. He'd been right. The chill of the former closet, paired with the tepid spray from the handheld nozzle, washed all excess testosterone down the drain. The increasing frigid flow made his lust more manageable.

Peeking his head outside the door to ensure the coast was clear, he snatched the miniature swatch of fabric these cabin owners passed off as towels and tucked it around his waist. He moved carefully in his bare feet across the hardwood toward the wood stove, where his clothes were neatly folded. Despite the brisk nature of the shower, he felt much improved.

Clearheaded.

Even though he'd shared a kiss with Francesca the night before, he sensed a renewed assurance that it wouldn't happen again. They'd make it out the next day and be able to put this whole series of unfortunate events behind them.

Chapter Thirty

Frankie

"**I**s everybody decent?" Frankie called from the cracked bedroom door. She'd listened to her roomie's shower progression through the thin slab of wood. Convincing herself that it was to ensure his privacy by not exiting the room until he was fully clothed did little to quell the shame she felt as she imagined what a sight that man would be.

Under a stream of water.

Naked.

She quivered at the thought and tried to focus on something unrelated to the stodgy professor in the other room.

"You're in the clear, Miss Miller." She could hear the smirk in his voice and assumed the rinse-off must have done him some good too.

Benjamin poured hot water from the kettle into a pair of mugs on the small table. He wore a one-sided grin that prominently displayed one of those mischievous dimples. A couple locks of still-damp hair hung over his forehead in stark contrast to his typical structured coif. Frankie imagined running her hands through the apparent silkiness and grabbing hold for leverage.

Benjamin glanced up for the first time after replacing the kettle on the stove, perusing her from towel-wrapped hair to cherry red toenails, eyes snagging briefly on the spaghetti straps of her undershirt. Her cheeks flushed under his appraisal, and then she forced herself back into a manufactured aloofness.

"I thought a nightcap might be," he searched for the right word, settling for "relaxing."

After their heavy discussion, no doubt he felt just as emotionally drained as she did—if not more. Frankie hadn't anticipated the tragedy of Benjamin's broken family. He'd embodied pretension, and she'd just assumed he came from money. A long lineage of "superior" men with fancy degrees and lifetime yacht club memberships. She hadn't been all that wrong. He had gotten his start in life under those parameters. But the unexpected—and from how he described it—sudden upheaval of his world would have cut deep, changing his entire view of the world in more ways than one.

Marriage is the most asinine institution ever created.
It has the capability to destroy people.

Honestly, Frankie wasn't sure about the whole marriage thing either. The complete inverse of Benjamin, her start had been rough. She'd learned quickly not to trust people in general. And while the Millers—whom she'd considered Mom and Dad since she was nearly eight—helped to restore her faith in a handful of people, that consideration didn't expand far beyond their immediate unit.

She perched in one of the chairs and inhaled the herbal fumes of her tea as Benjamin sat opposite her. "Thank you."

"You're welcome." He watched with eagle-eye sharpness as Frankie tugged the towel from her head, allowing damp waves to fall about her shoulders. She hung the cloth over the back of her chair to dry then proceeded to finger comb the tangles, doing her very best to disregard the laser beam focus coming from her temporary roommate.

"Can I help you?" she clipped, breaking the spell more for her sake than his.

"Apologies." He blinked rapidly but continued to analyze her from across the little table. "I can't help but wonder something."

Oh hell, this ought to be good.

"Shoot."

"Johnny hasn't really told me about the before years leading up to the adoption."

Frankie stiffened. "I'm not surprised by that."

"Why not?"

She scanned Benjamin's face. Long gone was the shrewd scrutiny of an uppity law professor who'd gone out of his way to make his class brutal just for the sake of booting her out. For once, those deep blue eyes and furrowed brows weren't being wielded in intimidation. Frankie found the concern that oozed off him and the resulting energy intriguing. Almost comforting. Talk about a big, fat shift in dynamic.

"Because he carried a lot of guilt about it." She shrugged. "Probably still does."

"Walk me through it." And then, so as not to sound too demanding, added a gentle, "Please."

Frankie dragged in a deep breath, expanding her ribs and puffing out her cheeks, then released it noisily.

"Fine."

Benjamin set down his mug and scuffed his chair to face her. His full attention settled on her like a cozy weighted blanket.

"Our birth parents died in a car accident when I was four and Jon was six. I guess we didn't have any grandparents left or they weren't interested in taking us. Either way, the result was the same. Foster care. They split us up because finding a home that had space for the two of us was a struggle."

Frankie only recalled flashes because she was so young. What stuck was the feeling of immense loss—first her parents, then her big brother.

"Jon ended up in a decent setup with a younger couple who already had a kid, a boy, if I recall, about my age. Anyway, they were nice. They made his lunch for school and bought him clothes when he outgrew his old ones. They even got him a bike secondhand the first Christmas he was there. Long story short, he was lucky."

She watched the calm waters of Benjamin's eyes darken like clouds blocking out the sun on the open ocean. He sat there. Attentive yet silent.

"I, on the other hand, got the shit end of the deal." Running her tongue along her teeth, Frankie engaged the practiced numbness she'd learned to build around her when necessary. "I bounced from place to place. To one family, I was a bit of a handful; to another, I was a *wildcat*. They could label it however they wanted, but it all boiled down to the same sentiment."

"Which was?" His tone was flat yet seeking.

"They didn't want me."

Benjamin cleared his throat and gripped his forgotten mug.

Frankie swatted away the thick waves of tension that vibrated off him, dismissing the niggling emotion that began to spark inside her chest.

"Anyway, I did finally settle somewhere. But it wasn't any better than bouncing around."

The whitening of his knuckles didn't go unnoticed.

"I was with a couple, the Garbers. They had that old school type of marriage where the man was the head of the household and 'what he said goes.' It wasn't like they beat me or anything like that, but their punishments were pretty harsh."

"Elaborate." The sharp demand echoed off the walls of the tiny cabin, resonating a touch longer than it should have.

"Their most common punishment was withholding food.

And not only going to bed without dinner—although that happened more often than not. Sometimes I'd go a whole day without more than a glass of water. I can remember the sharp hunger pangs in my gut as I'd lie in bed dreaming about the shitty cooking of the family I'd lived with before. The summer and weekends were the worst because I didn't have school lunch to fall back on. Once, Mrs. Garber took pity on me and snuck me a sandwich. I think she got beat for that. That's what it sounded like anyway.

"The only good thing about living with them was that it meant Jon and I were in the same school. I was able to tell him the Garbers' address, so he'd sneak out some nights and ride his bike over to bring me food. He got caught a couple times, and his foster parents started keeping a better eye on him. One night, he showed up to 'rescue' me and took me back to his house. The next morning, they found us snuggled up in his room. It was the best night's sleep I'd had in a long time.

"Anyway, the next morning, Jon refused to let me go. He stood in front of me shouting that he wouldn't let anyone take his sister away from him and that anyone who tried could 'go straight to hell.'" Frankie grinned at the memory, pretty sure that moment had triggered her older brother's fierce protective streak.

Her eyes collided with Benjamin's, the darkened depths now a swirl of storming waves. Anger simmered there, just below the surface of his once carefully constructed reserve. She glanced away, finding it very hard to keep her eyes dry in the wake of his apparent outrage.

"They called our social worker, this frazzled, burnt-out woman with way too many cases to manage on her own, and removed us both. She didn't know what to do other than take us home with her—which is a massive violation, by the way. But after a few days, she managed to find a middle-aged couple willing to take both of us." Frankie smiled. "The Millers. And the rest is history."

She recalled the sense of relief that she'd felt all those years ago as though it had just occurred. She and Jon were together again. Those years separated had been bleak, damaging Frankie so deeply that the ability to trust was next to impossible. Slowly and with much care, the Millers showed them what family was. And after three years, they asked Frankie and Jon if they could adopt them officially. She couldn't have manufactured a better set of parents, and justified that a few years of misery was a small price to pay to be a part of something so wonderful.

Chapter Thirty-One

Benjamin

Benjamin had to resist the urge to pull on his many layers and plow through the howling wind and snow in search of vengeance. The wind roared outside the little cabin, reminding him that he was not meant for colder weather and would probably die in a random snowbank after marching angrily in circles for a few hours. But it didn't keep him from fantasizing about finding the Garbers and repaying them for how they'd treated Francesca. The image of the petite, powerful, stubborn woman sitting across from him as a young child, alone and hungry, was too much to process.

"Hey, Benji." It took him a moment to notice the concern in her words and soft touch on his wrist. He met Francesca's amber gaze, fighting to set aside the massive weight crushing his chest. "At the risk of making the mistake of asking you if you're all right and then you biting my head off, I'm just going to say that it all turned out for the best."

He had done that, hadn't he? Punished her for showing concern in a rare moment of exposed vulnerability that day after class. Lashed out at her because he allowed her presence—her success—to get under his skin. God, he was a prick.

"Anyway," she said and sighed thoughtfully. "Maybe I'll write a memoir and make buckets of money."

"Is that why you want to be a social worker?"

"For the buckets of money?" she joked dryly.

"You know what I mean."

"Yes. Specifically, I want to work with youth who are underprivileged or in the foster care system. My ultimate goal is to open a nonprofit that exposes kids to nature. Hiking, camping. Perhaps some artsy classes where they sketch or photograph flowers or whatever. I found a lot of healing and clarity outdoors. Maybe I can help them find a way to channel their pain so they don't feel so alone."

"Francesca, I—"

"I know. You plan to wait with bated breath for me to bestow mercy upon your wretched soul." She teasingly tossed his recycled words back at him, but for Benjamin, they rang true this time around. "You've already apologized, and I've already accepted."

"I am, though. Sorry, I mean. I never stopped to think of your reasoning for being in my class. All I considered was how your presence upset my . . ." He struggled to voice his thoughts. Focus? Concentration? Dedication to nothing but law? After scanning through all the truths, one seemed the least damning. "Routine."

"You like order and predictability. I get that. Next time maybe pull your head out of your ass and ask a couple of clarifying questions first, yeah?"

"I can do that." He let a chuckle drift from his mouth, but the mirth didn't feel genuine.

"Well," Francesca groaned, squeezing one of her shoulders with the opposite hand and rolling her neck in a semi-circle. "I'm sore from yesterday's yard sale and drained from today's emotional purge. I'm going to bed. With any luck this storm will subside tomorrow. The second it does, let's get the heck out of here."

"Agreed." Benjamin rose and snagged their mugs, placing them in the empty wash basin for tomorrow. He watched her saunter toward the bedroom door, where she stopped and turned.

"It felt nice to clear the air with you today. Maybe after this is all over, we can be friends. Or at least friendly in each other's presence?"

"I'd like that," he said, though as she closed the door, he wondered how he could ever temper the heat in his chest enough to consider her in such benign terms.

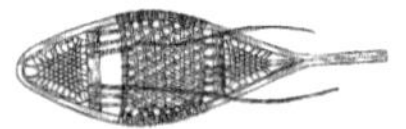

As night crept along, Benjamin lay on his bed of quilts, listening to the increasing howl of the wind. The storm raged around the little shelter, tearing at shingles and banging shutters like it was a living beast seeking out the tender morsels inside. At times, the gusts were so aggressive that the fire flattened out behind the glass stove door, threatening to lose its grip and extinguish. How long would the heat remain if it did? Would he or Francesca be able to get the logs burning again? Would they survive the night?

They had to get out of that valley tomorrow. Benjamin wasn't worried so much about dwindling supplies, because the people who stocked the cabin left plenty. There was a couple weeks' worth of dried food. No, his concern was his hold on control. Each interaction with Francesca chipped away at the delicate balance he managed between seeing her as his best friend's little sister/his student and seeing her as a sexy, compassionate firecracker. They'd kissed twice and that was enough for Benjamin to acknowledge that more would lead to all out addiction. And while losing his mind in her might sound like heaven, the hell that would reign upon him—from his friend and his boss—would not be worth it.

Probably not worth it anyway.

As another frame-rattling burst of wind flung itself at the cabin, the sound of shattering glass and a blood-curdling scream emanated from the bedroom.

Francesca.

Feet responding faster than his brain, Benjamin flew to the door, swinging it open to find a branch protruding from the tiny bedroom window. Snow, glass, and debris scattered the floor, discernible only from the steady glow coming from the main room. Francesca sat huddled on the far corner of the bed, pressed up against the wall, gasping for air and shaking.

"Stay there," Benjamin barked and bolted from the entryway. He roughly pulled his boots on, not bothering to tie the laces, and stalked back to the bedroom. He marched across the glass and, without warning her in advance, scooped the shivering woman and surrounding blankets off the mattress. She snuggled against his bare chest, curling into his warmth and thundering heartbeat. With her head tucked under his chin, he took a deep inhale of the fresh eucalyptus from the shower she'd taken earlier and removed her from the little room.

Still maintaining a death grip on her shuttering form, he toed off his boots and sat cross-legged in front of the stove.

"Th-thanks," she managed through chattering teeth. "Th-that scared the f-fuck out of me."

"Same." He hushed at his pulse as the initial jolt of fear devolved into something more carnal. Holding her like this, in his lap, against his bare skin, strands of silky hair catching on the thick stubble of his jaw, was nearly too much to handle. "You're still shaking. Are you cold?"

"No. Just startled."

Benjamin flexed his arms, raising her from his lap and sliding his legs out from beneath her. He settled her facing the wood stove between his veed-out thighs and slid his hands to her shoulders. The bunched muscle under her smooth skin amplified his desperation to calm her nerves. With gentle pressure, he began to knead the knots.

"Is this all right?" he asked, even as he felt her melt beneath his fingers.

"Better than all right," she hummed as her chin fell to her chest.

Her little moans and sighs tunneled through his ears and seeped intoxicatingly into his bloodstream. He was high on her. How could such a small touch cause his head to swirl like he was on a carnival ride? Dizziness took over, and he willed his palms to stop, but every sound of approval that slid from between her lips secured him more permanently to her. And while his aim was to steady her nerves and calm her after the window smashed in from the terrorizing storm, he could feel her pulse pounding rapidly along her neck. He considered kissing her where it beat so erratically, trailing his tongue along the thumping vein.

He almost jumped as Francesca settled a hand on each of his bare thighs, lightly sliding her palms up and down the dusting of hair on his tensed quads. Suddenly aware that he was in nothing but his boxer briefs, the proximity of her to his thickening erection made him squirm. She sat squarely ahead of him, a mere whisper away from pressing into his length.

Oh god, he'd never wanted a woman more than in this moment. But not just any woman, he wanted—no, needed—Francesca. Her hands, mouth, and legs all wrapped around him so he could lose himself in her.

She groaned deeply as he found an especially tight knot on her lower back. She'd fallen hard the day before, had taken such a terrifying tumble that Benjamin hadn't known if she would get back up from it. He wanted to make all her discomforts go away.

"Let me take care of you, Miss Miller," he teased, words low, whispering against the back of her ear. She shivered and scraped her nails along his thigh muscles. "Tell me where it aches."

Chapter Thirty-Two

Frankie

Heat and pressure grew and blazed within Frankie. Her skin had never been so sensitive. She needed him to touch harder, drag his fingertips to all the places that begged to be stroked. There wasn't even a hint of that nagging voice saying it was a bad idea, because her desire roared above it all.

She'd been so good, swearing off men and focusing on her studies for so long, that she deserved some release. And not just the kind that came from a buzzing toy. She wanted to be touched and tasted, and she wanted her former professor to use his tongue to soothe instead of lashing like he usually did.

She'd earned it, and he seemed to agree.

And so when he asked her where she ached, she gasped, "Everywhere."

The rumble that came from his chest was either a chuckle or a growl, maybe an amalgamation of the two. Either way, it buzzed down Frankie's back and to the tips of her toes.

Benjamin gathered her hair and draped it over one shoulder, grazing his knuckles along her skin with the sweep. He took full advantage of the bare shoulder after sliding the thin strap of her tank top out of the way. Hard teeth dragged toward her neck, her skin erupting in a wash of goosebumps. His slow, patient hands were everywhere, but he still managed to avoid the regions that begged for contact. Frankie squirmed beneath his teasing, and when he inched painfully close to one nipple, she arched in encouragement.

He retreated with a low chuckle. "No, no, Miss Miller. You have to tell me what you want. I'm not a man who enjoys guessing games."

Frankie's chest rose and fell in frustrated inhales and exhales, skin following his avoidant grazes like he was a magnet and she was made of molten metal. She wanted all of it: stroke, pinch, bury, sink, pull, glide. How could she possibly voice the myriad sensations she craved from him?

Benjamin slid a firm hand up between her breasts, settled it against her throat, and used the pad of his fingers to turn her face up to his. His lips lowered, hovering a nanometer from hers, zapping her with electricity. His hot breath puffed onto her lips as he spoke.

"I didn't take you for being so shy."

"I'm not," she panted as he held her there, using his other hand to play with the hipbone hiding just below the waistband of her leggings. "Normally, I'm—"

"Normally, you're what, Francesca?"

She felt the spread of heat as it flushed up her neck beneath his touch. Fuck, was this real life? Was she really in a secluded cabin, sitting between this man's legs, struggling to verbalize how she wanted him to satisfy her? And if so, what was with her sudden lack of boldness?

"Calling the shots. Doing the seducing."

"Oh, but you are," he groaned, pulling firmly at her hips so her ass pressed hard against his arousal. "You have been seducing me since you walked into my classroom, late and breathless. Do you know how often my mind drifted to you when I should have been lecturing? You couldn't know how many times I imagined, no, *fantasized* about dismissing class, locking the doors, and bending you over my podium. You said I tortured you in class.

Well, sweetheart, you returned the favor every *fucking* day."

The sensation of him cursing against her lips awakened Frankie from whatever meek daze she'd been hiding in. Suddenly, she needed him everywhere and felt zero shame about saying so.

"Touch me. Everywhere. Caress my breasts, pinch and tease my nipples, and slide lower and see how wet I am for you."

Benjamin grinned as he slammed a kiss onto her lips. He groaned in approval as she opened wide to the frenzied sweep of his tongue and matched him stroke for stroke. Doing as she'd asked, he slid both hands up her ribs and beneath her shirt, testing the weight of her sensitive breasts. He rotated between teasing each hardened peak and caressing the sensitive skin around the perimeter. Decadent sensation rolled through Frankie's limbs, and she arched harder, hungry for more of his touch.

He lowered a hand, trailing languid strokes across her soft abdomen, and stopped just after sliding a finger below the waistband of her pants. He raised his head, looking down at her.

"Are . . . are you not wearing panties?" he asked, the midnight blue depths of his eyes both icy and molten. His heaving chest pressed firmly against her back.

Frankie bit her lower lip and shook her head.

"*Fuuuuuck.*"

He hardened even more, nestling between her cheeks as she rolled against him. She needed his fingers to dip lower. Needed him to tend to the ache she'd been feeling for months.

"Touch me, Benjamin."

He needed no more coaxing after that. He reached farther, simultaneously sliding down and spreading her apart in search of that tiny bundle of nerves. Frankie jerked at the teasing flicks he administered, struggling to keep her ass on the floor as he circled, flicked, and retreated. Exquisite pressure built in her. She needed . . . needed . . .

But he knew. And he released her from her torment by sliding a long, searching finger into her, only to curl it and connect with just the right spot. A moan propelled from her, and she quivered and rolled her hips. More, faster, harder, but she couldn't get actual words to form on her tongue. His translation of her mumbles and gasps led to firmer strokes, and all she could do was grip his thighs and prepare to ride the wave as it came barreling toward her.

Until he stopped and pulled his hand from her leggings.

Her outraged whine had him chuckling as he soothed in her ear, "Not yet, sweetheart."

He kissed her temple and scooped her into his arms while she squirmed and tried to hold back the growls of her frustration. He'd taken her to the edge and let her dangle, writhing just out of reach of ecstasy. He set her on her feet, steadying her as she wobbled, then strode to her backpack a few feet away. She hummed in realization as he procured the red first aid bag and pulled out a condom.

"I'm glad I noticed these when I helped you bandage your head," he spoke into her hair then swept the locks back to inspect her little cut. Fortunately, it had been all bark and very little bite.

He dropped the packet on the table beside them and kneeled in front of Frankie. Slowly—inhumanly slowly—Benjamin slid down her leggings, kissing every inch of skin as it was exposed. With the garment discarded, he trailed his fingers up the backs of her ankles and calves, stopping at one knee to lift and settle it over his broad shoulder. The sight of that blue-eyed, raven-haired Adonis laving his tongue up the inside of her thigh and delving into her center was almost more than Frankie could manage. He was beautiful and sexy and so fucking good at what he was doing. She could barely stay on her feet, and so he cupped her ass, holding her in place as he explored and worshiped every inch of her.

The wave surged again, steadily gliding toward her as it loomed off the horizon. She could feel it, practically taste it as it drew nearer and nearer.

Until he stopped. Again . . . he fucking stopped.

Frankie's heart was going to explode. She pulled at his hair, dug her fingers into the bunched muscles at his shoulder, whimpered, and begged. But all he did was hold her hips mere inches away as he grinned up at her. "Almost."

Benjamin rose, standing close, crowding her with his size. He slid his palms up her side and tugged her shirt up over her head. As it landed on the floor, he gave her a gentle shove and she had no choice but to plop down onto the chair behind her. Again, he knelt down, meeting his lips to hers. Frankie could taste herself on his tongue, and the recognition was like a shot of morphine-laced adrenaline into her bloodstream. Bliss and fire licked at her skin, a blazing, near-crawling sensation that needed to be satisfied. She'd die if he didn't let her finish this next time; she'd never been so certain of anything in her entire life.

Frankie reached down and felt the swell of him straining hard against his boxer briefs. He groaned at her touch, thrusting instinctively as she slid her fingers below the waistband and gripped. Benjamin snatched the condom off the table, ripped the packaging open, and slid the sheath into place.

His strong hands pulled hard behind her knees, sliding her so her ass hung off the edge of the seat, the perfect hip level for him to gain access. He knelt there, poised and ready as he teased her with his blunt tip.

"Are you ready for me? Because this time, I won't stop."

"Yes," she whimpered, certain her desperation was loud and on display.

And then he said it. Those two tiny words, when combined, created a question—a *correction*—that plagued her fantasies night after night for countless weeks.

"Yes what?" he rumbled, brow cocked, pressing lightly against her entrance but sinking no farther.

Frankie grinned, knees shaking, all too happy to play along. "Yes, Professor Clark."

His sensual chuckle raked over her in heady sweeps. Then he thrust into her in one firm, solid movement. Her hips bucked and back arched as he pulled out and pushed deeply into her over and over again. She moaned and mewled at the pleasure of him stroking her with his solid strength while gripping her hips for leverage.

"Fuck," he groaned through gritted teeth. "I couldn't have imagined . . . fuck. You're so fucking tight. Goddammit, Francesca. You're ruining me."

The filth that curled from his mouth ratcheted up her arousal, and she recalled taunting him about his clean vocabulary. Teased him as she asked if he had ever cursed.

Of course I do. But there are only two very specific times, and you haven't been privy to either.

Oh, she had now.

She'd heard him through the haze after colliding with the boulder at the bottom of the valley. His panicked tone sliced the words into more than just their syllables. He'd been worried, scared for her. And now, as he tended to her needs, yet again, while also succumbing to his own desires. He swore all right, any time he let baser instincts possess him, bullying his sense of propriety to stand aside.

Benjamin dug his fingers firmly into the flesh of her hip as his thrusts became fevered, erratic. Frankie could feel the imposing pressure of release lingering back, waiting to be denied yet again. She met his eyes, and he grinned.

"I need to," she whimpered.

He slid a hand up her waist, chest, and neck then settled a thumb on her lower lip. She nipped at it then pulled it into her mouth and sucked. He moaned low in his throat.

"You don't want me to deny you again?"

She shook her head even as she felt the dip of low tide expose everything: desire, desperation, frustration. "Please. Please."

"Give me one more," he crooned, his smile dark and feral. "*Please.*"

Lowering his damp thumb, he stroked her clit, all the while thrusting faster, deeper. "Go ahead, sweetheart. Come for me."

The wave slammed into her, a crushing tsunami filling the space where the undertow had receded. Burying her in a flood of pleasure as he pushed hard then dove with her beneath the ripples and currents. Benjamin pulled her in tight, pressing her breasts hard against his chest as they heaved and gasped together. Shuttering in engulfing bliss.

Chapter Thirty-Three

Benjamin

The room was quiet apart from the crackle of the fire and the steady breath of Francesca sleeping beside Benjamin. He looked down at her, elbow propped to rest his head in his hand, tracing her rosy cheeks, thick lashes, and parted lips with his gaze. They'd managed a foundation-shaking orgasm together, linked, released into each other. The sex had been . . . indescribable. Something so engulfing and pleasurable that Benjamin was shocked he hadn't passed out in the hushed little room alongside his satisfied lover.

And yet his heart thundered violently in his ears.

He'd held back since they'd sought shelter. Doing his best to keep his distance and not give in to the desires he'd been harboring for her since day one. It hadn't been easy. They were sardines crammed in a cramped tin surrounded by a storm that screamed *touch her* with every gusty howl. He'd managed pretty well, considering the proximity, only slipping up once as she danced and swerved in his arms, singing one of his favorite songs with shameless abandon. She'd been so alluring and free and he couldn't help but take a taste. But the impulsive act had done nothing to scratch the itch.

No, that was all wrong.

She wasn't an itch.

No man could describe this multifaceted woman as some nagging ailment that needed to be cured. Francesca was perfection in a five-foot-two package, with thick honey hair and that cloyingly earthy scent of eucalyptus and lavender. Curled up and pressed against him, snoring lightly, she was utterly at peace. And he hated the corridor that his mind wandered through the moment they settled in to rest. Each door flashed him a glimpse of what could be.

Fantasies. All of them. Not a single one the reality of how something more permanent with her—with any woman—would go.

Because marriages were doomed.

He'd seen his father slowly extinguish his mother.

He'd helped wealthy men and women strip their spouses bare of their dignity and financial security.

He'd helped win custody battles, where one parent disparaged and ruined the other purely to flex their might. Mothers or fathers who never actually wanted to be the primary caregiver but fought, all the same, to make their former partner hurt.

He'd stood with the bullies and stomped on their castaway lovers like bugs under his expensive leather shoes, all while cashing enormous checks to pad his own security.

He'd single-handedly destroyed girlfriends without batting an eye; played with them for a while then tossed them aside.

He refused to subject Francesca to any of that.

Even if he was confident that they'd remain together, unbroken and functioning, he couldn't deny that he didn't deserve her. She was too good for him. Her aspirations to work with foster kids, to help them feel safe and heal, were admirable. She was determined to ensure no child felt discarded like she had.

His motivations had never been as selfless as hers.

Even now, as a professor, he had been looking out for himself. The claim that he was trying to mold students into honorable lawyers who contributed to society was shrouded in his own selfish desire for security—tenure.

Dean McCaffery dangled the carrots of prestige and job security over his head. And Benjamin jumped at every command as he stood beneath his boss's own Italian loafers, hoping the sense of power the older man gleaned from the interaction was enough to keep him from lowering his heel.

Either way—as a divorce attorney or a professor begging for tenure—he was perpetuating the cycle of power and control instead of equalizing it.

Benjamin looked down at Francesca, who slept so soundly, like she hadn't rolled down a valley, struck her head, then labored through the snow to be stranded in a tiny powerless cabin with her prick of a law professor. She didn't deserve his damage.

And she didn't deserve the chill that would come in the morning either.

Chapter Thirty-Four

Tuesday, 3 days before the wedding: Frankie

Before she opened her eyes, Frankie felt the blissful weight of her relaxed limbs. The dry, soothing heat from the stove enveloped her, leaving the quilt draped across her lower half unnecessary. Memories of the romp she and Benjamin had shared the night before sent delicious curls of satisfaction through her bloodstream. Who knew that when it came to banging, that uptight, stick-in-the-mud would be so . . . intuitive? Erotic? Masterful?

However his skills should be labeled, all she knew was that she wanted more. Surely, another round before vacating the cabin was reasonable.

Frankie rolled over, reaching for the sexy man who'd rocked her world the night before and found nothing. Her eyes popped open and she searched the room. Sunlight glowed in through one of the windows, evidence that the storm had passed and they would be able to get the hell out of the valley that day. She sat up and scanned the small room. Empty except for a *swish, swish, swish* coming from the bedroom. Wrapping the quilt around her, she stood and meandered to the door.

Inside, Benjamin swept the shattered glass into a dustpan. He was fully dressed, but that didn't keep Frankie from shivering at the recollection of what lay underneath his layers. Rock solid sex appeal. She grinned, watching him as he worked.

"Good morning," she purred, slowly letting the blanket slide low on her breasts, hinting at the rosy peaks beneath. "Care for a little breakfast to start your morning?"

The length of time it took Benjamin to turn his head after letting out a heavy sigh cooled her libido. He leveled his gaze on her eyes with no consideration to drift lower. Enveloping herself against the sudden chill, she cleared her throat. "Is ... Is everything ok?"

"Fine," he clipped. The sweeping recommenced. "I just want to get out of here."

"Yeah. Same."

Frankie hovered a moment then turned back and dressed hastily in the living room. It wasn't like she was expecting to cuddle up like a couple or anything, but she had expected a little more warmth. Perhaps a lingering hum of desire. A tiny crackle of want, like embers that hadn't yet burned out in a campfire. Not a fully extinguished flame that fizzled before it ever had a chance to roar.

Maybe he slept like shit.

It made sense and would explain a lot. She leaned into that scenario as she folded the quilts they used for their makeshift bed.

They worked around each other, erasing any evidence that they'd spent two nights in the cabin aside from the broken window and reduced supply of dried goods. In their silence, the process took about an hour, and as they hoisted on their packs and stepped out the door, Frankie wondered where the hell she'd gone wrong.

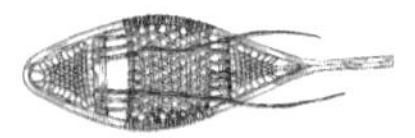

The sun hovered blindingly in the cloudless winter sky. It shined cheerily down upon the undisturbed snowfall that coated the trees and boulders meandering along the valley. The blanket of crystalline flecks covered the dips and mounds like fistfuls of iridescent sanding sugar on a white cake. Every now and then a delicate breeze drifted through the trees, kissing the branches together with the tinkling chime of ice against ice. The air smelled fresh. Long gone was the musty scent of autumn with its fallen leaves and earthy mushrooms. Winter had arrived despite what the calendar said, and typically, Frankie would have been overjoyed.

Typically.

Instead, the sour tang of rejection sullied her tongue as she tried to enjoy the leathery piece of jerky that was her breakfast. Even without the breeze, it was cold. The temperature likely hovered around the high teens, but she didn't feel much of it.

What she felt was pissed.

And a little used.

The humor in that wasn't lost on her; it just didn't land like it should have. Typically, she was the one doing the using, although the men she played with were always happy to oblige, so could she really call it that?

Neither she nor Benjamin had spoken beyond a quick "you ready" and a "yep" as they left the life-saving shelter. And then, with the trudge in knee-deep snow on what Frankie was pretty sure was the trail that would lead them to a trailhead along Highway 2, the silence was loud. Deafening. A distraction.

Unable to hold her ire back any longer, she spun around.

"What the *hell*, Benji?"

His eyes widened behind foggy glasses as he popped his head up in surprise. "What?"

"Don't play dumb, *professor*." She air quoted his title as the scorn dripped with her words.

"I *am* a professor."

"What?"

"I am a professor," he said exasperatedly, removing his crooked frames and buffing out the lenses with his undershirt. He replaced the smeared result on the bridge of his aristocratically masculine nose. "Air quotes imply satire or sarcasm when applied to a phrase, but since I do, in fact, teach at a university—"

"Ohmygod, stop." She retraced a few steps using established footprints and lumbered angrily back to him. "You know what I am talking about—last night. We had sex—great sex, actually—and now you're enacting the silent treatment like I . . . I dunno . . . like I switched your lecture USB drive with one loaded full of dick pics or something."

His lip twitched, though Frankie couldn't be sure if it was while suppressing a smile or a frown. Either way, it was a reaction.

Finally.

Anger would be fine.

Amusement would be fine, even if it were at her expense. But what she couldn't handle was the reinsertion of an aloof chill, not so soon after they'd . . .

"It's not personal," he finally said.

"Well, I should hope not. I know I didn't do anything wrong." She crossed her arms, recalling the way their bodies molded together, how filthy words flowed from his characteristically proper mouth.

Goddammit, Francesca.

You're ruining me.

She shivered despite the sweat that trickled down between her shoulder blades.

"It's complicated," he huffed, brushing past her—trying to at least—to continue down the trail.

"So use little words, and maybe I'll be able to keep

up." She bounded past him like a ridiculous golden retriever puppy because, surprise, surprise, it was impossible to march purposefully in knee-deep snow. Taking the lead, she stopped ahead of him again.

"It doesn't matter. What happened happened. It's over. Done."

"I still don't get it." Impulsively she raised a hand and settled it on his chest. "Last night was incredible. And just so you know, I'm not one to stroke a man's ego. The key is to let them go home thinking they need to work just a *little* bit harder the next time—"

His deepening scowl cut off her words.

Focus, Frankie.

"My point is," she continued, "we were amazing together, and that's not only my self-inflicted-fall-quarter-vow-of-celibacy talking."

"Francesca," he said, exasperated. She was wearing him down. Just a little more. She needed to know what went wrong and why he didn't want an encore of last night.

Why he didn't want her.

"Look," she pushed. "I'm not looking for anything serious, but it would be foolish to ignore the chemistry we have. Why not relinquish control and see what happens?"

He trained his especially icy eyes on her face, scanning for answers like he was some artificially intelligent robot trying to solve a riddle. Then he pinched the bridge of his nose, looked to his feet, and puffed out a ragged breath. Frankie waited for him to look back up at her, allowed him the time to organize his thoughts, to come to the same conclusion that she had. But all the heat fled her body as he leveled a frigid expression on her.

"Last night was a mistake, Francesca," he stated coolly with his Professor Clark mask secured in place. "I take full responsibility for my actions. It should not have happened and it will not happen again. Period. Out of respect I will keep our interaction to myself. I hope that you will extend me a similar courtesy and do the same."

Chapter Thirty-Five

Benjamin

Benjamin longed for a fissure to crack open below his feet. Cowardly, sure, but it would be a quick escape so he could stop hurling cruel lies at Francesca. Unfortunately, he was stuck there. Forced to face this woman who he'd touched and worshiped and brought with him to the brink of bliss. They'd shared something deeply passionate last night, and he would have given his law degree to live in that rosy world of passion forever. But he knew the truth.

What he was capable of doing to her.

And so he decided to do her a favor and shield her from a potentially hazardous fate.

Not *potentially*. Inevitably.

So why didn't he feel any relief from shooting her down? Protecting her from a miserable future? Was he making a mistake? He ached to reach for her. Apologize for being so weak and beg to keep her with him. Maybe he could be careful. Intentional. Remain diligent through the nights and weeks and longer. Should he even be considering this? He began to lean forward but halted as a smile sprang to her lips but didn't reach her eyes.

"Ok," she said with a suit-yourself tone.

"Ok?" What was happening?

"Yes. O. K.," Francesca said pointedly and shrugged. "It was a one-time thing, and we can both go our merry ways."

She turned and continued the laborious trek through the

snowy terrain.

"You're over it? Just like that?" Benjamin was taken aback by her easy acceptance. Was she really all right with things ending on this note? "Francesca—"

"You act like I haven't had a one-night stand before. I've had plenty." She paused and looked over her shoulder with casual concern. "But you might want to consider being a tad more upfront about your game plan with your next sexual partner. Chicks can get pretty pissed when they think there will be more than one round only to be left hanging with massive lady-wood the next morning."

"You've got to be kidding me," he muttered, frustration simmering just below the surface.

"I'm not," she continued as if he'd been talking to her, lowering her tone to mimic his. "A quick 'You'd better enjoy this fuck, sweetheart, cuz it's the only one you're gonna get' would have been nice."

"Stop." His command echoed along the walls of the valley but barely penetrated the pulse-pounding between his ears. He just wanted her to quit with the attempted retribution, not because he didn't deserve it, because he really did, but because he was desperate to explain that he wasn't like that. He didn't screw around. He didn't get hooked on other women and call them pet names. It was all her. Only her. And he was doing what needed to be done.

"One last thing," she said as she spun around and wagged a finger in his face, cheeks suddenly pink from more than just the cold. "My brother and Lucy's wedding is in three days, and I swear if you screw with it by either leaving quietly the night beforehand or acting all weird about this . . . this non-thing we had, I will go straight to the dean and *actually* ruin you. Am I crystal clear?"

At least they were in agreement on one thing: preserving

the joy of Johnny's big day. He nodded because he wouldn't do anything to jeopardize his best friend's happiness.

Satisfied, Francesca fell silent and Benajmin trailed behind, still reeling from the turn of events.

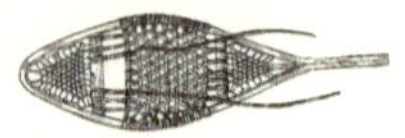

"I see them!"

The bellow broke through the awkward silence like dropping an armload of pots and pans in the middle of a library.

They'd spent the better part of the morning crunching through the smooth snow in a southward direction. Benjamin followed Francesca unquestioningly because he knew full well that she was going to be the one to lead them to safety. Maintaining a distance so as not to distract her or cause any more turmoil, he felt like dead weight as she surveyed the terrain, consulted her compass, and tested channels on her radio every few minutes. Eventually, as the sun beat down and their water supply dwindled, voices obscured in thick static sounded through the walkie-talkie.

Francesca's beaming grin was short-lived, however, because the moment she turned back and glanced at her "snowshoe buddy," the edges of her lips pulled down into a remembering frown. The way she looked at him pierced like a spear to the heart, and Benjamin wished ferociously that he could turn back time and keep his hands to himself.

Two bundled forms wearing snowshoes moved steadily toward them, sunlight reflecting off their jackets just as brightly as the surrounding snow.

"Any injuries?" a man in his early forties wearing a bright

green jacket with reflective stripes across the chest called. Was his name Miguel? Benjamin recognized him from the welcome dinner and the start of the snowshoeing trip two days ago. God, had it only been forty-eight hours ago?

"None, aside from the little cut I got on my head from rolling ass over teakettle into the valley on Sunday."

Maybe-Miguel nodded then stumbled to the side as Johnny, wearing a similarly flashy coat that was clearly too small, shoved past him, barreling straight for Francesca.

"Frankie. Holy hell." He swept his sister up and hugged her tightly, her feet dangling a few inches above the snow. "We've been freaking out. I'm so glad you're ok."

"Woah there, big brother," she coughed, arms pinned at her side. "Air's super important."

"Right, sorry." He gave another squeeze and set her back down. "God, I kept playing out the worst-case scenario. It took Lucy, Miguel, and Zac to keep me from searching for you two in that storm."

"I know the feeling," Francesca said as she looked up at her brother with a sad grin. Was she referring to last year when Johnny had gone missing?

"And you," he pushed past his sister, marched over to Benjamin, and wrapped him in an equally impassioned hug. "Thank you for taking care of my sister."

All three men turned at Frankie's offended scoff.

"She's right." Benjamin patted his friend's shoulder. "She did all the work. I followed along and did what I was told."

Johnny grinned. "Way to go, sis."

"Thanks." Her smile pulled tight with words unsaid.

"Here." Miguel handed each of them a spare pair of snowshoes then relayed into the radio at his shoulder that they'd found the missing hikers and were due back in about an hour.

"This reunion is lovely, Jon, but I'm sure these two want to get back to town sooner rather than later."

"You can fucking say that again," Francesca groaned, glancing over at Benjamin then quickly back to the straps of her snowshoes as she clicked them in place.

Her expression said it all: The last two days didn't happen.

And while he craved to take back everything he said about their encounter being a mistake, he knew he couldn't. Because even if he decided to take the leap and risk her downfall, it was crystal clear he'd done irreparable damage. Francesca was hurt, angry, and perhaps even a little embarrassed. But fiercer than that, the loathing that danced in her eyes proclaimed her opinion.

He was nothing to her.

Benjamin let his gaze linger, taking in Francesca's rosy cheeks, pink nose, and tangle of honeyed hair. He recalled contributing to those wavy snarls as he licked and touched then thrust into her. Imagined the heady passion rippling over her face as she threw back her head and moaned into the warm air.

A throat clearing beside him dissolved the memory.

Johnny studied him with raised brows, glancing from the surly professor to his younger sister. "Do we need to have a discussion?"

If he only knew. The discussion would be light on the words and heavy on the fists.

"No." Benjamin shook his head and secured his last clip. "It . . . it was a lot. That's all."

A swirl of amber flowed in his best friend's eyes, an almost identical match to the set he'd gazed into the night before. "Benji."

"Johnny. Nothing happened." At least that's the way Francesca wanted it.

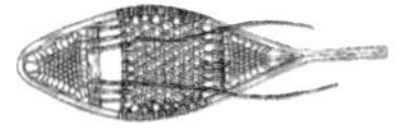

As the rescue party reached the trailhead with their mission in tow, Benjamin heaved a sigh of relief. A dozen people scurried around in the plowed parking lot under pop-up tents, talking on cell phones, prepping supplies, and folding blankets. An ambulance waited near the road, ready to cart an injured snowshoer to the hospital with the flick of a blaring siren. Miguel had called ahead and relayed the status of the two missing hikers, and having explained that they were both in good shape, the energy was less frantic panic and more casual damage control.

A cheer erupted as they were spotted coming around the bend. Other search and rescue volunteers gathered around to tend to whatever orders their fearless leader, Miguel, directed.

Benjamin accepted a heavy woolen blanket and a hot cup of coffee pressed into his hand. The caffeinated fumes and motor oil consistency warmed him from his belly outward. He watched Francesca accept a cup and snickered as she scowled after a tiny sip. Despite the upheaval between them, he was beyond relieved that she was back in safe and loving arms.

"Frannie!" A deep voice boomed from behind the ambulance.

Frannie?

Benjamin scowled at the massive brute loping across the parking lot. The man's face screamed relief under his angular, clean-shaven jaw as he scooped up Francesca and held her tightly to him. Before he could reconcile the uniform and holster, Benjamin watched in horror as she intertwined her legs around his hips and arms around his neck, fingers plunging into his surfer-blond curls. One bulging forearm braced supportively under her rear while the other hand settled comfortingly against the back of her neck.

"I've got you, princess. I've got you," the sheriff cooed as he swayed with Francesca in his arms.

The few sips that Benajmin had managed prior to the *heartwarming* display threatened to come up. He swallowed to keep the coffee and his growing rage down where they belonged. He had no claim to her. In fact, he'd discarded her that very morning, not a handful of hours prior. Still, the sight of her finding comfort in the arms of that Goliath was nearly enough for him to march over to the good sheriff, slap him across the face with his glove, and demand a duel. But seeing as how only one of them had a firearm, and this wasn't 1833, he clenched his coffee cup and turned away instead.

"Ya have a few minutes?" came the calm, steady voice beside him. Benjamin looked up, face to face with friendly brown eyes and a salt and pepper crew cut. Miguel settled a hand on his shoulder and squeezed. "I have a few questions I need to ask; all standard stuff. Figured now would be the best time."

Benjamin pretended not to notice when the search and rescue lead glanced pointedly over his shoulder at the sappy reunion a few yards away.

With a sigh and a hopefully convincing grin, Benjamin nodded. "My calendar's wide open."

Miguel squeezed once more then led the way to the pop-up tent furthest from the scene.

Chapter Thirty-Six

Thursday, 1 day until the wedding: Frankie

"I thought my toes would never be warm again." Frankie sighed dramatically as she allowed the rolling massager of her chair to thump at her sore muscles. At first dip, she was convinced the basin at her feet contained lava, but after adjusting to the scalding swirl of perfumed water, she realized it was that her feet had yet to be relieved of their winter chill.

"If you hadn't insisted on sleeping for two days straight after the snowshoe incident, we could have done this a lot sooner," Lucy said beside her, sighing with content as the pedicurist massaged her calves.

"This is my third time here. *Merci,* Tamera." Todd flashed a winning smile to the salon's receptionist as she refilled his champagne flute. "Your lashes are on point this morning."

Tamera smiled as she topped off Lucy's and Frankie's glasses. "Let me know when you're ready for another bottle on me. A little thanks for showing me how to properly apply the damn things without them falling off halfway through my shift."

"Aren't you the sweetest?" As the receptionist sauntered off, Todd leaned over. "My second day in here, Monday, I think it was, she hadn't noticed that one of her strips had gone rogue and landed on her lip. Poor thing looked like Groucho Marks with that little stick-on mustache."

"Thank god she had you to save the day." The bride-to-be

giggled and squirmed as the pumice stone destroyed her callouses.

"Wait, Monday?" Frankie scoffed. "That was the day after I went missing."

"Yes," Todd said.

"And you went to the nail salon?"

"That is correct."

"Glad to see you were real torn up with worry for me."

"Some people stress eat or drink or pace around wildly." Todd shrugged. "I happen to stress pamper."

"Why didn't you invite me?" It was Lucy's turn to be incredulous.

Todd lowered his glass mid-sip and eyed his friend. "Like I could have gotten you away from Captain America and the rest of the Avengers trying to devise a snowstorm rescue mission."

"I *was* really freaked out." Lucy turned back to Frankie and death gripped her soon-to-be sister's hand. "Jonathan too."

"Aww. I appreciate that," Frankie teased, trying to bury the memories—and subsequent emotions—that inevitably crept up whenever the snowshoeing incident was mentioned. "But like I keep saying, it was no biggie. Like a vacation, really. A vacation where I happened to be stuck with my dick of a professor."

"Speaking of dick," Todd interjected. "Are you sure nothing happened between you two?"

"Positive."

"Because I've watched no less than five different pornos that start that very same way, only the dudes weren't half as devastating as your professor."

"I can objectively agree," Lucy added. "Not about the porn part, but about the hunk you were shacked up with. *Woof.*"

"Bullshit, Luce!" Todd barked out a laugh, reaching over to pinch the bride's elbow skin. "You sent me the link to the raunchiest video I'm thinking of, you little hussy."

The flush of pink trickling over Lucy's cheeks had Frankie biting back her own laugh. She'd spent enough time with her brother's fiancée in the past year to know that deep down, the sweet and cutesy brunette managed to hide a respectable level of filth. It just took a few margaritas and some girl talk to shake it to the surface. On more than one occasion, typically after one shot too many, Lucy would shift from hypothetical scenarios to real-life recounts of her experiences, which would be all fine and dandy if the other half of Lucy's torrid encounters hadn't included Frankie's older brother. That's when Frankie would usually settle up the tab and call for a rideshare.

"Hands off my weenus," Lucy squealed, batting at her friend's large hand and attempting to poke him in the ribs simultaneously. Water sloshed onto the floor as Todd's whole body jerked from the tickling jab.

"Oh, Martha." He emphatically apologized to the sturdy woman who'd been exfoliating his feet. "Shit, I'm sorry for my heathen friend. She doesn't get out much. I'll help with the cleanup when we're done."

Martha chuckled, shaking her head. "You think you're the first ticklish person to come through here? Tamera! Mop."

The receptionist scurried over, and with two quick swipes, the puddle was gone.

This was exactly the therapy Frankie needed after the fallout between her and Benjamin. She'd spent the first two days back—after putting her mother at ease with a few hugs and a promise to come by after she rested—holed up in her hotel room. Sustaining off of her mother's leftovers and *Love it or List it* reruns. She'd cried once when *Judge Judy* came on, but instead of admitting to herself that the show reminded her of Benjamin, she convinced herself she must be PMSing two weeks early. And even if she had shed a tear over the cabin situation, it had nothing to do with feelings beyond the embarrassment of rejection. It wasn't like she wanted to date her former professor, but she had been open to swapping orgasms while in her hometown—and the occasional romp once they returned to Seattle.

Eventually, Lucy and Todd barged in, claiming to be housekeeping, and forced her to shower and go to the nail salon with them. In the harsh light of day, and with the help of a blended chocolate peppermint mocha frappe and an almond croissant, Frankie found clarity. She'd been moping over something insignificant: a one-night stand. She'd had plenty of those in her adult life and had never balked at not hearing from a guy after parting ways.

There were two reasons this was different (and only two). First, she had been dry for months. Of course abstaining from sex would make her clingier when she finally re-popped that cherry. Second, the proximity. She and Benjamin had been through a traumatic event together then stranded in a sexy little cabin with nothing but a wood fire stove and each other's genitals to keep them warm. Not only did many a porn flick start that way, but also countless romance novels and movies.

"My nookie senses are tingling," Todd drawled, glancing at Lucy. "I'd bet money there's something she's not telling us."

"Mm-hm." The little brunette nodded, green eyes narrowed on Frankie.

Jesus, can't a girl catch a break?

She was used to her future sister-in-law hounding her about her sex life (when she had one to discuss), but the two of them together were like The Inquisition.

"You pervs know real life doesn't play out like adult movies, right?"

"Not if you aren't doing it right, it doesn't," Todd murmured with a wink. Lucy snorted into her mimosa. "Ok, ok, we'll leave you and Kylo Ren alone for the time being."

"Kylo Ren?" Frankie scoffed.

"Brooding, deep voice, black hair, a temperament that shouts, 'test me one more time and I'll use The Force to choke you a little.' The man has overt First Order vibes."

"What about Sheriff Howards?" Lucy offered. "From what I heard, there was quite a reunion the other day when search and rescue found you and Benji."

Oh, right. Frankie would have been perfectly happy to forget that little public display of humping. Rational thought had played zero part in her decision to jump into Clint's arms at the trailhead. Her ego was wounded and her instinct was to dole out just as much discomfort to the person who'd bruised it. However, she had no clue if she'd been successful because, by the time she glanced over her shoulder, Miguel had Benjamin across the parking lot, facing away from the whole sappy display. At that point, she'd dismounted the sheriff, who was completely unaware that her motivations had little to do with him and more to do with injuring her snowshoeing buddy.

Guilt and regret crashed onto her periodically over the last couple days, like waves on a pebbly shore. She didn't like to play emotional games, and Clint deserved none of it. He'd been nothing but patient and respectful as she expressed her need for rest and solitude.

"We're picking up where we left off in September." She hoped her claim satisfied her skeptical friends because it did little to convince herself.

"That's great," Lucy chirped out a little too encouragingly as though she were trying to make a child feel proud of an honorable mention ribbon when they'd set their sights on taking home the trophy. "Clint's got that golden retriever boyfriend material thing going on."

"Yeah, but will a PB&J be as satisfying after having a fat, juicy cut of steak?"

No, it absolutely would not. But Frankie's two best—and most meddling—friends didn't need to know the whole story. She sniffed and flipped through the nail color swatches on her lap. "I'm sure I wouldn't know."

Todd and the bride-to-be exchanged an irritatingly knowing look and sighed in unison.

"Fine, have it your way." Lucy shrugged.

Frankie settled back in her chair, noting her back muscles were sore all over again. She didn't want to think about Benjamin, let alone discuss what they'd shared in the cabin a few days ago. Eventually, she'd fill those two nosy Nellies in on the details, but not while everything felt so raw and tender. For now, her focus was needed elsewhere—namely, the rehearsal dinner later that night then the wedding the following evening. As maid of honor, her job was to attend to anything the blushing bride needed, and she wasn't going to let a little drama get in the way of her brother's happiness.

Chapter Thirty-Seven

Benjamin

B enjamin followed Johnny up the rickety steps to The Rooftop Tavern on the edge of town. The old establishment was just as his friend had described while recounting numerous stories from youth to adulthood: walls loaded with photos of surrounding landmarks and adventurers who'd summited, rafted, or climbed them. Various antique snowshoes, backpacks, trekking poles, and lanterns adorned the shelves above and around the bar, which housed an impressive array of liquors. Twinkly, festive lights and bits of greenery framed each window and doorway. An updated version of "Jingle Bell Rock" played gently over the speakers.

The smell of warm, dry wood sent flashes of a cozy little cabin tumbling through his mind.

Last night was a mistake, Francesca.

A quick 'you'd better enjoy this fuck, sweetheart, cuz it's the only one you're gonna get' would have been nice.

He couldn't keep going there, bringing himself to the brink of madness by replaying the hurt he caused over and over. She'd encircled herself in armor so quickly that the shift had given Benjamin whiplash. So easily she'd pretended that what happened between them had been meaningless.

But it wasn't.

And it was killing him to play along with the façade.

He hadn't seen Francesca since she wrapped herself around

Sheriff Beefcake two days ago. What he couldn't determine was if she'd meant for the display to induce jealousy—which it had—or if it was for her own comfort. Neither was preferred, and it took everything in him not to bang on her neighboring hotel room door and ensure the living action figure wasn't warming her bed. Touching her. Kissing what Benjamin had so recently kissed.

The rehearsal dinner would be starting in a few minutes. An affair considerably smaller and more casual than the fancy welcome dinner Jonathan's mother, Patty, had insisted upon in order to "set the tone" for the week. While a more intimate gathering was typically preferred, Benjamin had reservations about there being fewer people to run interference between him and Francesca.

"Beer or scotch?"

His friend's glittering amber eyes—so similar to *hers*—skimmed over Benjamin's face, likely noticing the distressed clench of his jaw. Willing his expression to soften, he said, "I'll have what you're having."

Jonathan held up two fingers to the bartender, who nodded, returning with a couple bottles of Dogfish Head 90 Minute IPA. They clinked and drank. The strong, hoppy flavor was comforting in a familiar way. While it had been a regular in the rotation of libations he and Johnny enjoyed back in their college years, he hadn't had one since his friend had moved back to Leavenworth. It felt so long ago.

It had been so long ago.

"It's great to have you here, Benji." His friend settled a heavy hand on his shoulder and squeezed. "Not to sound too sappy, but I've really missed you."

Shame nipped at Benjamin's chest.

"I'm sorry I haven't made it out here sooner."

"Hey, you don't owe me an explanation," Johnny soothed,

brows pulling together.

"I feel like I do, though. I haven't been there for you in so long. Why," Benjamin's voice caught a little in his throat. He threw back a swig of beer to steady his emotions. "Why did you even ask me to be your best man? I'm glad you did, but surely there's someone who deserves it more."

Benjamin had played it over and over again in his mind. But no matter how he reconfigured it, it just didn't make sense that Johnny would have chosen an absent *friend* to stand beside him at the altar.

Johnny's face morphed into a knowing smile—a very fatherly gesture. Golden eyes scanned the darkness that shrouded Benjamin's face. He'd always been able to do that, see into others, deduce what they were worried about or dwelling on without having to be told. Johnny had some serious people-reading talents. An impressive party trick in the past. Currently, Benjamin found it unsettling. What if his friend figured out how he'd behaved with Francesca? Would he be as reassuring if he knew how his sister had been used and discarded with little concern?

"I'll be honest," Johnny said as he shrugged, "I almost didn't ask you."

The admission burned but wasn't surprising. "What changed your mind?"

"Not what. Who. Lucy convinced me to reach out."

"Really? Your bride doesn't even know me."

"Ah, but she's heard enough of my stories that she kind of does. She knows everything we've shared." Johnny barked out a laugh at Benjamin's cringe. "Before you ask, yes. She knows about all of it."

"And she still pushed you to call, huh?"

"She did. It was something about how I 'lit up' when I talked about our shenanigans and how we've been there for each other—the way brothers should. Said if I didn't do it, she'd snatch my phone and meddle." Johnny's eyes crinkled so hard that Benjamin suspected he did so to push back a few tears. "God, I love that woman."

"I owe her a thank you."

"You do. Zac too," Johnny scoffed and took a pull of his beer.

Benjamin recoiled. "Why Zac?"

"If he hadn't been such a flake over the last few years, you would have been runner-up to his Miss Leavenworth."

Benjamin chuckled and shook his head. He glanced at his beer bottle and traced a drip of condensation rolling down the logo. "I am sorry. I mean it. I've been a piss-poor friend. I promise to start visiting you more often. But, uh, in the summer."

A mirthful bark of laughter ricocheted off the weathered tavern walls. "Not everyone's built for the snow. Take my lovely almost-wife for example . . ."

He followed Johnny's gaze to the back entrance, where the woman in question practically skipped through the door. Todd followed close behind, moving with breezy, self-assured strides, and two bridesmaids whom Lucy had introduced, though their names momentarily escaped him. Benjamin held his breath, heart thundering in his ears as he waited anxiously for the maid of honor, bringing up the rear of the cavalcade.

When Francesca entered the dimly lit dining room, the glow of the disappearing sun set fire to the golden waves swept casually behind one ear. Dressed in tight jeans and a cozy green sweater, she looked positively adorable. In an instant, the room brightened and warmed.

But the moment her amber eyes snagged on Benjamin, they dulled, and the glow faded. She looked away and replaced the genuine grin with an expertly manufactured version.

I did that.

I'm the reason she has to pretend to be comfortable in a room where she shouldn't have a single care.

"—despite the Costco-size jar of hot fudge and my impersonation of the Swedish Chef singing 'Thong Song,'" Johnny finished, shoulders heaving with laughter.

"What?" Benjamin hadn't heard a word his friend had been saying.

"Exactly." He chuckled, wiping away a tear. He took a swig and then jabbed out his elbow. "Hold my beer, will ya?"

Before he could ask for clarifiers, Benjamin's hands were full, and the happy couple embraced for a quick yet slightly inappropriate kiss. He set both bottles down and strode to where the wedding party had begun to congregate. Without meaning to, his feet led him to stand beside the maid of honor. He rationalized that it was because of their roles and nothing to do with what happened in the cabin.

"You look rested." He stuffed his hands in his pockets, rocking back on his heels.

"Let's not. With the small talk." She pivoted slightly toward him, arms crossed.

He nearly grinned at her effort to remain aloof. Despite her rigid shoulders and flat expression, he could practically feel her buzzing. "All I was saying was that you look nice."

"Thanks," she scoffed quietly.

Her fresh herbal scent accosted his senses as she ran a hand through her honey waves. Brain fogged with decadent memories, he reached forward and slid a lock aside to inspect her forehead. Surprisingly, she allowed the contact. His fingers grazed her skin while taking care not to touch too closely to the small, puckered cut she'd received the other day. Flashes of her tumbling, careening down the embankment stuck thickly in his throat, and he swallowed to banish the intrusive image.

"This will be a fun memory in the wedding pictures," she lamented, gently brushing his hand away.

"A souvenir to remember our little adventure."

Her lips pulled down in a scowl. "Sadly, I didn't keep the receipt."

"Francesca, I—"

"Food's ready." Miguel's booming voice halted the hushed conversation and directed attention to the steaming taco bar along one of the walls. It was just as well, because Benjamin had no idea where his sentence was going, but he'd wager it wouldn't have led anywhere productive.

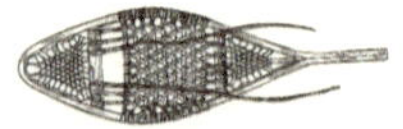

"Has anyone tried his cell?" Miguel asked the rest of the group once dinner was done and the table and chairs had been pushed aside.

"I've texted and called a number of times." Jonathan crossed his arms over his chest and shrugged. "Haven't seen him since last night, though."

"Should we take bets on whether he's in jail?" Francesca's melodic yet husky chuckle heated Benjamin from the inside out as he allowed his attention to be drawn to the petite blonde. She stood with hands braced on her hips, wearing an exasperated expression that also proclaimed her lack of surprise. Her cropped sweater shifted up as she combed her hair back with delicate fingers, flashing a patch of smooth, pale skin above her jeans.

He licked his lips, recalling how sweet she'd tasted, how soft she felt, writhing beneath his touch.

A rumbly throat clearing to his left snapped Benjamin out

of the memory. Todd stood shoulder to shoulder beside him, displaying mild boredom at the fact that no one could locate the missing groomsman. "Eye fucking the groom's little sister is not a good look."

Benjamin turned abruptly, bumping into the Christmas tree he'd been hovering near since dinner had finished. A few baubles fell to the ground, and he crouched to retrieve them. "Eye . . . what? No, I'm just—"

"Salivating over our girl like a cartoon wolf does a chick wearing a red hood?" Todd turned to face Benjamin head-on. "Look, everyone else here is so focused on finding Zac that it's given me plenty of time to size you up."

Burying his momentary shock, Benjamin arched a brow and affixed his most smug smirk. "And what have you deduced?"

"That you've got it bad." Ignoring the protesting scoff, Todd turned and watched Francesca. "Pretty sure she does too, and before you ask, no, she hasn't said anything. I can just tell."

Great. He needed to reign it in because if some stranger could spot his lust, then it would be a matter of time before Johnny did too. And the last thing he wanted was to cause an issue at his friend's wedding.

"Care for a little advice?"

"No."

"I'll take that as a yes," Todd hummed with a smile. "If she's having as big of an impact on you as it appears to the casual observer, then fight for her. She's worth it. There's no one like Frankie."

"It's not that easy." He absently hung the plastic balls back on the tree.

Clearly unimpressed by their placement among the branches, Todd shifted the ornaments around and then nodded in satisfaction. He turned his gaze back to Benjamin, boring his eyes deep then letting his lips curl into a mischievous grin. "Benji. It's *always* that easy."

"Ah, hell." A deep, raspy voice drifted in on the frigid night air as the back entrance opened. Zac clomped in, kicking snow off his boots, and pulled off his down jacket. "Did I miss dinner? I'm starved."

"Finally," Johnny groaned, walking over to the tardy groomsman. "Where were you, man?"

"I lost track of time." Zac shrugged, removing his scarf to hang it on the rack along with his coat.

"Nice hickey," Johnny chastised.

Nostrils flaring, Francesca marched over and stepped in front of her brother then flicked the angry cluster of purple welts on Zac's neck.

"Ow!"

"You selfish, unreliable sonofabitch."

"Jesus, Frankie. Calm down," he huffed, massaging the multicolored splotch on his neck.

"How hard is it to show up on time, especially for something important?" she demanded.

"Maybe I was doing something equally important," he said with a smirk, waggling his eyebrows. "Jealous?"

In response, Francesca flicked Zac again.

"Shit, ok, ok. *Uncle.*"

"I swear to god, if you're late tomorrow, you will have me to answer to. And while you may have enjoyed how you got those marks on your neck, you won't love how I administer my damage." Pride puffed up in Benjamin's chest, though he knew he had no right to the feeling. She continued in a tone denoting violence. "This wedding isn't about you. This is about your friend. You need to quit being a vengeful baby and get over the fact that you aren't the best man. Show up for him like a fucking adult or you will spend every day hereafter wishing you had. Am I clear?"

Sporting a fresh wash of red across his cheeks, Zac nodded sheepishly.

"Great!" Francesca slapped her hands together and turned to the group. "Let's get this show on the road."

She barked directions until everyone was lined up where they needed to be. The processional walked through the routine twice before calling it a night. Each time, Francesca stood with a gap between her and Benjamin, and it took everything in his power not to touch her.

Chapter Thirty-Eight

Friday, the wedding day: Frankie

"You're telling me you aren't even the teensiest bit nervous?" Todd asked Lucy as he secured a few rhinestones in her expertly sculpted hair. Glossy chocolate waves cascaded down her back while delicate wisps played about her face. Todd truly was a master craftsman when it came to beautification. He'd plucked, shaped, teased, painted, and pinned the bride within an inch of her life, all the while managing to enhance her natural features into something ready for the runway.

"Looking this good, how could I possibly be nervous?" Turning her head this way and that, she inspected her friend's handiwork, smile beaming with unfiltered joy. "I look like me, only airbrushed," she said with a giggle.

Frankie watched her almost-sister rise from the chair and hug the only man allowed in the bridal party's dressing room. "You look stunning, Luce. My brother is one lucky SOB. In more ways than one. You're way too good for him, and if you ever figure that out, it will be too late. You've already been claimed by the Miller clan."

Lucy grinned, mist gathering in her eyes and embraced Frankie in one of her notoriously bone-crunching hugs.

"Enough of that, ladies." Todd marched over, handing a tissue to the bride and lightly pinching Frankie's side. "You'll sully my masterpiece. Go pee so we can get you into your gown."

Gingerly dabbing at her eyes, Lucy scurried off to the

bathroom.

"I'm surprised you went with a suit," Frankie mused, perusing the tall, slim man from head to toe. Dark hair swooped and secured in a *GQ*-worthy fashion, custom-tailored suit grazing every inch of lean muscle, ridiculously expensive shoes buffed to perfection, Todd looked every ounce the stunning male specimen that he was.

"Our girl told me Dirty O'Feelya was welcome at the shindig, but I declined. She's a performer, a show stealer. And as you so rightfully pointed out last night when that walking louse showed up late—today is about Lucy and your brother. It's not about the rest of us."

"You'll still turn heads in this getup." Frankie nodded in admiration, appreciation warming her words.

"Well, it's not like I'm *dead*."

They both laughed as Lucy emerged from the bathroom. With the assistance of the other two bridesmaids, Lydia and Kylie, the group draped the bride in her long-sleeved lacy wedding dress. Frankie had begun the arduous process of fastening the thirty-thousand buttons that trailed from nape to just below Lucy's rear when there was a gentle yet adamant knock on the suite door.

"I got it." Todd walked over and greeted whoever stood on the other side with a low voice. After a little back and forth, he shut the door, reapplied a winning smile, and said, "Frankie, dear. Duty calls."

"What's wrong?" Lucy asked, voice wobbling for the first time all day.

"I'm sure it's nothing," Frankie reassured Lucy. "Probably the caterers asking where to put the chocolate fountain or something."

"But we didn't get a chocolate fountain—"

"I'll handle it. Want me to bring back a snack for you?" She crammed every shred of calm she could manage into her expression and practically breathed a sigh of relief as Lucy smiled and nodded. "Great. Bourbon and a packet of fruit snacks coming right up. Lydia, can you take over the buttons? My fingers were about to bleed from the sheer number of them anyway."

"Bite me," the bride said as she laughed.

Frankie winked and joined Todd at the door.

"If you need backup, text me, and I'll come running," he rumbled, one perfect brow arched mischievously. "Oh, and I'll take a bourbon."

"I already planned to bring back the bottle," Frankie drolled then slipped out the door.

She lifted her gaze and froze at the laughably sexy display of male beauty leaning against the opposite wall. With nothing in her mouth, she still managed to choke and cough.

"You all right?" Benjamin stepped forward and gently patted her back. His hand singed through the ice-blue velvet of her bridesmaid gown. The heat rippled across her skin and quelled the onslaught of shock that had taken her aback.

How?

How was he this devastatingly handsome in real life? Practically poured into his dark navy blue tuxedo, the fabric stretched seductively across his shoulders, tapering down to a trim waist. Her gaze lingered on his hips, recalling how they'd moved in ways that could ultimately lead to her destruction.

She shrugged his hand away and got ahold of herself.

"Fine. What is it?" She aimed for clipped but winced at how snotty she sounded.

"Zac," he said after taking a moment to conduct his own perusal of her.

"Fuck," she cursed sharply and started down the hall to the

groom's suite. "You can fill me in as we go."

She stopped and turned when she realized he wasn't by her side, catching him in the middle of a shameless stare. Perhaps he had all the time in the world, but Frankie needed to fix whatever clusterfuck the groomsman was causing and get back with Lucy's hanger prevention as soon as humanly possible.

"He's this way." Benjamin jerked his thumb over his shoulder, biceps straining against his jacket sleeve. Frankie grumbled then followed closely behind as they made their way down to deal with the chaos the soon-to-be-dead man was causing.

The massive tent, brimming with long white tables, twinkling lights, and plenty of space heaters to chase away the December chill, hummed with activity. Caterers prepared the serving station for dinner and dessert. The wedding planner and her swarm of assistants buzzed around tables, putting the finishing touches on the centerpieces. The bartender glanced around nervously as Zac and some woman stood at the little bar, preparing to take shots of tequila.

"Zackariah Sebastian Hartford the third," Frankie bellowed, eliciting a physical jolt from everyone nearby. "You put that shot glass down right now or I'll cram it down your throat."

The lanky redhead behind the counter breathed a sigh of relief and made himself useful by stocking cans of beer in the small fridge behind him.

"Busted," Zac chortled, setting down his tequila and wiping the salt off the back of his hand with a cocktail napkin. "Frankie, you look sexy as hell. Can I interest you in a shot?"

"What are you doing?" Her lethal glare oscillated between Zac and the woman standing beside him. Either he'd convinced one of the employees to shirk responsibility and throw back a few, or this was the groomsman's date.

"Bethany's my plus one—"

"It's Bethanne, actually," the woman tried to correct around Zac's shoulder.

"And she rode here with me. We're having a couple drinks to kill time before the ceremony."

"You should be with Jonathan. Not 'killing time' out here."

"What's the big deal, *Francesca*?" He flicked a spiteful glance at Benjamin. "It's not like groomsmen do anything besides walk a hopefully hot bridesmaid down the aisle. I don't hold the rings. I don't give a speech. I didn't even get to help plan the bachelor party, for Christ's sake. Not that Jon had one. He didn't 'feel up to it' since you two were too busy fucking in the woods."

"I'm sorry, what did you say?" Benjamin stepped forward, but Frankie stretched out an arm to block his path. She watched in shocked outrage as Zac clinked glasses with his date and threw back the shot. Thankfully, Bethanne, accurately reading the escalating agitation, had the good sense to set her own shot down and shrug into her coat.

"Maybe I'd better grab a seat. Let you get back to. . ." She trailed off, turned, and scurried away.

"Well, that was rude," Zac snorted. "You scared my date away."

The nerve of this guy. Frankie was reaching her boiling point and judging by the vibrations coming off Benjamin, she was in good company. She hadn't quite realized until this point how bitter Zac was over not being Jonathan's best man. Ever the casual, roll-with-the-punches-while-wearing-a-smarmy-grin kind of guy, his reaction seemed so out of left field that Frankie almost felt sorry for him.

Almost.

Still, she softened her expression—or at least made her best attempt. It was her duty to de-escalate the current drama so they could have a stress-free, happy wedding.

"Look. Your feelings are hurt." She ignored Zac's scoff and continued, "But Jon is counting on you. Will you please go to his suite and be there for him? Put aside whatever this is and deal with it tomorrow. He's your best friend."

He looked pointedly at Benjamin. "It just sucks that I'm not his."

Frankie watched Zac slink out of the tent, relieved to have avoided the situation becoming a bigger deal than it already was. She turned to the bartender and requested a bottle of J.P. Trodden and a few tumblers.

"Weren't you just giving Zac the business about drinking before the wedding?" Benjamin's husky voice prickled the back of her neck. His warmth permeated their shared space. He was so close.

Too close.

"Lucy requested it. Besides, having a drink as a group before the wedding is one thing. Throwing back a few shots with your date when you should be attending to the groom is completely different."

Accepting the bottle and stack of glassware, Frankie turned to Benjamin. "Thanks for letting me know what was going on."

"Honestly, I was more worried about what I would do if I didn't have you as a witness." He grinned fiendishly and stuffed one hand in his pocket. "Can I help you carry that?"

"Thanks, no."

She turned to make her way out of the tent. Then turned. "Another thing."

Benjamin inclined his head. "Anything."

"What Zac said about us in the woods. I don't need someone defending my honor."

Chapter Thirty-Nine

Benjamin

Over the next hour, Benjamin did his best to project an air of calm pleasantness despite the array of emotions parading through him. Even when he'd made it to the groom's suite and found Zac stalling out in the hall. Reaching around the wounded groomsman, he'd pushed open the door. They both entered.

"Zac," Jonathan exclaimed, voice rife with relief and irritation. "Nice of you to show up."

Zac nodded sheepishly, shoulders slumped in a way Benjamin had yet to see from the usually confident man. A twinge of understanding tugged at the back of his mind. The groomsman wasn't the only man in the room to have let Johnny down. Benjamin hadn't exactly been the poster child for the perfect best friend.

"He was handling a few essential things downstairs." Benjamin clapped Zac's shoulder. "I had to remind him that there was an entire army of people making sure the day goes smoothly and that his services were needed up here."

The groom looked between the two men, smiling in appreciation and wearing a hint of doubt. Clearly, as long as the people he cared about were there, he'd accept whatever excuse they gave him.

A knock sounded on the door. Todd strode in with an air of confidence that put Zac's usual display to shame. The man was beyond comfortable in his skin, not an ounce of insecurity. He knew who he was and what he stood for.

Benjamin decided he liked the bride's best friend.

"Well, well, well, isn't this a room brimming with devastation," Todd whistled, casually appraising all four tuxedo-clad men. "We're ready for you, Mr. Miller."

Jonathan beamed at the newest arrival with the affection given to family. But that's what Jonathan did; he collected brothers.

A short while later, Benjamin found himself congregated at the back of the building, just inside the door leading to the deck positioned to face the snow-capped mountains that surrounded the little Bavarian-themed town. The sun idly drifted down toward the peaks, preparing to set and wash the landscape in a haze of purples and pinks.

Beaming with joy, Jonathan stood beside Todd under a bough-woven arch, sparkling with white fairy lights and silvery, glittery things. Patio heaters encircled the altar, doming the space in comfortable warmth. A quiet murmur hummed through the crowd of about two hundred guests dressed in an array of clothes ranging from glamorous dresses to flannel shirts and puffy vests. The invitation had read *Come as you are*, and the interpretation varied greatly yet worked with the rustic theme of the whole affair.

"Ready, professor?"

Her warm touch seeped through the fabric of his jacket sleeve, quickly venturing a direct line to his chest. He turned, taking in the wintery goddess at his side. He'd seen her before when they'd handled the wayward groomsman and his date, but the second sight of her was just as moving as the initial glimpse. Her icy blue velvet dress appeared to have been custom-created to glide along her decadent curves. The long sleeves added a demure quality that offset the seductive plunging neckline. Woven into a thick, understated updo, her honey-golden hair glowed and shimmered with bits of sparkles strategically placed to catch the waning sunlight. A whisper-thin silver chain hung at her neck with a tiny infinity pendant resting gently in the hollow between her collarbone. Benjamin imagined sneaking a taste of her skin just beneath the shiny twist.

Francesca was beautiful. Strong. Steady. Filled with adoration for her family.

She was . . .

Everything.

Everything he wanted.

Perhaps he could make her happy.

Maybe if he was very careful he could have her and not destroy her like his father did his mother.

Benjamin shook his head, banishing the romantic flights of fancy. His focus should be on the wedding. He could dissect his feelings tomorrow and go from there.

He glanced at the maid of honor on his arm. Despite the joy wafting off of her as a result of the upcoming nuptials, Benjamin couldn't help but notice the strain of tension in her eyes. She was keeping it together, but the happy day held a swath of shadow—undoubtedly caused by his reckless seduction back at the cabin.

He sobered, stilling his reaction to her nearness.

"A better question is whether the bride is ready," he teased.

Francesca rolled her eyes. "Lucy's been chomping at the bit since last night. Practically tried to shimmy down a trellis to get to her groom. Speaking of. How's Jon holding up?"

"Same," he said with a chuckle. "Exactly the same."

"I guess that means they're making the right choice."

"I guess so."

Lingering, eyes full of meaning, Benjamin couldn't help but understand the translation.

We would never work.

"I like your glasses," she offered casually.

"Oh. Thanks."

"They aren't as harsh as the last pair. You look more approachable."

Benjamin readjusted the wireframes on the bridge of his nose. He'd been fortunate that the local optical shop had the option to rush order a new pair; otherwise, he'd be stuck wearing the same scratched lenses with an arm held together by sticks and tape. The style was different than he was used to, but after Francesca's assessment, he didn't mind the change so much.

"Who's running this thing?" came the singsong complaint behind them. "I've got a hottie to marry and a buffet to destroy."

Benjamin glanced over his shoulder at Lucy, who was indeed jittering around like a racehorse, ready to blast through the starting gate and gallop down the aisle. He sucked in a snicker.

"See what I've been dealing with?" Francesca bit her lip, holding back a burst of laughter. "I'd better check on things and figure out when we can start. Can you make sure people are lined up properly?"

He nodded and watched as she glided off, the picture of calm. His chest ached as though his heart were reaching out between his ribs for her retreating form.

Todd was right. He had it bad.

It was high time he admitted it to himself. Francesca was exquisite. She was the woman of his dreams, which would make the remainder of his time here in Leavenworth unbearable. Being this close and not having her was just too much.

Mustering all his focus and resolve would take everything in him, but what other option did he have?

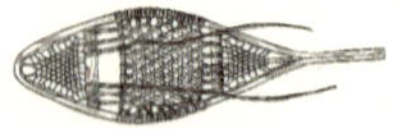

As expected, the ceremony went off without a hitch, filled to the brim with expressions of love and devotion and splashes of humor throughout. Benjamin managed to only look at the maid of honor a couple dozen times, which felt like quite an accomplishment considering how radiant she was.

He sat alone at the wedding party table, dinner having been cleared away, toasts given, cake cut. The room was alive with music and dancing, laughter and cheers for the bride and groom to *kiss kiss kiss*! Swirling the glass of scotch he'd barely consumed, he watched with hawk-like intensity as Francesca swayed in the arms of Sheriff Howards. The overgrown Boy Scout dwarfed the petite woman, despite her sky-high silver heels.

It may have been his imagination, but with every attempt Clint made at pulling her close, she managed to shift and maintain a sliver of distance between their synchronized bodies, and Benjamin was eternally grateful for that.

Torture seemed like too meek a word to describe the way he felt watching those large hands graze the small of Francesca's back, lips move close to whisper some sweet nothings in her ear, eyes rake over her dress like he knew what lay beneath despite the fabric's heft.

Jealously was a useless baser emotion, one Benjamin refused to entertain.

Typically.

Nonetheless, it bloomed aggressively in his chest. The heat of it rose in his throat, and for a moment, he believed that fire would shoot from his mouth at any moment. The unsettling realization that she might end up warming another man's bed made Benjamin sick. He wanted to smash something: his glass, the sheriff's face.

With another subtle press, Francesca was flush against Clint's hulking chest. Glancing away from her dance partner, her eyes scanned and found Benjamin's. In one look, he read her discomfort, and he didn't stop to translate the nuance. Mechanically, he threw back the rest of his scotch, wincing slightly at the burn slashing down his throat, and stood. Long strides quickly ate up the distance between him and his target, giving very little time for his rational brain to reboot and take control of his body.

Fortunately for him and his lack of self-control, the second his hand came down on Clint's large shoulder, the sound of shattering glass and resounding slap rang out in the large tent. A hush settled over the crowd as everyone, Benajmin included, strained to see what all the fuss was about.

Chapter Forty

Zac

The sharp sting of what he was sure was a hand-shaped welt prickled across Zac's cheek. He tracked the angry sway of Bethany's hips as she marched through the tent exit.

Fuck.

Bethanne.

He'd struggled with her name the entire time he'd known her but gave himself a little slack since they'd only met forty-eight hours ago. He'd tried to bestow the moniker Beth, but she *did not* like that, and since his goal had been to get in her pants, he avoided doing anything that would piss her off. Fortunately, she enjoyed it when he referred to her as beautiful, sexy, and lovely, so he stuck with similar terms of endearment.

The struggle had come when others approached them at the wedding. Since introducing her as his "friend" seemed to cool her jets, and he couldn't very well call her his bang buddy, privates pal, booty call, or (*gulp*) girlfriend, her name was the safest bet.

Or *would* have been if he could freaking get it right.

She must have slid to the end of her rope because when Stella, the smoking hot server at The Rooftop Tavern, came over to say hello, everything got out of hand.

To be honest, Zac couldn't really say with any real certainty what had gone wrong because Stella's dress was so low cut and her tits were more buoyant than usual, so he'd been pretty distracted. He could have called Bethanne Bart or Bradley for all he knew.

Whatever came out of his mouth deemed him worthy of a drink in the face and a slap.

"It's all in a day's work," he chuckled to the wide-eyed bartender, whose mouth hung open like something shocking had just happened. Zac licked the lemon drop from his lips and used a couple napkins to dab the rest of the sticky drink as it dribbled through his trimmed beard. "Shot of tequila. Make that two."

A solid hand clamped onto the back of his arm and Zac prepared himself for the brotherly razzing of his best friend. But when he turned, instead of Jonathan, Miguel stood there with a dark scowl and some pretty impressive nostril flaring.

"Can I talk to you privately?" At nearly forty, Miguel was the oldest member of their friend circle and never missed an opportunity to act like the patriarch of the group. The frequency of his advice and heart-to-hearts had increased since he'd become a dad last year, as though knocking up his wife gave him infinite wisdom that he felt compelled to bestow on the rest of them.

"Later, pops. I'm about to down these two bad boys and make my way to the dance floor."

"You really think that's a good idea?"

Zac inclined his head and gave a wink as he shot back the tequila in rapid succession. Spitting the lime rind into one of his napkins, he hissed at the campfire burning down his throat. "Best idea I've had all night."

Brushing past his friend, bumping shoulders just enough to not be taken as an overly aggressive gesture, Zac settled his eyes on the pint-sized target he'd been trying to nail for years: Frankie Miller.

The blonde bombshell stood a few feet away, hands on her hips, face contorted in a chastising scowl fit for an uppity school teacher. He'd be all too happy to take a ruler to the knuckles if it meant she'd be the one doling out the punishment. The day she'd turned twenty-one was the day Zac had launched Operation Nail Jonathan's Little Sister. And while the mission name lacked a certain finesse, his various attempts had run the gamut from exceedingly clever to downright blunt.

Unfortunately, nothing had worked.

But imbued with numerous doses of liquid courage, despite the rage that radiated off of her like cartoon squiggle lines, he saw the virtue in making another attempt.

Even though another woman had just thrown a drink in his face.

Even though two large men were holding a subdued pissing contest to win her.

Even though he already knew what she would say.

Because either she'd finally crack or it would be another humorous rejection to file away under "Zac's Failed Attempts."

"I must not have made myself clear earlier." Her sharp words landed like a soft leather flogger on his chest. Stinging yet offering tingles of pleasure with every scolding syllable. The ice in her usually warm amber eyes complemented the cool velvet of her incredibly sexy maid of honor dress. Cut low and slit high, the getup showed off the lush curves she'd brought back with her from her first term at NWU. He'd always found her tight and sexy, fit from hiking, climbing, and rafting, but her new, more shapely design made his mouth water. "What the fu—"

In a hail Mary, he swept his arms around her and twirled her onto the dance floor. Shocked at his boldness, she didn't pull away. Instead, she gripped his arms with nails clawing through his button-up shirt, his tuxedo jacket abandoned somewhere long ago.

"There. Isn't this better?" he crooned, eyes sweeping over her lovely—if fuming—face, the pulse pounding in her neck and chest heaving against the confines of her dress.

"What is your problem?" she all but shouted, but remembered she'd been about to chastise him for making a scene, so she lowered her voice. "You are behaving like a damn child, and you need to knock it off. Now."

"I'm no child, Francesca," he smirked. "Just a man going after what he wants time and time again."

"You're immature and insane." He bristled at her sneer.

"I prefer youthful and optimistic."

"You can prefer all you want, but to everyone else, you come off as a useless ass."

Zac casually glanced around the room. Everyone watched them. Including Benjamin.

Fucking Benji.

The "best man" who swooped in after years and years of being a shit friend to Jonathan. Zac had been there, day in and day out, standing by Jonathan through the good and bad. He should have been the best man, not some snooty law guy who gets everything he wants. Taking everything Zac had been working so hard for.

"I have to know." He plastered a grin on his face, knowing full well his eyes displayed more bitterness than warmth. "Did you fuck him?"

"Excuse you?" Frankie recoiled as though she'd been slapped.

"Your professor. In the cabin. I wouldn't blame you. Life and death situations make people do irrational things all the time."

"I'm going to give you the benefit of the doubt and assume you're concussed from Bethanne's slap earlier and let you retract your words and apologize." She shoved at his chest then practically growled as his hands stayed firmly planted at the small of her back.

"I imagine you need a pallet cleanser after subjecting yourself to the rigid and unimaginative sex that walking wet blanket gave you. Maybe that's why you've been throwing yourself at Captain

Clint over there. But you're fooling yourself if you think either could compare to what I'd be able to—oof!"

What could only be described as an actual polar bear paw landed hard on Zac's collar, flinging him around. Head swirling with drink and his own callous words, he looked up at the large sheriff in question. He wasn't in the mood to come to blows with local law enforcement, especially with one who outweighed him by a good fifty pounds, but he'd be unable to back down if it came down to it. Sometimes fighting—or getting your ass beat, which would more likely be the case—was the only answer.

"What the hell is your malfunction, Zac?" Jonathan barked from beside Clint.

Zac's attention snapped to his friend, whose face held so much frustration and disappointment that it made his head hurt. "Jesus . . . I. I'm sorry, brother—"

"I think it's best if you leave," Clint interrupted, still gripping Zac's drink-stained collar in his mighty meat claws. "Avoid any more of a scene."

Anger spiked Zac's blood as though he had taken another shot of that smoky tequila. "It's not your call, sheriff. What are you? The hired security now?"

"Zac, please." Jonathan's quiet plea was sobering.

Scanning the crowd, Zac's eyes settled on Lucy. Jonathan's fiancée—er, wife—who usually glided around town with endless warmth and joy, now stood wearing a hurt expression similar to her new husband's. Miguel and Benjamin hovered nearby, arms crossed over their chests, ready to assist with the ejection if necessary. His eyes snagged on Patty Miller, the surrogate mother who had looked after him like he was her own since he became friends with her son all those years ago. There, he saw similar disappointment, and it wrecked him.

He needed to get out of there.

Immediately.

"I'm going." His words were quiet but triggered Clint's hands to release and lower. Zac strode past Jonathan, pausing momentarily to take the jacket his friend held out. "Congrats, man."

Zac wasn't quite sure exactly when he'd been labeled an unreliable fuck up, but he was pretty certain it was a gradual development as opposed to any one event. But as he strode from the tent, where he could hear the DJ attempting to gloss over the disruption by calling the crowd to the dance floor for the "Cupid Shuffle," Zac was certain that he'd finally hit rock bottom.

Chapter Forty-One

Frankie

"Are you all right?"

Frankie's perked up as the rich baritone pulled her attention from Zac's sheepish departure. Benjamin stood beside her, head cocked to the side in exaggerated concern.

No, not exaggerated.

Genuine.

"Yeah." She glanced back to the happy couple, trying their best to rebound from the momentary disruption and enjoy the rest of the evening. Clint and Miguel talked in animated yet hushed tones near the bar, no doubt debriefing the incident and making further plans should the troublemaker decide to rejoin the party. She shrugged, still taken aback by the entire altercation. "That was a lot."

It hadn't been the first time that Zac had come on to her. In fact, she'd become a pro at sidestepping his advances. But this was the first time he'd ever been cruel about it. His typical play was a smooth-talking ladies' man, not an aggressive, vulgar bastard. Something was up. Part of her wanted to ignore it, to chalk his behavior up to too much tequila, but that didn't feel accurate. There was more to it than that.

"Want to get some air?" Benjamin's large hand hovered upturned in front of her, and her unfocused attention zeroed in on it. With a nod, she took hold and followed him out of the tent through one of the rear entrances.

A refreshing gust of cold mountain air calmed Frankie's nerves as she and Benjamin stepped out onto the small, vacant patio. The December chill contrasted with the ambient warmth the two large space heaters pumped out into the space. She approached the wooden railing that overlooked the Wenatchee River as it coiled around Enchantment Park. The moonlight glittered on the rippling current, refusing to wash downstream with the rest of the water. Clouds hovered in thick patches, steadily converging into a solid mass, promising snow but not giving away when or how much.

She shivered.

An instant later, Benjamin's tuxedo jacket settled heavily across her shoulders, smelling strongly of a crisp fall afternoon. The scent, more intoxicating than the sparkling sweet wine she'd been slowly sipping all night, soothed her anxieties about Zac's earlier antics.

"Can I get you anything?"

Benjamin stood beside her while also ensuring a solid foot of distance.

Frankie shook her head.

He nodded, matter-of-fact, and said, "I'll let you be."

Turning on his heels, he strode back to the entrance.

But she didn't want to be alone. She needed company, but more than that, she wanted *his* company. "Stay."

"I'm not sure that's wise," he mumbled, still facing away.

"And why is that?"

"Self-control."

"Too much or not enough?"

He turned and lit up her insides with his pointed stare. "Oh, come now, Francesca. There's no need to tease."

She shrugged, feigning a nonchalance that she knew he'd

never believe. "I'm not the tease, Benji."

Like a whip, he was in front of her, consuming the air she exhaled with each fragmented breath. That cinnamon and sandalwood scent intensified, feeling warmer and more vivid from the source.

"Oh, no?" The endless sapphire of his irises tipped over, cascading into the widening black of his pupils as they jerked from her eyes to her lips and back.

"Nope."

He dipped his chin, settling his mouth a whisper away from her ear. Hot breath played on the shell, tickled her lobe, and descended in silky swirls along her neck.

"How do you think I felt watching him touch you?"

"Which one? Zac or Clint?"

He responded with a growl and curled his solid fingers around her hand. Lifting, he slid her sleeve down her forearm and danced a gentle kiss along the inside of her wrist—something in her belly leapt at the contact. She thought about all the places those plush lips had been on her, dying to feel them there again. Ached to explore his body with her own.

"Both." His hoarse response held a tortured quality at its depths, but why?

In the cabin, he'd practically devoured her, teased her, withheld release until she truly believed she'd come undone. He'd murmured sweet nothings about being ruined by her. But that's just what they were.

Nothings.

They didn't mean anything.

"Look." She sighed, sliding her wrist from his gentle grasp. "I'm not sure what you're doing. Either you're a little buzzed or don't like that another dude touching a toy you threw away prematurely. Maybe it's both, but either way, your *dismissal* the other morning was heard loud and clear."

His shoulders tensed at her words. She'd struck a chord, and for that, she felt a drifting flutter of satisfaction, but it was short-lived as she slid his jacket off and handed it back. The chill overtook her, and she backed toward the tent.

"Francesca." An apology, a plea? It didn't matter. It was too little too late.

"Thanks for taking me to get some air. I didn't realize how much I needed to step away." Smiling weakly, she turned and rejoined the reception, leaving a dejected Benjamin out in the cold.

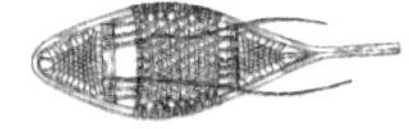

"Should we request 'The Electric Slide'? Or the 'Macarena'?"

Frankie's eyes went wide at both of Lucy's awful suggestions. Lydia and Kylie nodded emphatically. As the maid of honor, it was her job to humor the bride no matter what, but this was a bit too much.

Surveying the crowd, she spotted her brother. Jon glanced down and pulled back his sleeve, checking the wristwatch that was once their father's. A tinge of sadness bloomed in Frankie's chest.

I wish Dad could have been here.

Catching her expression, her brother strode over, wrapping her in a strong hug. "Me too, sis."

He always managed to do that. Scan someone and read their thoughts like some psychic freak of nature. Typically, his little parlor trick wigged her out, but the embrace and words were exactly what she needed.

"Screw it. We'll do both," Lucy called over her shoulder, a bridesmaid in each hand, as she sprinted barefoot to the DJ. As the first few bars of "Macarena" rang out, a few of the remaining guests scurried out to join her on the dance floor.

"Dad would have loved her," Frankie said wistfully.

"They would have been insufferable together. She has the same power of persuasion that he did. Same genuine warmth too." The weight of his arm settled casually around her shoulders. She instinctively leaned in, watching with amusement as their mother—also barefoot—danced right alongside her new daughter-in-law. "It's probably why Mom glommed onto her so quickly."

"Can't say that I blame her."

Jonathan squeezed tighter at the wobble in her voice. He sighed heavily. "It's been an emotional day."

"That it has." Frankie nodded.

"So emotional, in fact—"

"No, Jon," she warned uselessly.

"—that even the cake is in tiers."

"You're the worst."

"And you love me anyway." He squeezed her again.

"You got me there."

One song bled into another, and Jonathan winced.

"That's about enough of that, I think. Night, sis."

Frankie watched her brother's long, purposeful strides as he made his way onto the dance floor, weaving fluidly between a handful of electric sliders in various states of intoxication. Lucy shrieked gleefully as he scooped her up in his arms like a proper bride, and then she snuggled against his chest.

"Bye, everyone. Thanks for coming," the newest Miller called hastily as the couple left the venue.

Frankie gathered her handbag and turned toward the door. Her warm bed was calling and she wasn't willing to deny it a moment longer.

Until a deep voice stopped her in her tracks. "Care for an escort?"

Chapter Forty-Two

Benjamin

Benjamin leaned against the bar, sipping on his second drink of the night and watching the venue staff stack chairs and roll away tables. He wasn't typically a heavy drinker; he'd been favoring water the whole night, allowing himself a single finger of a perfectly aged scotch during the round of toasts immediately following dinner.

But when he caught sight of a certain blonde wrapped in blue velvet leaving the reception, wrapped just as tightly around the bulging bicep of the largest man in the room fifteen minutes prior, he'd decided a second drink wasn't outside of propriety. He could use a little relaxation. Unfortunately, the fiery liquid had the opposite effect: souring his stomach almost as much as the thought of hearing Francesca's moans of pleasure from the next room.

Moans he wouldn't be causing this time.

He abandoned the barely touched tumbler on the bar with a hundred-dollar bill tucked beneath and strolled out of the tent.

"Night," the bartender called.

The very December crispness in the air provided more relief than the drink. A stroll around town as the bars closed down would help. The holidays were in full swing along Main Street. He took in the glow of the Christmas lights, twinkling between the silent flakes of snow drifting from the clouds. A giant tree in the middle of town reached higher than the rest, proudly displaying twists of ribbons and lights. The scene was beautiful but left him with a bitterness he couldn't shake.

He'd messed up.

Spectacularly.

And there was no going back from the error he made. He'd slept with a student. One of *his* students and jeopardized his career and potentially her scholarship in the process. Not only that, but he took advantage of his best friend's little sister like an opportunistic villain. He risked his most cherished friendship, and if he had the opportunity to go back . . . If he had the chance to undo every choice he made, every touch and taste . . .

Who was he kidding? He would do it all over again.

That's why when he spotted the good sheriff clomping to his truck just outside of the Wilhelm Haus Inn, he breathed a sigh of relief. Before he could second-guess anything, he found himself at the door of the room just beside his and knocked.

The creak of the hinges reverberated in his ears, and the sight of Francesca still dressed, hair neatly in place, lipstick unsmudged, left him breathless.

"Oh, thank god," she gasped the instant she registered his presence.

Benjamin needed no further invitation, stepping across the threshold and into her seeking arms. His lips met hers in contact rife with so many unspoken thoughts.

I'm sorry.

Forgive me.

God, I need you.

His mouth slanted feverishly over hers, pushing hard as though he had the power to will the words from his mind to hers. His fingertips pressed into her waist and firmly dipped to the small of her back. Benjamin whispered an oath of gratitude for whoever designed her dress because the high slit at the front allowed perfect access to reach through and cup her ass. Effortlessly, he lifted and Francesca settled her bare legs around his waist, hooking her ankles at his back.

He didn't mean to crash her so violently into the entryway wall, but her satisfied groan doused any worry that he'd hurt her. Her needy fingers gripped at his hair, now fully out of sorts and rumpled, as she did her part to pull him even closer.

This woman.

Francesca.

He was drowning in her: her lavender scent, the soft prickle of her goosebumps under the drag of his teeth. The realization that he might never come back up for air again—and the fact that he took pleasure in the notion—made him rumble a quiet laugh.

Pulling back, she looked at him quizzically. Her eyes filled to the edge with expanding pupils and questions. "What is it?"

The hesitation in her voice burrowed into his chest and flattened his heart—so much subtext in those three little words. The loudest concern centered around whether they were making a mistake. So badly he wanted to offer her everything. Promises and vows to touch and protect and care for her until the day he died, but they would be empty. Because odds were, he would destroy her in the end. In his experience, things like love and commitment did not last, and despite the joy and happiness in the beginning, the very display he'd witnessed mere hours before, he knew deep down that there was no truth in *happily ever after.*

"I can't give you what you want—"

"Give me tonight." Her words came out raw and vulnerable. "That's what I want."

His flattened heart split down the middle. He should have set her down, straightened his jacket, and marched to his room, but Benjamin was a weak man. *She* made him weak. And so, despite wishing for the strength to do the virtuous thing, he rolled his hips into hers, pressing her more firmly against the wall. She shuddered and dashed her fingers down his shirt, frantically unhooking buttons until his chest was bare.

"Are you sure?" he croaked, legs shaking as she pressed against the erection that stiffened against her core.

"Mm-hmm," she hummed, practically groping his pecs, nipples, and abs with her hungry eyes.

"*Francesca*," Benjamin chided in his most convincing professor voice. "Focus, please."

The blaze of desire emanating from the golden rim of her irises nearly knocked him back. Straight white teeth worried her plump bottom lip playfully before she said, "Yes, professor. I'm sure."

Groaning in relief, he nipped at her jaw and followed down the length of her neck, all the while pressing his hips against hers. The silky roughness of her velvet dress abraded his bare chest, scraping against his nipples with every single shift.

Too much clothing; she was practically swimming in the heavy fabric. Gripping harder with one hand to ensure she stayed in place, Benjamin slid his other up her side then slowly cupped her breast. She trembled as he curled his fingers around the edge of her neckline then grazed her nipple with his knuckles as he pulled the dense fabric aside. The lace of her bra matched the darkening swell of her pupils as they edged out the lingering amber ring.

Still, it wasn't enough. The tiny glimpse ratcheted his lust, and he feared his own demise if the torture continued.

"Hold onto me," he demanded.

"Aren't I already?"

He slapped her ass in warning, the muted clap making her giggle, but she obeyed, clamping her legs harder against his waist. Pushing off the wall, he marched her to the bed and landed on top of her. He pushed up onto his hands so he hovered above her. She reached for him, and he casually swatted her hand away. Sweat glistened on her collarbone and just between her breasts. The flush of her cheeks and the heaving rise and fall of her breasts announced her response to his gaze, his touch.

"What do you need, Francesca?" He teased his tongue along her collarbone, and she arched in response. "What do you want me to do to you?"

He couldn't have missed her cheeky grin if he tried. What crossed her mind? Whatever it was, anything, all she needed to do was ask, and he would do it to her. For her.

"I'm the boss," she said as she giggled.

"Oh, are you now?" he teased, tracing along the black straps of her bra.

"That's what I want." She propped herself up on her elbows and arched a challenging brow. "I want you to do as I say and only as I say."

Intriguing.

Benjamin swirled the idea around in his head for a moment. It was not an outlandish request, but he tended to prefer being the one in control. In all aspects of his life. And typically women were happy—thrilled even—to oblige. Francesca had done just that in the cabin. But something about the idea of being her willing plaything had a certain appeal.

"All right, Francesca," he growled, sucking lightly on her neck and rolling his hips against hers in one final display of power. "I'll let you take over, but fair warning. I may not be able to follow directions as well as you expect."

"Even if you get a reward?" She licked her lips, and he nearly died.

Chapter Forty-Three

Frankie

*T*hank you. Thank you. Thank you.

The sentiment chanted through Frankie's mind from the second she opened her door and found Benjamin standing there wearing a mix of hope and shame. She'd tried to stop wanting him, tried to put him out of her mind or at the very least categorize him as "completely unavailable." Her efforts even extended to welcoming another man into her hotel room when he'd escorted her back from the reception.

"Alone at last." Clint's words—brimming with implication—crawled over Frankie in an unsettling way she didn't understand. In all measures, Sheriff Howards was a good man: kind, patient, hard-working. And to say he was attractive was the biggest understatement since Mercutio claimed his stab wound was just a scratch. Because at six-foot-four, jacked with solid muscle, unruly surfer boy curls, and jaw sharp enough to cut glass, the dude was ridiculously hot.

And yet the thought of him touching her, kissing her, pleasuring her, made her cringe, which would be a very inconvenient reaction given the circumstance. Enough of one that she'd let him down easy and turned him away before he had the opportunity to land his perfect lips on hers.

Clint's disappointment had been clear, but he hadn't pushed or pressured. He'd simply suggested she call him if she changed her mind then ducked out the door.

Her self-flagellating thoughts—*He's perfect and available. What's wrong with you?*—met a hasty end when a knock sounded at her door.

While she knew there wasn't a future with Benjamin, she'd met his arrival with relief and body-shuddering lust. Tonight was all she'd get. She could accept that.

But she was going to make it worth it.

And leave an impression in the meantime.

Standing in front of Benjamin as he lounged on her bed, she dragged her gaze up and down his body and came to a stark conclusion. There was a huge problem, one that needed to be remedied immediately.

"You're wearing too much," she scolded, gesturing lazily at him. "Strip."

He grinned, that cocky, seductive, flashing blue-eyed grin of his, and rose from the mattress. She watched, mesmerized, as he slowly slid out of his unbuttoned shirt. The gray-toned tattoo of Lady Justice peeked from his side, rippling against the expanse of well-crafted obliques. Next, he handled his belt, button, and zipper steadily until his immaculately tailored trousers slid to the floor.

How could he possibly be so cool and collected while Frankie's body shivered and hummed in anticipation?

Because this means something different to him.

Shaking her head to dispel the nagging thought, she caught Benjamin's frown.

"Not to your liking?" he teased, though there was an undercurrent of something else in his voice.

Redirecting her attention, she shrugged. Her thoughts were hers, and she wasn't going to share them with a man who would be gone by sunup.

So, she lied, kind of. "I feel overdressed now."

She stepped closer to him and gave him a tiny shove to sit on the bed and then turned. He slowly unzipped her dress, planting luxurious kisses along each vertebra he exposed. The elegant garment fell heavily from her shoulders into a pool of icy velvet at her feet.

A low rumble emitted from Benjamin's throat, clearly approving of what he saw. He reached out to touch, but she sidestepped him. "Ah-ah. I'm the boss, remember?"

His hands dropped to his sides with a playfully menacing look. A thrill fluttered at the thought that such a commanding man would be so obedient.

She stepped closer, standing between his knees, and dipped her head enough to kiss his perfect lips. His hunger matched hers, taking the contact as an invitation to touch much more of her. And he knew exactly how to touch her. Fingers dug into her flesh, squeezed and pinched sensitive peaks; fingernails gently scraped from her nape to the crescents below each cheek at the top of her legs. He licked and kissed and nibbled. Frankie moaned approvingly, praising his work as he thoroughly roamed her body.

His erection strained aggressively against his black boxer briefs. All manner of naughty ideas of what to do with him crossed her mind. A ripple of heat rose up her neck. She knelt, and he sucked in an audible breath.

"Francesca." She couldn't tell if he said it as a prayer or warning, but both possibilities imbued her with heady power. Smiling up at him, she laid a trail of wet little kisses down his belly until she reached the top band at his hips. He'd let go of her, instead gripping the linen beneath him, but as soon as she dipped a fingertip below the only garment he still wore, he plunged his hands into her hair.

She pulled, releasing the full heft of him, and met his wild, unblinking eyes. Except for the ragged rise and fall of his chest, Benjamin sat frozen as though any twitch would cause her to flee. Frankie had to bite back a giggle because the stark, wicked anticipation was broadcasted across his handsome face.

Slowly dipping down, she trailed her tongue around the tip. His hips jerked on instinct.

"Fuck, sorry," he said through a clenched jaw, throat bobbing as he swallowed hard.

"Stay put," she warned with a grin. He nodded.

Frankie lowered again, repeating the movement but with agonizingly slow strokes. The hold on his self-control was admirable, and she rewarded him by taking him into her mouth as far as she could. His hands tightened to fists in her hair, eliciting from her a pleased moan that she was certain he could feel against his smooth rigidity. She slowly retreated to the tip and then advanced, hands joining in to touch and grip more of him.

"Holy fuck, Francesca. Your smart little mouth. It's so hot . . . so wet. You're killing me, sweetheart, oh, but please don't fucking stop."

She began to bob up and down more rapidly, thoroughly enjoying the vulgar words that crept through the cracks of his usually so-composed exterior. His taste, his low voice encouraging her—praising her—all swelled inside of her, skyrocketing her own craving for more of him. Soon, she noticed him start to tense beneath her attention and chuckled to herself because as soon as he neared climax she pulled away, stopping him just shy of release like he had done to her in the cabin.

Gripping her hair tighter, he turned her face up toward his, amazed at the fire that seemed to dance on the turbulent ocean blue of his eyes. She could see it written all over his face. He knew exactly what she was trying to do, and he battled internally over whether he should return the favor.

"Need I remind you that I'm the one in control tonight?" Frankie hadn't realized how fun and heady it would be to play with fire until that moment. Power surged through her as though she were superhuman, and she found herself intoxicated.

He growled—actually growled—but loosened his fists. "Thin ice."

Detangling him from her already wild hair, she reached for his discarded pants. After fishing through his pockets and finding them empty aside from a keycard, she grumbled and flung them aside.

"What are you searching for, Francesca?" His composure, at least in part, had returned as he watched her curiously.

"Looking for something," she mumbled.

"Inside jacket pocket."

She eyed him suspiciously then dug her hand into the silk lining, procuring a strip of condoms.

"You're lucky," she purred as she slowly walked back over to him, hips swaying.

"I have a lengthy list of reasons why running through my head." He chuckled huskily. "But tell me why *you* think I'm lucky."

"Because I would have sent you out to the nearest drugstore if you hadn't brought protection." She dropped the foil packets on the nightstand and stepped across to straddle his hips. "Dressed just like this."

"Sweetheart, there are no bounds to the lengths I'd go for you."

As he said it, his eyes glinted playfully, but before she could focus on the lie in his words, she got back to her original mission.

"Lay back."

He did.

So, she rewarded him by straddling his hips and removing

her bra. "Touch me."

He did.

She arched into his strong hands, grinding hard against his straining erection. He cupped her ass and pulled her up toward his chest. She understood and shimmied so her knees rested on either side of his head, pretending all the while that it had been her idea. "Lick me."

And, holy fuckity fuck, he did. Hooking a finger and pulling aside her panties for better access, he swirled and dragged and flicked his tongue until she was quivering and shuddering. All the while, she undulated her hips above him, desperate for even more contact, more friction. This position was great—fantastic, really—but she wanted him to slide into her, claim her, even if it would only be for one more night. She didn't mind so much because she was aware of the circumstances this time.

"Benjamin." The wobbly quality of her voice startled her.

"M-hm?" The hum against her most sensitive spot sent quivers out to the tips of her fingers and toes.

"I want you to bend me over and slide into me until I'm begging to come."

The hum turned to a growl, and with deft action, he flipped her off of him. Strong hands gripped her hips, turning her onto her belly and tugging her panties down with one surprising swipe. She tingled, hearing the condom wrapper. But before she could say anything cheeky about him hurrying up, the press of his solid tip tested her, finding no resistance because of the wetness they'd both provided. Suddenly, with her hips in the air and cheek pressed into the mattress, he drove into her.

She screamed, but not one of pain. No, there was only agonizing fullness and stretch and bliss. He felt perfect inside her, and she had no idea how she had forgotten how good he would feel.

"Did I hurt you?" Her heart filled too as he checked in with her, still testing her with tiny, gentle thrusts.

"No. No, it was perfect," she assured breathlessly.

"Thank god."

The relief in his voice almost made her laugh, but the chuckle morphed into whines and whimpers because he pulled out fully and pushed back in. Over and over, he thrust with increased speed and force. Every plunder pressed her deep where decadent pressure began to build.

His hands were everywhere. Playing with her nipples, the tight bundle of nerves between her legs, squeezing and teasing her with playful smacks on her ass.

"So. Fucking. Perfect. So tight. So exquisite. Oh god, Francesca, squeeze. Yes. Oh fuck, yes." Benjamin's words were a chant, tumbling out as though he were in a trance as he pumped harder and harder. "I'm going to make you come so hard, and then I'm going to lose it. When you squeeze and flutter around me, I'm going to give you everything."

He reached around and cupped her breasts, pulling back so she was upright against his chest but still kneeling on the bed. A large, solid hand stroked up and settled at her throat. His other fingers spread and teased just above where he pumped into her over and over.

"I can feel you. You're about to come. Oh fuck I can feel you tensing."

What were words? They might as well be something as complicated as theoretical physics because Frankie couldn't form a single one as she barreled toward a lethal orgasm. Just another thrust, another flick, another squeeze, and . . .

She toppled over the edge, riding a roller coaster through a cavern of blisteringly bright stars. Shocks of light flooded her senses as she wailed in shameless pleasure.

"That's right, sweetheart, that's right. Come for me, squeeze me tighter. I can take it." Benjamin's thrusts became more erratic, which only magnified the encompassing bliss strobing through Frankie as he neared his own completion. Louder rumbles and grunts rode out of his mouth with each strangled breath until he slid in hard and held her tight to his body.

The throb of his orgasm pulsed inside Frankie, playing against the wildly sensitive parts of her as she barely hung on to her sanity. He heaved raggedly against the back of her ear, planting lazy kisses against her neck and shoulder.

He carefully pulled out of her. "Give me one moment. Please, stay right here."

She couldn't refuse such a gentle request and was instantly rewarded by being swept into his strong arms not a few seconds later. Pulling back the blankets on her bed, he settled her in the warm comfort and tangled his limbs with hers.

Perfection.

That's what the last hour had been. Her chest ached for a moment, knowing that there wouldn't be an endless supply of similar encounters, but quickly schooled herself. Not now. She could mourn the loss of this delicious, bliss-delivering man in the morning.

Chapter Forty-Four

Benjamin

"Are you asleep?" Benjamin asked after some time had passed and his heartbeat resumed a normal cadence. Francesca settled across his chest, her honey hair and limbs draped all over him.

"Not sleeping. Dead, maybe." The husky quality of her voice shot a spark of renewed lust into his bloodstream.

"I'd better revive you with some mouth-to-mouth, then." He tilted her chin delicately up and swept a kiss over her swollen lips. The flutter of her heart tickled against his chest, and her breathing—like his—spcd up. "She lives."

"It's a miracle."

Her chuckle puffed out against his sweat-damp skin as she nuzzled back against his neck.

This.

This right here was heaven—something he'd never experienced with another. And unfortunately, never would again after tonight. Because he knew one thing above all else.

He couldn't keep her.

The desire to claim this singularly incredible woman nearly overrode the reality that, over time, he would snuff out any fire and vivacity she held. He wouldn't mean to of course.

It was purely . . .

Inevitable.

It'd happened before.

Perhaps not on the same destructive level as what his father did to his mother, but it wasn't negligible either. In those times that Johnny played wingman, Benjamin had gone home with countless women. Occasionally, those connections would deepen into something more than a one-night stand. But always in a disproportionate way. They would get attached and he would have to callously cut ties the second he caught wind of their *feelings* for him. Most of his exes moved on quickly. A few, though, did not.

Benjamin had been so heartless with so many that he'd never experienced a healthy relationship, and the idea of trying to have one, especially with Francesca, seemed out of his expertise. Beyond reach.

No. Dating her would not end happily because he didn't know how to break the cycle of use and dismissal.

"Can I ask you a question?" Francesca asked softly.

"Anything." He brushed a kiss on her temple.

"I don't want this to come off as an insult or anything."

"Spit it out, Miss Miller," he teased, retrieving his glasses off the side table and hooking them over his ears. "No need to beat around the bush."

She pushed up and sat cross-legged with the blanket wrapped around her shoulders. Benjamin desperately wanted to tug the comforter away and feast his eyes on her lithe body, but the urge to give her what she wanted won out.

"I don't get it," Francesca blurted.

"That's not a question," he smirked, sliding a hand beneath the covers to play with her knee.

She swatted his fingers away. "Would you let me finish?"

Benjamin sighed and sat up, mimicking her posture. "Apologies. Please proceed."

"Why does my brother love you so much? You . . . you

haven't been here. You didn't show up for either funeral. You two don't chat on the phone. He doesn't even know that your mother died or that you made a huge career change. Those are all things friends share. For all intents and purposes, you two aren't friends. So . . . why?" Her voice held a certain tone of protectiveness, and it felt corrosive against Benjamin's heart.

"I asked him that very question yesterday at the rehearsal dinner." He chuckled dryly.

"And what was his answer?"

"Nothing profound. Nothing that satisfied my conscience, anyway." He looked into Francesca's eyes and lost himself in their emotion. In a few short hours—maybe less—he wouldn't have the luxury of having her look at him like that ever again. The moment he walked out of her room would be the last time he would ever feel whole. Yet he knew what needed to be done. "But after what I witnessed at the wedding, I understood."

Her face contorted in confusion. "Understood what?"

"Jonathan. He collects damaged men and turns them into brothers. Once he's deemed someone worthy of redemption, he never lets them go. Zac, Miguel, me."

"Miguel's not damaged. He's the most solid one of the group."

"You've been preoccupied with the wedding and your asshole of a professor. It's understandable that you haven't seen it.

"And Jon kicked Zac out."

"Of the reception, yes. He didn't kick him out of his life. He'll continue to believe in Zac. Continue to love him like a brother."

Francesca took on a distant expression as she put all the pieces together. "Huh."

"My point is that your brother is a rescuer. And he refuses

to let someone go once he's cataloged them as family. No matter what."

A little smirk tugged at her lips.

"What?" Benjamin asked with narrowed eyes.

"Even if they slept with his little sister?"

He dropped his head and sat back. The truth was, he didn't know if he'd be losing one Miller or two when he went back to Seattle. So, he decided to take the coward's way out. "I suppose it all depends on if you tell him or not. The choice is yours, Francesca. And I won't harbor ill feelings either way."

Benjamin watched Francesca ruminate for a while. He wished she'd say her thoughts out loud. If he knew what was going on in her mind, then he'd know her true wishes and perhaps they could align with his. She'd agreed to tonight just being tonight. But perhaps she would want more. And perhaps if they went into it all as partners, a united front, facing the expected challenges head-on together, then maybe, just maybe . . .

"No. I'm going to keep it. Jon doesn't need to know what we have—or had." Her sad smile plunged a dagger deep into Benajmin's heart.

"I respect your choice." He nodded curtly, and her smile faltered.

"So, what now?"

The one-shoulder shrug he managed zapped all his remaining energy. "Would you like me to leave now? Would that be easier?"

"Would you . . ." she murmured then swallowed. Shy eyes peered up through dense lashes as she tried to conceal her emotions. "Would you stay with me the rest of the night?"

I would do anything for you. You only have to ask.

"It would be my pleasure, Francesca."

Chapter Forty-Five

Saturday, the day after the wedding: Frankie

*B*ang. Bang. Bang.

Frankie's eyes popped open, unsure whether the noise came from the hotel room door or inside her pounding head. *Water.* Her mouth was so dry, likely because all the drool had fallen out and soaked into her pillow. God, her breath could probably melt plastic. Maybe she should sneak off to the bathroom for a quick brush and rinse before a fourth round—

Her mind flatlined when she peeked over at the other side of her bed only to find it empty.

When the hell had Benjamin left?

She slept like the dead (especially after a sex marathon), but surely she would have felt him get out of the bed. Heard the creaky front door. A chill washed over her even as she pulled the heavy comforter up to her neck.

Bang. Bang. Bang.

Nope. That came from the door and echoed in her hungover skull. Who the hell was bugging her at—she squinted at the side table clock—eight-forty-three in the damned morning? An evil son of a bitch, that's who.

Unless . . .

Maybe Benjamin changed his mind.

Maybe he had snuck out to grab coffee and breakfast for them.

Bounding from bed then pausing momentarily to steady herself against the spins, Frankie snatched a robe off the ground and tugged it around her. "Coming."

After a quick glance in the mirror that left her cringing at the rat's nest on her head, she shrugged. It was his fault anyway. Their particular level of enthusiasm would surely leave a mess. She peeked through the peephole and caught a fisheye view of a dark-haired head tipped down as he steadied two travel coffee cups and a paper bag she hoped contained some kind of pastry. Striking her sexiest pose, complete with knee popped out through the slit of her robe, she pulled the door open.

"Are you trying for extra credit—"

A startling pair of brown eyes above a mischievous grin stopped Frankie dead, while the inferno igniting her cheeks reminded her that she was very much alive.

"Someone's been ridden hard and put away wet." Todd pushed past Frankie as she instructed herself to close her slack mouth.

"Thanks," she murmured, peeking out to see if anyone else happened to be in the vicinity. The external hallway was depressingly vacant.

So that was it, then. No *see ya*. No *it's been fun*. No *please don't tell anyone what went down because I could lose my job*. He stole away in the night like a coward.

"Jesus. It smells like sex in here." Todd grinned as he flung the curtains wide, unleashing the bright-as-fuck sun on her room. "How was he?"

"How was who?"

"The sheriff of course."

"Oh, Clint. Yeah, he was a gentleman." It wasn't a lie. It was the god's honest truth. It wasn't exactly the whole truth, but whatever.

"Doesn't smell like he was a gentleman," Todd said as he cracked the window for a bit of airflow. Spying a small pile of empty condom wrappers on the side table, he nodded in approval. "Glad to see you used protection. Now spill. You don't have to give me every tiny detail, but give me every tiny detail."

Frankie accepted the offered paper cup of what smelled like a chai latte and inhaled the spicy-sweet scent. The notes of warm cinnamon conjured fresh flashes of Benjamin all over her—touching, kissing, nibbling. She shook the images from her mind. It was over and done. She needed to take it all at face value and move the hell on.

"Ok, fine. Paint me a blurry watercolor instead." Todd settled into the threadbare chair in the corner of the room, perching an ankle on his opposite knee. He wore black socks with Christmas lights winding around the ankles. The tacky footwear was in such juxtaposition to his cool, fashionable aesthetic that Frankie finally cracked a little smile. "Was he tender? Did he toss you around like the brute he is? What was he packing? I'm not referring to the Glock on his hip, so don't be coy."

Her friend sought vicarious action, and she wanted to deliver. He'd bought her coffee and a chocolate croissant after all. Talking about the whole thing would probably make her feel better. But how much should she divulge?

"Can you keep a secret?"

"I am a master secret keeper." He leaned forward, propping forearms on his splayed knees. Pointing to his lips, he assured her, "Like a steel-trap."

"All right." She shrugged, sinking cross-legged onto her bed with the pastry in her lap. "First off . . . I sent Clint packing last night."

"Was this after the coitus?"

She choked on a flaky bite. "No. No coitus with the sheriff."

"So then who helped you aromatize your room?"

Frankie worried her teeth along her bottom lip, while Todd's demanding stare burned a hole through her face.

"Benjamin."

"Professor Prick?" It was her friend's turn to choke. She waited patiently as he found his bearings. "Oh wait. Never mind. I get it." He settled back against the chair and took a sip of his coffee.

"What's there to get?"

"You guys hate fucked."

"What? No." One thing was certain: She didn't hate Benjamin. Was she disappointed that they wouldn't hook up again? Yes. Were her feelings hurt? Maybe a little. But she wasn't exactly harboring stabby feelings toward the guy either. "I don't hate him."

"Was this your *first* time together?"

Frankie glanced away and took a long swig of her chai, despite how the scalding liquid decimated her tastebuds.

"I knew you were holding out at the nail salon. I have half a mind to take back that half-eaten pastry," Todd scoffed with mock offense. He rolled his eyes as Frankie dragged her tongue up one side of the croissant to lay claim. "It's cute you think that would stop me."

"We agreed the cabin hookup would be a one-time thing, but then last night . . . Whatever. It was just a meaningless fling and now it's over."

Todd sucked his teeth and narrowed his eyes, the word *bullshit* hiding on the tip of his tongue, then his eyebrows raised. "You *love* him."

Frankie barked out a hysterical laugh. "No, I don't!"

"But you definitely have feelings for him. Warm, sexy, make you tingle kind of feelings." He waggled a finger at her, confident in his assessment. "Admit it. I can smell a liar. Even in this sex dungeon candle shop. Yes, I'll take a triple wick mason jar of the Spank & Spice, please."

"You're so dumb," she mumbled, taking another giant bite to avoid confession. Alas, her flaming cheeks responded for her.

"Are you going to be seeing him again?"

She shook her head, barely registering the buttery flake of her usually favorite treat. While she wouldn't be seeing him intentionally, the truth was she'd probably run into him on and around campus. Their paths did have a tendency to cross after all.

"Why the hell not?"

"Come on, Todd. You know why."

"I really can't come up with a single, solid argument."

"Then please allow me to list them for you." Frankie brushed the crumbs from her hands, ignoring the snide judgment on Todd's face as he watched the wayward flakes tumble to the carpet. "First, he's a professor at the college I attend—"

"Ah, but he is no longer *your* professor. You won't even be affiliated with the same department."

"Sure, but fraternizing with a student could still cost him his job security. He told me he's up for tenure and something like this could derail the whole thing."

"Sounds like a him problem," Todd mumbled.

"Second," she said forcefully, choosing to ignore him. "I am on full academic scholarship. Funny business like banging my teacher could jeopardize that. And I don't know about you, but I don't have a cool fifty grand floating around to back me up. And since I'm not going into social work to get rich, I'd be paying off the resulting student loans well into retirement."

"I'm sure there are people who would help you if it came to that. Jonathan or your mom."

"I could never ask them to do that, especially after being so reckless with the scholarship to begin with."

Her friend shrugged but deflated a little. "That's fair."

"Three, Benjamin is damaged, and while I'm the last person to ever judge, he doesn't do relationships. Something about how it would end badly."

"I love a brooding academic."

"Then have at him, be my guest."

Lounging back in his chair, Todd appeared to consider the idea then swatted away the words like a circling gnat. "Nah, I don't think he'd ever swing that way."

"Finally, my animalistically protective older brother probably wouldn't be too thrilled."

"Understatement of the century." He rose and walked to Frankie. The weight of him next to her caused the mattress to dip, and she allowed the excuse to snuggle into her friend's side. "You're sure there's nothing you can do to make it work?"

"You mean if he would have stuck around to discuss it instead of disappearing like a thief in the night?"

Todd screwed up his face. "Ok, that's not a good look. But look on the bright—ouch! What the fu—"

He squirmed, raising a hip to pull something out from under his butt cheek. He held his hand open to find two glimmering baubles in his palm—Benjamin's cuff links.

"Now I guess you have to see him again."

"Because he left some jewelry behind? Whatever. Toss 'em or keep 'em."

Todd's shrill laughter matched the frantic clamp on Frankie's wrist. He dropped the twin bits in her hand and stepped away. "While those are not my responsibility, please, please, please, on all that is holy and fashionable, don't throw them away. Those antique babies could pay for a month of our rent. Plus utilities."

She eyed the mother of pearl inlay set inside a ring of

obsidian, and the word Bvlgari repeated twice around the surrounding silvery metal—though more likely white gold or platinum by Todd's dramatic response.

"What makes you think they're antiques?"

"Call it a hunch, but you need to return those. They might be important to him, and I don't just mean because they're pretty and expensive."

He was right. What if they had been a gift from his mother? While Frankie had zero intention of continuing her involvement with Benjamin, she also didn't resent him enough to toss out a potentially sentimental heirloom.

"I'll drop them by his office at the start of the next quarter." What she didn't say was that she would easily avoid actually seeing him and slip them quickly into the mail slot on his door.

Chapter Forty-Six

First day back in the office after the new year, Seattle: Benjamin

Benjamin dragged his fingers along his jaw, wincing at a couple spots where he'd nicked himself with a razor that morning. The three weeks' worth of growth he'd negligently allowed to accumulate hadn't gone quietly, leaving ample angry bumps behind as a reminder. He couldn't remember the last time he'd had so many ripped pieces of toilet paper scattered across his face, but he'd wager it had been sometime before high school graduation.

As he approached Dean McCaffery's office, he performed a final exploratory swipe to ensure any lingering tissue had been removed then knocked firmly.

"Come in," the older man called. He sat in his oversized desk chair, alternating between squinting at his computer screen through his glasses and above them.

"You wanted to see me?" Benjamin schooled his voice and features in the cool, unemotional affect he perfected in his time as a professor beneath McCaffery. While his boss proudly displayed everything that tumbled through his mind, Benjamin quickly learned that his own emotions could—and would—be used against him.

The dean raised a finger and then pointed to one of the two intentionally low chairs sitting in front of his desk, all the while not bothering to glance in Benjamin's direction.

With nothing to do but wait, Benjamin lowered, choosing to ignore how his knees raised to the level of his nipples—freaking intimidation tactics. He'd been no stranger to them, especially when he'd been working at Hewitt, Moser, and Pratt and wanted his opponent to feel extra small. Lawyers from an opposing firm, the occasional colleague, even spouses who were about to lose their shirts—and, more accurately, most of their dignity. He cringed as the faces of powerless targets flipped through his mind like microfiche in a public library.

The highlight reel ended with thoughts of Francesca. He'd done his best to lord over her the previous quarter, to bully her into dropping the class. Fortunately, she was too tenacious. But how many other students in the past had he dressed down, belittled, or intimidated to the point of fleeing his classes? Shame crept up his cheeks. He'd left the law firm to redirect his skills and efforts into positive change. Over the years, he'd even convinced himself that he was making a difference, but the realization that he merely exerted his power in yet another tyrannical way made him sick.

"Are you quite all right, Clark?" Benjamin blinked up at McCaffery, who wore a quizzical expression. "You look a little green around the gills."

"I'm fine. Just . . ." He searched around for some explanation that wouldn't reveal the soft underbelly of his internal conflict. "I haven't had breakfast yet. Too anxious to get into the swing of things again."

Satisfied, the dean gave a perfunctory nod and leaned back against the pompously maroon leather of his chair. "Understandable."

"You wanted to see me?" Translation: Get on with whatever this is so I can brood in solitary peace.

Benjamin's boss silently buffed out his wire-rimmed glass

with an old handkerchief he'd pulled from his breast pocket. After careful attention to the lenses, followed by a quick inspection of the hinged arms, the sparklingly clean eyewear found a home atop a crown of thinning white hair.

"I assumed you would know what this is about." The thin line of McCaffery's mouth gave nothing away.

Benjamin found he didn't love this more emotionally reserved version of the older man and wished he would get on with it. "I do not."

Wiry white brows peaked. "Hmm. I don't know if that should be alarming or comforting."

This game of cat and mouse was nearing the edge of his patience.

"A young woman came by my office yesterday," he began.

"A young woman . . ."

"Yes, one of whom we are both acquainted," he said, casually tapping arthritic fingers on the oversized desk. "Perhaps one of us more than the other."

Oh no. She wouldn't have. Benjamin schooled his features while anxiety churned in his gut. He never would have thought Frankie would tell Dean McCaffery about their affair. Yes, he'd disappeared from her bed like a spineless cad, neglecting to call a proper end to their rendezvous, but surely that wouldn't trigger her to take steps that would ultimately end his career. He'd read her incorrectly in the beginning, but that was before he knew her.

So, what woman was his boss talking about?

"And who might that be?" *Good, good. Aloof is good.*

"Mrs. Clarice Brinnoman."

Thank god. Benjamin nearly relaxed enough to sink into his chair, but he quickly remembered who sat across from him and steadied his spine. Brinnoman. Brinnoman. Why did that name sound familiar? Wait! "Mrs. Brinnoman, as in the head of the board of trustees?"

A sanctimonious smile curled across the dean's thin lips. "The very same."

This was about tenure. Be cool. Be calm.

"And what did she have to say?"

"That you've been approved for tenure." McCaffery reached his hand across the desk. "Congratulations, my boy. You're officially one of us."

Automatically, Benjamin returned the gestures, noticing only the cool and dry fingers pressed into his larger, warmer hand. The dean chattered on, but his words were a muted jumble as though Benjamin's head was underwater.

I got it. I finally got tenure.

That meant prestige and job security in a position that allowed him full autonomy to teach as he saw fit. To assist in creating lawyers who could go out into the world and make a difference.

Like *he* had?

He should have been jumping for joy, and yet the excitement he expected to feel was completely absent.

"This is wonderful," he murmured because perhaps he could force himself to believe it.

"You should be thanking me, Clark." Benjamin's eyes finally popped up to meet his boss's. "After all, it was my little stunt with Miss Miller that properly greased the wheels."

Francesca.

He pictured her sitting in his class, front and center. Hands poised and ready to type, amber eyes challenging him as he prepared to pepper her with impossible questions. Remembered the chill of snow and the flush of anger pinkening her cheeks as she tried to out hike him during the snowshoe excursion. Flashes of honey golden waves sliding through his fingers and the heady scent of lavender and eucalyptus invaded his memories. She'd been so much more than he'd ever thought to give her credit for.

"—could do it. But you both proved me wrong."

He'd missed what McCaffery was saying. "I'm sorry, what was that?"

"Francesca Miller. I hadn't thought she'd be capable of surviving your class. But you must be doing something right because if you can teach an MSW student law—without the basics of civil procedure—well, let's just say you earned your tenure." McCaffery had come around the desk to clap him on the back, to congratulate not only Benjamin but himself in his clever scheme.

The scuttle of dread clawed up Benjamin's neck. He'd wanted tenure for so long and he'd been convinced all along that he deserved it. But by the dean's own admission, it took the success of an interdisciplinary stunt for the older man to go to bat for him in front of the board.

Benjamin made Dean McCaffery look good and in return he tossed a bone to the lab rat that had made it happen.

"What do you say we get your papers signed and dropped off with human resources? I'm sure you are excited to get your pay bump as soon as possible." The charred laughter scratched at Benjamin's ears, reminding him of the snide way his father used to laugh after he'd won particularly life-crushing settlements for his stupidly rich clients. After he'd helped to destroy lives of those with shallow pockets and limited power.

She wasn't like us.

We're strong. Resilient. I'm proud of you for making something of yourself.

Just like your old man.

The dean returned to his chair and pulled out a thick manila folder. "Sit down, son. I've got it all right here."

With eyes flitting between his boss's drawn brows, the pile of papers on his desk and back, Benjamin inched toward the door. This wasn't right. All of this felt very, very not right.

"I'm sorry," he choked out between thick swallows. "I need a minute. There's something I—"

The raised voice from the office followed Benjamin out the door, but he didn't stop. Not when he exited the building nor when he reached the edge of campus. His feet quickened, and while dress shoes weren't exactly conducive for such activities, he succumbed to the urge and ran.

Chapter Forty-Seven

A few days later, Seattle: Frankie

The cuff links sat heavily in Frankie's jacket pocket as she marched through campus toward the law building. Having a few grand worth of accessories clanging together in a small envelope at her side made her antsy, paranoid even. She'd never been mugged, but Murphy's Law dictated that today would be the day, what with her carrying around an entire month's rent in pawnable goods. Footsteps a couple feet behind had her throwing guarded glances over her shoulder. She released a sigh, doubting the middle-aged guy in tweed and the chipper young woman bounding around him like an excitable chihuahua were planning to jump her.

Climbing a few steps beside wooden arbors covered in dormant lilac vines, she reached the law school courtyard and entered through the glass doors. Students meandered around, talking quietly in groups. The ensuing murmurs hovered around her, creating a sense of safety. More witnesses inside than out on the open sidewalks.

She'd spent the last few weeks with her family, making up for time she'd lost being married to her schoolwork during fall quarter. She'd also chipped in quite a bit at her family's business. Since Jonathan and Lucy were on their honeymoon in Belize, it had been all hands on deck at Off the Beaten Adventures. Frankie was glad for the distraction. And in no time, her attention was redirected away from the misguided dalliances with a certain professor of law.

Misguided dalliances? Oh god, she'd spent too much time with that man.

The initial sting of Benjamin leaving cut deep, but she wasn't deluded enough to think a few rounds of sex would have kept him bound to her side—despite how toe-curling their interactions had been. The distance helped, as did the flow of activity she took on in support of the newlyweds' absence.

But now, with every step leading her closer and closer to his office door, her heart pounded more ferociously in her chest. The twenty-minute walk to the building had given her ample time to fantasize about how things might go down. Would he pretend nothing happened, reverting to his original cold Professor Prick persona? Would he address the elephant in the room and offer an apology? Would he leap over his desk, slam the door shut behind her, and crush his lips to hers? Her mutinous lady parts tingled in want.

"Quiet you," she murmured downward, ignoring querying glances from a couple students in the hushed office hallway.

The scenario she hoped for most (logically speaking) was that his office would be empty. In theory, it was the most likely, because after creeping on the online registration platform, she'd managed to learn that the family law class was beginning at that very moment. And since he was allergic to being late . . .

Her heart and vagina hoped things would play out differently. When had her libido become such a traitor?

Case in point: Clint had invited her out last week for New Year's Eve. It seemed like a great plan. The best way to get *over* a guy was to . . . well, you know. However, the moment he leaned in for a kiss, she turned her cheek, shuddering at the indescribable cringe she felt deep to her core. Images of Benjamin, with his impossibly blue eyes and mussed black hair, hovering over her invaded her mind.

Goddammit, Francesca. You're ruining me.

Right, who ruined who?

Anyway, Clint called her out on it—in the most respectful and concern-filled way possible of course—then took her home immediately after. She'd apologized to him, mentally cursing Benjamin in the process, then watched Sheriff Howards' truck drive away. As his taillights disappeared around the corner, she knew that would be the last time he'd come sniffing around her. Not that she could blame him; a dude can only be politely turned down so many times before he moves on to other interests.

Room 310 loomed before her, unassuming yet potentially holding something powerful behind it. But even if he was in there, it more than likely wouldn't end happily. But maybe she'd get closure and finally shed the mental chastity belt she'd been wearing since the morning he'd left.

She approached, staring at the black placard with white lettering that read Prof. Clark. A few deep breaths and she raised her hand to knock but noticed a little mail slot. Pushing aside her fleeting bravery, she pulled the sealed envelope from her pocket and shoved it through the slot. She breathed a sigh of relief and started down the hallway then froze as the door pushed open.

Busted.

As she turned, Frankie quickly realized that she hadn't run all the scenarios through her head prior to coming, because she hadn't expected the woman on the other side.

"Excuse me, miss." The woman smiled warmly behind oversized glasses that crept down her long, thin nose. Kinky strays of dark blonde hair escaped every angle of her ponytail. She wiped her brow with the back of her hand and held the envelope out to Frankie. "I don't think this is meant for me."

Puzzled, Frankie stepped closer, peeking at the room

number again. "Three ten. Isn't this Professor Benjamin Clark's room?"

"Yes." She turned and tapped the nameplate of the door with her knuckle then settled both hands on her hips. "Er, well, yes, it was."

"Was?"

"Yes."

"But now it's yours?"

"Yes." She beamed proudly and offered no more than that.

"Did he switch offices?"

"No, at least I don't believe so."

Good grief, woman. Were they playing twenty questions and Frankie hadn't been looped into the game?

"Do you know where I can find him?"

"Sorry, no."

"Okay," Frankie dragged out the word, ready to be done with this particular exchange. "I guess I'll just wait outside the family law class and catch him there."

"Oh, you won't find him there."

"Why not?"

"Because I teach that class. Professor Dalton." She gestured to herself. "Just transferred in."

"You mean you teach the class that started"—Frankie glanced at her watch—"seven minutes ago?"

Professor Dalton's eyes flew wide with panic. "Balls, I knew I was forgetting something."

Before Frankie could get any more information, the cryptic conversationalist scurried past with an armload of papers and a mason jar of iced coffee.

So, there was a new family law professor in town. What did that mean for Benjamin? Did he still work there? Had he quit? Been fired? And what the hell was she supposed to do with the cuff links now?

Frankie wrestled around with the idea of calling him. That's what an adult would do, right? Dial his number, and say, "Hey there, former sexual partner. You left your fancy schmancy cuff links in my hotel room just before you bolted. Do you want them back, or have you become less pompous and only buy shirts with buttons now?" Yeah, that would be smooth.

The devil on her shoulder provided a whole host of alternative ideas: pawn them and pay for textbooks, donate them to charity, bury them in the park for some metal detector enthusiast to make the find of a lifetime.

Her conscience won out. What if they were important to him? Perhaps his deceased mother had given them to him or they were an heirloom or something.

Before she could overthink, she pulled out her phone.

Frankie:

Hi Benjamin, I have your cuff links. If you send me your address, I can mail them to you. Thanks.

Perfect. Cool, matter-of-fact, and zero invitation to connect face-to-face. To reward her bravery, she decided to stop by The Java Judge in the law school lobby. Surely, she deserved a congratulatory treat.

She jumped when her phone buzzed almost immediately.

Benjamin Clark:

I don't want them.

Frankie:

Are you serious?

Benjamin Clark:

When am I not?

Fair point.

She advanced in line, attempting to focus on the pastry case and earthy scent of roasted coffee beans. Why did it seem so weird that he didn't want them back? Why wouldn't he need them? Surely, he had other occasions where wearing cuff links made sense. Frankie couldn't exactly think of an example since she'd never owned a pair. Correction: She'd never owned a pair until now. So what should she do with them? It felt awkward keeping them. It wasn't like she wanted a keepsake to remember her time with Benjamin. She'd much rather forget it ever happened and move the hell on with her life. He was the past and needed to stay firmly planted there. Her phone buzzed again.

Benjamin Clark:

How are you?

A weight settled on her chest, and warmth rose to consume her cheeks. Red flashing lights with the word "danger" illuminated down that path. She pulled up his contact, thumb hovering over the screen.

"What'll it be?"

Frankie looked up and into the warm brown eyes of the barista. "Can I please have an almond croissant and a mocha?"

The aproned woman nodded, punching the order into the register.

Frankie took the opportunity to press a few buttons on her phone too.

Contact blocked.

Chapter Forty-Eight

Three months later, Leavenworth: Benjamin

Pulling into the town of Leavenworth, Benjamin drummed nervously on the steering wheel in tune with the frantic beat of his heart. Long gone were the twinkling Christmas lights and poinsettias, and while only a dusting of snow remained in town, the jagged peaks around him were practically coated. The white tips shimmered crystalline against the backdrop of bold blue sky and glowing sun. Even in his heightened state of apprehension, he could admit the view was remarkable. A far cry from the gloomy remains of winter that still lingered on the western side of the Cascades.

He'd debated with himself about stopping by unannounced like this, but his best friend's new wife insisted that he was welcome anytime. Lucy, with her cheerful disposition and hospitable nature, had explicitly said, *No need to call, our door is always open to you.* And so, here he was, following his phone's GPS to the charming Bavarian town that held haunting memories in hopes of finding some closure.

That wasn't completely accurate. He'd accept closure, but what he hoped for was a new beginning.

Pulling into the gravel lot outside Off the Beaten Adventures, Benjamin inhaled a series of deep breaths, intending to calm his humming anxiety.

Through casual texting and cunning conversation, he

learned that Jonathan and Lucy were both at the office that morning.

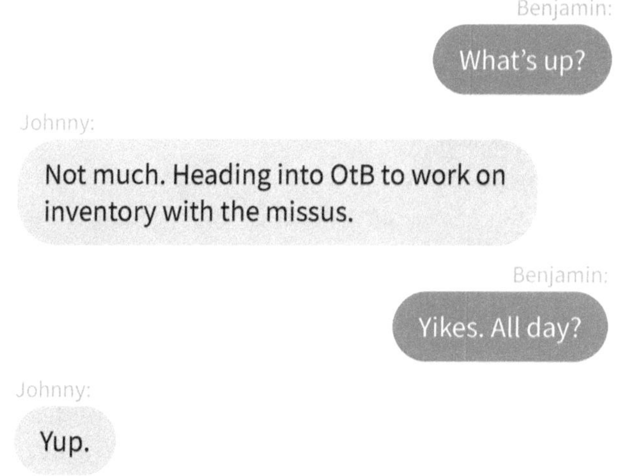

All right, perhaps Sherlock wouldn't have been impressed, but it had done the job.

After signing a few documents and finding his Friday suspiciously open, Benjamin had acted on instinct and taken the day off. Bizarrely enough, that wouldn't have been his first (second or third) reaction to an empty calendar three months ago before tendering his resignation to Dean McCaffery. But there he was, a duffel bag full with zero expectations for the long weekend.

The bell above the front door chimed as he entered the front lobby. The small space boasted poster-sized photos of people engaging in a variety of outdoor sports: hiking, kayaking, white water rafting, and rock climbing. But instead of the cheesy, posed postures and grins, the pieces looked authentic. Clearly, someone with an artistic eye had taken these because passion—either for the act of photography or participating in the adventures themselves—radiated off the images. He stepped closer and found signatures in the bottom corners of each: Z. S. Hartford.

Zac. Huh. He was the last person Benjamin would have

expected to possess the talent to produce these. Especially since there wasn't even a whisper of cleavage nor a single "artistic" butt shot among them.

"How can I help—oh!"

Benajmin looked up in response to the melodic voice and grinned. "Hey, Lucy."

"Finally, someone takes my 'the door's always open' comment at face value," she said with a laugh, gliding around the front desk and wrapping the much taller man in a fierce hug.

One thing Benjamin had learned very quickly was that for such a petite package, the little brunette was way stronger than she looked. "I could sense the honesty in your voice."

"Good. Because I meant it." She bounced on her toes, clapping her hands, barely containing her joy. "Jonathan is going to be so excited. Hey, husband!" she barked loudly over her shoulder then turned back, giggling. "Calling him that never gets old."

"Yes, *wife*?" Johnny crooned with a laugh that carried a slightly exasperated tone, like he did, in fact, find the moniker to be losing its luster. He turned the corner and stopped dead.

"Look what the cat dragged in," she said, gesturing to Benjamin.

Advancing toward each other, the two men embraced in a back-patting hug.

"What brings you here, Benji?" A grin split wide across his bearded face and crinkled eyes glittering.

"Can't a guy drop everything and drive three hours east for a beer and giant pretzel? I came to see you. How much more inventory do you have?"

Johnny flinched. "Hours worth."

"But he's about due for a lunch break," Lucy cut in, snatching his coat from the nearby rack and thrusting it into her husband's arms. Shooing them out the door, she called, "Bring me the biggest bacon burger you can find, will ya?" then retreated into the back room.

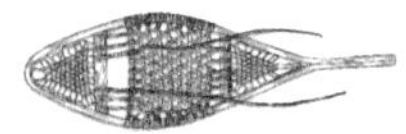

A short while later, the two men sat at a bistro table in The Rooftop Tavern, beers in hand as the server, Stella, dropped off a couple BLTs.

"What really brought you all this way on such short notice?" Johnny asked, chewing thoughtfully on a thick-cut fry.

"We didn't get a chance to catch up in December." Benjamin shrugged. "You were understandably preoccupied."

"Very true. But so were you." He scowled and tossed another fry into his mouth.

Gulp. He hadn't mentioned anything about his sister, but that doesn't mean he didn't know something had happened between them. Still, it was probably best to play dumb.

For a little while at least.

Try for nonchalance.

"What do you mean?"

Nailed it.

"You and my sister." Johnny's eyes never left Benjamin's as he took a long pull from his frosty glass.

"Yeah, about that . . ." Ok, maybe playing dumb wasn't the best plan. He could practically feel the dirt accumulate under his nails as he dug his hole deeper.

"I don't know how you survived being alone with her without either of you murdering the other," he said with a chuckle. The glitter returned to his amber eyes, warm and humorously empathetic. "From the looks of your initial meeting at the welcome dinner—well, I guess it wasn't the first time you'd met, was it, Professor Prick?"

The corner of Benjamin's mouth ticked up, and he let out a snort. He deserved worse than that nickname.

Then and now.

"Anyway, you never did find yourself in her good graces, did you?"

"I wouldn't say that," the husky murmur was out of his mouth before he could stop it.

"Meaning?" The warning in Johnny's voice was unmistakable, and Benjamin had to tread lightly if he hoped to mend things with Francesca while also keeping his friend's head level.

"There's a little more to it than what you've witnessed."

"Again, I say: meaning?" Beer and sandwich abandoned, the man who'd been like a brother sat leaning back, arms crossed, gaze sharp and calculating.

Benjamin's assumption had been accurate: Francesca had remained tight-lipped about their affair. Did that comfort him? Or did it worry him that she'd gone through considerable efforts to move past the encounters, perhaps even going so far as to pretend nothing happened? Regardless, she would most likely be quite upset once she learned he confided in her brother that they'd had sex. And yet it had to be done. He was done closing himself off from those he respected and cared about. Life's too short and true friends don't come along easily.

"Francesca and I . . ." How exactly was he supposed to explain what they'd shared together? They'd had sex, yes, but it wasn't purely physical. She'd overwhelmed him. Seeped into his bloodstream and after making the unilateral decision to go cold turkey, he went through withdrawals. He was still going through them. So much so that he'd turned his life completely upside down and forged a new path. One that she'd hopefully be proud of. He hadn't done it all for her, but she was absolutely in the back of his mind the entire time. Benjamin held his friend's heavy stare, one that waited patiently while also measuring. "We were intimate."

Johnny's amber eyes dimmed, losing their usual friendly glimmer. "Intimate how?"

"We had sex at the cabin and then again the night of your wedding."

A swirling storm of sand and lightning cracked in his friend's narrowed gaze. He said nothing, only stood, pulled a hundred out of his wallet, and slid it under his barely touched plate of food. Footsteps landed heavy on the wood floor as he strode from the table.

Benjamin hung his head. He'd really made a massive mess of this whole thing. First with Frankie and now with his best friend. How could he be so careless?

"You coming?" The gruff call came from the tavern exit.

Benjamin slid off his seat and followed Johnny down the rickety stairs and into the parking lot.

"Look, Johnny, I know I messed up but that's why I'm here—Oof!" The collision of a massive fist on his jaw caught him off guard. Stumbling, he landed on his knees. He heard birds chirping overhead and hoped he wasn't imagining the cartoon version of them flying around his head, though after a solid blow like the one his friend just delivered, he wouldn't be surprised. Squinting into the high noon sunlight, he shook off the haze of the hit. The large man loomed over him, stepping slightly to the right to block out the sun. Benjamin prepared for another blow—he deserved it after all—but one never came. Cracking an eye to take stock, he flinched at the open hand hovering inches from his face.

"Get up." The growl was unnatural coming from such a gentle guy. He'd hurt his friend and his friend's sister. He deserved what he got and he wouldn't fight back.

"I might as well stay down here."

"Oh for fuck's sake." Johnny stalked around behind him and scooped both arms under Benjamin's armpits, hauling him to his feet. "I'm done."

Benjamin rubbed his jaw. The lumberjack threw one hell of a punch, there's no way there wouldn't be a mark. Despite his better judgment, he chuckled as Johnny shook out the hand that had done the clubbing. "What? Did you break your hand on my face?"

"No." Cramming both hands in his pockets, Johnny shrugged sheepishly. "I thought it would make me feel better. Then I thought of what my father would have said if he knew I punched someone."

"Way to go, slugger?"

He snorted. "More like 'cut that alpha shit out, son, you're a grown-ass man.' And then he'd probably mutter all day about his man-child of a son having a tantrum. It'd be a whole thing."

"I'm sorry I didn't show up for his funeral." Benjamin hung his head.

"It's all right."

"And then again for Cynthia's." God, he was a horrible friend.

The same large hand that did the hitting settled on his shoulder. "I'm sure you had your own shit going on. Plus, I know if I had asked you outright, you would have come flying over the pass in an instant."

"It shouldn't take you asking, though. And I'm sorry."

"Apology accepted. Now, about my sister."

"That's actually the main reason I came out here."

"You cut me deep," Johnny groaned, pressing a palm over his heart and leaning back in mock agony. "I thought you came to see me."

"I did, but mostly, I need to make things right with Francesca. And I need your help finding her so we can talk things out. How I left—without saying goodbye—well, I doubt it went over well with her."

"Why not call or text her?"

"I tried, but she must have blocked me because I never heard back."

A knowing smile played along his friend's lips, the kind of smirk that said that the reunion wouldn't be as easy as that.

"Is she in town?" Benjamin asked.

"Yep."

"And you know where she is?"

"Oh-ho yeah."

"Then let's get going."

"Hold on, buster. Let's go finish our sandwiches first." He turned and took the wooden steps two at a time.

"I'd rather get this handled—"

"You're going to want to eat first. Trust me." Just as Johnny turned into the door, he chuckled and said, "You'll need the calories."

Chapter Forty-Nine

Frankie

Why did she insist on doing this to herself?

There were dozens of other snowshoe routes she could have taken that didn't conjure feelings beyond awe and the standard appreciation of Mother Nature's vast beauty. But no, she had to do things the hard way and twist the knife a little bit more.

At the very least, the weather conditions along Highway 2 were impeccable. Cloudless cobalt sky, no wind, a balmy thirty-nine degrees. The weather was so perfect, in fact, that it made Frankie that much crankier. She wanted a good old-fashioned sulk. One final mope about the last time she'd clomped along Skyline Lake Trail and ended up stranded with the most infuriating asshole she'd ever met.

Convincing herself to move on had been more challenging than she'd anticipated. She'd never been dumped, always the one to break ties when a "relationship" had run its course. She'd also never had sex quite like what transpired between her and Benjamin. And his total disappearance from the college should have been helpful in putting the extremely sexy past behind her. But for whatever reason, this struggle was outside of her wheelhouse, and his eyes and smirk and uninhibited sexual utterances flitted through her mind nightly.

Who was she kidding? They plagued her daily too.

She even took drastic measures and said yes when one of the

students in her MSW cohort asked her out for drinks at a local trivia night, but then she chickened out. She wasn't sure if he believed her strep throat claim. Probably not, since she moseyed into class fit as a fiddle the next morning. He hadn't approached her since then.

Just as well. She should be focusing on her studies anyway.

So she trundled through the winter quarter, acing every exam and paper the professors threw her way. She'd worked so hard that her advisor recommended she apply for an internship with the Community Youth Justice Council, the most coveted placement organization among her peers. Despite being flattered, she couldn't help but want to spend her time with the family resource counselor at the local Boys & Girls Clubs. Since her goals involved working closely with foster kids, the experience shadowing and assisting the FRC made much more sense long term.

Spring break had snuck up on her, but she was happy to head home and help out at the family business. Focusing so much on school, she'd, again, neglected her ingrained sense of adventure and needed a big hit of the outdoors before the final leg of her program.

And since Jon didn't need her to lead a group until the following morning, she found herself with a wide-open blue-bird day.

Naturally, unapologetically torturing herself seemed like the thing to do.

Huffing and puffing up the final switchbacks, bursts of cloudy breath erupting from her mouth, she felt like the little engine that could.

I think I can make myself suffer a bit more. I think I can make myself suffer a bit more.

Frankie stopped as she reached the fork leading to the lake.

The banks of the small body of water would likely be frozen all the way around. The center would be thawed but flat as ice from the lack of wind. The sun would glisten off the surface. There'd probably be birds chirping as they fluttered from branch to branch. She might even spot a couple critters hopping around the snow, digging for new shoots and leftover seedpods they'd buried the previous fall but hadn't been able to find in time for hibernation.

Sitting on a log, taking in the beauty, and basking in the lingering chill would do her some good. It would help her collect her thoughts so she could return to Seattle clearheaded and whole.

And yet.

Begrudgingly, like habitually poking at a canker sore inside her mouth, Frankie turned right instead, following the path past the lake turnoff. Her feet led her without conscious control.

Clomp. Crunch. Clomp. Crunch.

The rhythmic progression toward where she and Benjamin shared their first kiss urged her onward. In no time, she stood at the drop-off, scanning the wide-open view of glittering white peaks and peppered splotches of green trees and bare grass in the valley. It was beautiful.

Seattle had been an interesting change, but she was excited to return home after graduation in June. Once her MSW program ended, the real work would begin. The three thousand experiential hours she'd need to complete to be able to gain licensure from the state of Washington was only the beginning. Fortunately, Child Protective Services in Wenatchee was always on the lookout for interns. Double fortunately, they paid their interns—modestly, but she could supplement her income by guiding for OtB a few times per month.

Clomp. Crunch. Clomp. Crunch.

Someone approached from behind. The intrusion sent a

twinge of irritation rippling up Frankie's neck but abruptly dissipated. With the day being so stellar, it was foolish to think she'd have the trail to herself. But that didn't mean she'd have to stick around and chitchat with the newcomer.

She stood, preparing to turn, wave, and stride briskly past the approaching snowshoer, when a deep voice froze her in place.

"Francesca." Her name was spoken so heavily, like the weight of his future hung in every syllable.

She didn't need to turn to know who had invaded her solo trek. His voice was ingrained in her memory—and fantasies—and continued to plague her thoughts. Unprepared to face him again, she considered her options for escape. Upon finding none (unless tumbling down the embankment again was an option. Spoiler: it wasn't.) she steadied her shoulders and turned.

Laughter bubbled up inside her at the sight of Benjamin. His choice of winter wear was ridiculous, and not just because he had borrowed her brother's beloved knit hat, complete with ear flaps and a bushy pompom on top. He clearly had not been prepared to snowshoe, nor had he deemed it necessary to change before descending upon her peace and quiet.

Tailored brown trousers clung to his long muscular legs, along with a white button-down shirt stretched against broad shoulders, sleeves rolled up to reveal corded forearms dusted with dark hair. His navy blazer slung across his hips, tied at his waist like a grungy plaid a Nirvana groupie would have worn in the 90s. But of all that, this fish out of water's footwear was the most ridiculous because Frankie had no idea that snowshoes could be strapped onto perfectly buffed loafers. His feet had to be soaked, toes frozen, while sweat collected at his chest and armpits.

The sight of Professor Prick in such a state of disarray was too good for words.

Still, she schooled her features, warning her lips to quit their smiling and start frowning already.

The scent of heated cinnamon and fresh perspiration clouded her senses as Benjamin stopped an arm's length away from her. His chest heaved, cheeks flushed, bare hands curled tightly around his trekking poles.

"Well?" he gasped through ragged inhales.

What was he looking for? A high five for making it to the end of the trail in the stupidest outfit imaginable? Hugs and kisses and tears saying how much she missed him? She had, but he would never hear it from her lips.

"Well, I'll be off. Enjoy the rest of your hike," she deadpanned, brushing past him.

She halted when his large hand encircled her wrist. The brush of his cool fingers against the exposed strip of skin between her weather-appropriate coat sleeve and mittens tingled in response. His thumb found her traitorous pulse as it hammered frantically at his touch.

"Francesca," he pleaded with a little more warning than supplication.

All right, fine. I'll bite.

"What are you doing here, Benji?" Sliding from his grasp, she crossed her arms—no small feat with a ski pole in each hand.

"Out for a stroll. Thought a tromp through hell was in order," he teased. The swirl of stormy blue scanned her straight face, taking measure in a way that made her squirm. One side of his mouth quirked. "I came to find you."

"Clearly. Why?"

"To apologize—"

"Good."

"—among other things." The heat in his words was unmistakable. His once unreadable face, one so skilled in maintaining a flat, neutral expression, hid absolutely nothing from her now.

Her disloyal lady parts screamed their consent for the "other things," while logic, self-preservation, and pride battled valiantly to be heard above the horny protests. She refused to get sucked into this cycle. The night of the wedding was the last time she would allow him to fuck and then leave her in the same breath.

"Here." He reached into his pocket and handed her a little white business card.

"Let me guess, subtle coloring, tasteful thickness? Has a watermark, perhaps?"

He chuckled, and the sound was like warmed maple syrup. "Does that make me Patrick Bateman?"

"Might as well be."

"Read it," he urged, pressing the bit of card stock into her palm.

She sighed and scanned the words.

The Family Law Offices of
Benjamin Clark, Esq.
Attorney & Counselor at Law

Frankie shrugged. "So, what is this supposed to mean? You left NWU and got a new job? Neat. Good for you."

"Francesca," he said as he accepted the card back and replaced it in his pocket. "This is because of you."

"I'm not following."

"After my mother died, I left divorce law behind. It broke me knowing I was helping men like my father get away with destroying the lives of their spouses. So, I redirected my efforts and began teaching, all under the guise of creating quality lawyers who would do some good someday. To offset the damage I'd done."

"You told me all of this in the cabin." She shifted from foot to foot, feeling antsy and ready for the interaction to end. She didn't understand what any of this had to do with her. He'd been crystal clear about his intentions. Looking toward the trail, she considered how fast she'd be able to tromp out of reach, but knowing Benjamin, he'd figure out a way to outrun her.

"You're right," he said, tracking her twitchy eyes as they mapped out an escape route. "Please don't bolt. If you want to leave, I won't stop you, but please let me explain something."

The bitter part of her, the part that resented him for dipping out on her twice immediately following sex, wanted to make him feel the same way she had. She longed for him to know how blatant rejection like that felt. But the other part of her, curious and foolish as it may be, needed to hear his explanation. If nothing else, perhaps listening to him would provide something she'd been grasping at for months: closure.

Chapter Fifty

Benjamin

"Fine. Out with it." Frankie's arms recrossed over her chest. Standing there with her hip popped, Benjamin knew he had a limited amount of time. Perfect; he could work with a ticking clock because, if nothing else, she was listening.

"Sharing your—for lack of a better term—origin story made me see how unbelievably strong you are. You were dealt an awful hand early on. Juggled from one home to another, landing in a hellhole with the devil's minions to watch over you. And after all that, you maintained your empathy. There isn't a hint of bitterness, nothing that leads me to believe you would trade your situation for anyone else's. Instead, you plan to use your experiences to help others in similar scenarios. You, Francesca, are going out of your way to make the world a better place, and there is no limit to the impact you'll be able to make in the lives of so many children."

She squirmed uncomfortably and chewed on her bottom lip as though the analysis of her struck a tender chord. She cleared her throat. "We can't all be saints."

Her quip held no mirth and perhaps a touch of judgment.

Judgment that matched what he'd been directing at himself since he left her hotel room last December. The self-criticism only grew the more he compared what he'd contributed to versus what he'd received in return. The fact that he only backed off in family law once he knew there was something in it for him. And when

Dean McCaffery finally bestowed the honor and job security that Benjamin had worked so hard for, the thought of accepting tenure had made his mouth taste like ash.

Dry and foul and bitter.

"No, you're right. Some of us will work the rest of our lives in an effort to make up for the havoc and injustice we've caused and never be able to offset our past choices." His heart grew heavy with regret and shame, and part of him hoped he'd never become so complacent that he'd forget the sensation. "I was offered tenure—"

"How lovely for you," she deadpanned.

"—then I walked out and never looked back. I'm tired of climbing on the backs of others in a quest for my own prestige. I played others like pawns in a game of chess, hoping I never got the rug pulled out from under me like my mother did when I was a kid. What I was doing felt wrong, and so I quit. I thought of you as I packed up my office. I conjured your bravery as I resigned. Considered your selfless efforts in forging my next path."

"So what? You start your own business and I'm supposed to be impressed? It's supposed to excuse away how you treated all those people?"

Her subtext screamed: *How you treated me?*

"No." He took a step closer, ignoring his frozen toes and the chill he'd developed now that he wasn't marching uphill. He considered throwing on his blazer but was afraid that if he took his eyes off her for a second, she'd be gone. "I can't change the past. The only thing I can do is make amends going forward. And I didn't leave the university for you. Though you were my inspiration. I changed my trajectory because of you.

"Francesca, I cannot promise you that life will be perfect. Or that we wouldn't fight. Or that my mind will ever change regarding marriage. But what I can promise you is that from here on out, I swear I will do nothing but try to be a better version of the man you once knew."

Silence.

Absolute. Agonizing silence.

Until finally . . .

"How long did that little speech take you to prepare?" Her eyes were as flat as her expression. "A few days or the last half hour of the drive over?"

"I *was* a litigator before I became a professor," he said as he chuckled and shrugged. "Old habits of grandstanding die hard."

"It's scripted," she huffed, finally allowing emotion to trickle into her response. "I don't want some bullshit, carefully constructed speech that sounds like it came from AI software. It's not real. It's manufactured. You spend so much of your time meticulously organizing your thoughts that they never contain what's most important."

"And what's that?"

"You! Benji. Don't you get exhausted being this haughty, emotionless, never-swears robot? Can't you just for once let loose and show the real you?" Frustration vibrated through her body, causing her to shiver in a way that begged Benajmin to hold her.

"I can try." He shrugged.

"Then do it again."

"What?"

"Rewind. Make your declaration, and this time," she pleaded, "don't hold back."

He dragged in a breath and looked beyond Francesca to the sunlight glittering off the packed snow. The last time he'd been here with her, he'd felt the most terrifying fear of his life. He'd acted then without thought or concern for how he might sound or be perceived, and nothing bad had come of it. In fact, he ended up making a connection with her, one he'd never anticipated could happen. She was asking for the unfiltered version of him again.

Was that the key to successful relationships?

Being vulnerable?

Allowing oneself to be seen as exactly who they are and no less?

The notion was terrifying, but as he looked into Francesca's flickering amber eyes, so full of hope and caution, he knew.

"Francesca, I . . ." Words caught in his throat just as tears pricked the corners of his eyes. "*Fuck*, I don't think I know how to do this."

"Then don't. Think, I mean. Just talk."

"I've spent every day since my parents' divorce erecting this shield. I was determined to never end up like my mother. Anything that could be considered weak went out the window. Emotions. Slacking on anything. Any kind of vulnerability.

"In all those years, Johnny had been the only one to pry anything out of me, and that's only because he allowed me to see him first. I was there with him when he got the call about your father's cancer diagnosis."

Francesca's throat bobbed as she swallowed. Benjamin desperately wanted to wrap her in his arms and hold tight, but he had to get this off his chest.

"I'd never seen a man break down like he had. He sobbed and sobbed, and at first, I had no clue what to do about it. Until suddenly, some long-buried instinct jumped up to the surface and told me to hug him. I sat there, holding my friend—my *brother*—while he cried in a way that I'd never done. Was never brave enough to allow myself to do.

"Johnny was the first emotional connection I had since I was twelve years old, and I clung to him. But when he moved back home and I stayed in Seattle where my life was just starting to take off . . . I don't know . . . it's like the fire he sparked in me faded. Like it became folklore of a time that existed long ago. I know that makes no sense."

Francesca shrugged and dashed away a tear as it slipped over her bottom lashes. "It makes some sense."

Benjamin smiled weakly and continued. "And then you sauntered into my lecture hall and turned my world upside down. Francesca, you made my world explode with emotions and disorder and vibrancy. You live in a way that is so unapologetically authentic and I hate that I tried to snuff that brightness out. I am so sorry for how I treated you, not only as a professor, but as a lover. I was callous and malicious and I am so fucking sorry. I don't deserve your forgiveness—"

"But you have it anyway," she said simply.

"What?"

"I forgive you."

"Just like that?"

"Yes."

"But why?" There was no way it could be that easy. Benjamin had only begun to grovel.

"Haven't we been over this before? Because you mean it. What you're saying is *real*."

Benjamin's chest split wide from the way his heart swelled. He pulled Francesca into his arms and hugged her tightly. His hand swept into her hair, and he inhaled the lavender and eucalyptus scent he'd been longing to smell for months. She pushed slightly back from him and looked up then spotted the developing bruise on his jaw. Her eyebrow quirked as she tried to contain her humor.

"Who beat me to the punch?" She removed her glove and gently trailed a warm finger along the angry splotch. The heat was exquisite despite the tenderness of the raised lump.

"Oh, I'm sure you have an idea."

"Miguel?" she teased.

"No, though I doubt he would have stopped at one."

"Lucy?"

"No, but she definitely would have been the one to deliver the hit if she'd been there."

"What did you say to my brother? He's protective but not the punching type."

"I told him what I did to you."

Eyes flying wide, Francesca gasped. "In the cabin? Jesus, I'm surprised he didn't run you through with a ski pole!"

"No, no," he soothed, shaking his head and chaffing her arms, partially trying to calm her but also aiming to regain feeling in his chilly fingers. "I did tell him we slept together, but it was more about me leaving and not contacting you again. And, I guess, that I slept with his little sister."

"Are things tense with you and Jon now?" She winced.

He allowed a husky rumble to slide from his lips while attempting to swallow the emotional lump that remained in his throat. Was it really that easy? Was she really going to put aside her hurt and forgive him for being cruel and dismissive? It was the last thing he deserved, but that didn't mean he didn't hope.

"Things might be weird for a short time, but I think hitting me vented most of his anger. He's the one who told me where to find you and lent me the gear. And this sweet beanie."

Swatting at the poof sitting limply at the top of the hat, she grinned.

"So what comes next?"

"Well, that's the thing. Now that I run my own law firm, I can technically work from anywhere. I'm licensed in Washington state, so I can settle down wherever. Seattle, Wenatchee, Leavenworth. There will be work regardless of where I go. For now, I plan to stay in Seattle to be near my . . ." He gestured to her, not sure yet what he should refer to her as. "I figure we can take it day by day from there."

Smiling, she leaned closer. Benjamin shuddered at her warm breath on his lips.

"I meant . . . *now*. What should we do right now?" The molten amber of desire swirled in her eyes. He didn't deserve her forgiveness, not that easily. He deserved to suffer, to wait out in agony for weeks before she decided to put him out of his misery. Yet there she was, welcoming him with open arms, just like that. He vowed then and there to be everything she deserved.

He lowered his lips to hers, slanting over the plump heat of her mouth. God, that sweet taste of her solidified everything for him. She was where he belonged. She made him better, made him want to be better. And the least he could do was be everything she needed, happily, for as long as she wanted.

Epilogue

Three months later, Seattle: Frankie

Frankie was running late.

At least it wasn't her goofy flip-flops tripping her up this time.

She glanced down at her polished toes, noting the cherry red perfectly matched the lingerie set she wore underneath her sensible black dress. The scandalous set was meant to be a surprise after the ceremony, but when Benji walked in on her a couple hours ago just as she snapped the last garter in place, the surprise was ruined. She struggled to find even a shed of disappointment in her spoiled plan, but flashes of him laboriously exploring every exposed inch before delving beneath the lacy fabric left her with nothing but a matching flush on her cheeks.

Where is he?

She glanced at her watch—again—and peered out the large paneled glass at the entryway, searching for any sign of Benji.

Finally, she spied him, sprinting up the walkway with a large black square in his hand.

"Cutting it a little close, are we, *professor*?" she joked breathlessly as he wrenched the door open.

"You're welcome, *Miss Miller*," he drawled, handing over her graduation cap. They sped down the hallway side by side.

A light sheen of sweat speckled Benji's forehead. He hastily pulled a handkerchief from his breast pocket and swiped at his face. Rumpled black waves hung playfully over his brow. His coif had been so immaculate when he'd walked into the en suite. But Frankie had buried her fingers into his thick hair the second he'd knelt in front of her and grabbed her thighs. One thing had led to another (sex, snack, more sex, then a lightning-fast shower to wash off the residual lust), and he never did get a chance to restyle it.

"Where did you find it?"

"Behind the stack of boxes by the closet," he purred, conjuring the graduation role-play they engaged in the night before.

"I can't wait to get to our new place and settle in," Frankie managed through hurried pants as they turned at the end of the corridor. The next forty-eight hours were going to be a mad dash. This time tomorrow, the moving truck would be loaded, and she and her soon-to-be-live-in-boyfriend would be on their way to a little condo in Wenatchee. The digs were temporary. Once she finished her internship, they'd start hunting for a house closer to Leavenworth. Jon and Lucy had offered to sell a chunk of their land to Frankie and Benji so they could build the house exactly the way they wanted. While the gesture was appreciated, Frankie wasn't so sure about living *that* close to her big brother.

They stopped at the double doors leading into the large auditorium. He wrapped her in his arms and danced a gentle kiss along her glossy lips.

"Let's get you graduated first. I am so proud of you. Proud of your hard work in the face of adversity."—he glanced away sheepishly, fully acknowledging that *he* was the adversity—"Proud to call you my partner. Savor this accomplishment. You, Francesca, deserve every ounce of pomp and circumstance of this graduation and all the honors you racked up." He ran his fingers along the stole and cords draped over her shoulders. His ocean eyes danced merrily as Frankie smiled up at him.

"I love you, Benjamin Clark."

Frankie thought she spied a glistening of moisture gathering behind his lashes. "I love you, Francesca *Stanley* Miller."

Her peal of laughter bounced off the walls around them. She leaned in for one more kiss, then shooed him away to join their friends and family in the crowd.

It was hard to believe that nine months ago as Frankie started her fast-track MSW program, she would come out the other side with a lover, a partner, and a new best friend.

The End

Love on a Ledge

Stranded in Leavenworth, Book 3

Stay tuned for Zac's story.

For fans of
enemies to lovers,
second chance,
and (of course) forced proximity.

Coming
February 2025

Acknowledgements

Thank you so much for following Frankie and Benjamin's journey in Love Under Snowfall.

I was excited and nervous to write this love story for a number of reasons. First, I fell in love with Lucy and Jonathan (my OG MCs) and wanted to do my best to create another set of characters that you, as readers, would root for just as much. Second, I have to be transparent. I hate the snow and cold weather. I admit it . . . I'm a fair-weather adventurer, which helped me write Benjamin's distaste for snowshoeing. (I get it Benji!) Finally, I received so much positive feedback from Love by a Landslide that I was nervous about disappointing all of you. Hopefully, Love Under Snowfall allowed you to seethe and swoon in equal measure while also giving you an opportunity to check in on Jonathan and Lucy.

Thank you to my meticulous book editor, Michelle. You made my words sparkle. I can't wait to send you my next manuscript.

Thank you to my book cover designer, Ashley. Your creativity brought another set of characters to life. I still can't stop staring at these beautiful books.

About K. L. Parsons

LOVE UNDER SNOWFALL is K. L. Parsons's second novel. When she isn't writing sexy, swoon-worthy romcoms, she can be found hiking, rock climbing, and generally exploring the natural wonders of the Pacific Northwest. Her hope is that her readers fall in love with the region as much as she has. She lives among the lush evergreens of Washington State with her husband and son.

Learn more about K. L. Parsons and come say hello:

www.klparsonsbooks.com

Instagram.com/klparsonsbooks

Twitter @KLParsonsAuthor

TikTok @klparsonsauthor